four

Four Week Fiancé

Cover design by Louisa Maggio of LM Book Creations
Book design by Inkstain Interior Book Designing
Editing by Lorelei Logsdon
Proofreading by Marla Esposito
Text set in Cochin LT.

HELEN COOPER

NEW YORK TIMES BESTSELLING AUTHOR

MORE BOOKS BY THIS AUTHOR

One Night Stand
Falling For My Best Friend's Brother
Falling For My Boss
Illusion
The Ex Games
The Private Club
The Forever Love Series
Crazy Beautiful Love
Everlasting Sin
The True Diary of That Girl
The Prince Charming Series

acknowledgments

They say that no man is an island. And I say that no writer does it all by themselves. Four Week Fiancé has been in the works for years. It was originally intended to be a four-book novella serial and now it is a full-length two-book series.

I want to thank all the readers that messaged me for Mila and TJ's book throughout the years. If it wasn't for your encouragement and want of this book, I'm not sure it would have happened.

I would like to whole-heartedly thank my beta readers: Tanya Skaggs, Katrina Jaekley, Kathy Shreve, Stacy Hahn, Barbara Goodwin, Emily Kirkpatrick, Cathy Reale, Cilicia White, Chanteal Justice, Kanae Eddings, and Tianna Croy, for all of your help. Your feedback and support has meant everything to me and has helped me to write a better book. I consider you all readers and friends.

To the members of the J. S. Cooper and Helen Cooper Street Teams, thank you so much for everything you do to support me emotionally, mentally and physically as a writer. It makes me feel amazing to know I have so many awesome women in my corner.

To my cover designer, Louisa Maggio, thank you for all you do and for being a friend.

To the readers, thank you for reading my books. Thank you for loving my characters and for emailing me and telling me so. It's hard to be a writer and waiting for feedback, but it is the reason why I love going to work so much.

To all the bloggers that have showed me support and helped to promote my books, thank you for what you do for me and other authors. You read because you love to, but you spread the word because you want to help and you're excited about books. Keep being excited and keep spreading the joy that you feel. I know all of us authors appreciate you.

And last, but not least, thanks be to God for all of my blessings.

—Jaimie
XOXO

A NOTE TO MILA

The sun sets late in the corners of my mind.
I think of you when I go to the lake.
I think of you when I close my eyes.
I think of the girl who changed my world.
I think of the heartbreak that changed your world.
And I'd make one wish to take all your pain away.

TJ Walker

Prologue

TJ

PRESENT DAY

"I CAN'T MAKE YOUR decision for you, Mila." My voice was deep, some might say husky, as I looked down into her wide eyes. She was gazing at me with a question in her big brown eyes and her lips were slightly parted. "What's your answer?"

"Why are you doing this?" she asked me softly as she stepped towards me, licking her lips nervously. Her long blond hair hung around her shoulders and small runaway wisps blew into her eyes. I leaned over and moved them gently behind her ear. She blushed at my touch and I made sure to let my fingers linger on her cheek for a few seconds. I could feel the heat emanating off of her skin onto my fingertips.

"I want you to experience the happiness, the joy, the goodness that you deserve." My voice sounded too serious and I wasn't altogether sure why I'd chosen those exact words. I wasn't really sure why I was here myself, with her, about to do something I knew I shouldn't do.

"I wish I could control what happens next," she said, her voice breathless. I gazed down into her eyes and my heart stopped as I saw the emotion there. She was letting me in, baring her soul to me in a naked, vulnerable way. Her eyes reminded me of a young, innocent doe I'd seen in the woods one year when I'd gone deer hunting with a friend's family. I'd felt guilty then and I felt guilty now as well.

"There's not much that is going to happen next." I sounded harsher than I'd intended. I didn't know how to tell her that I was mad at myself, not at her. She wouldn't understand my inner turmoil. "We're going to kiss and then you're going to dump that loser of a boyfriend." I put my hands on her waist and stilled them from going higher.

"He's not my boyfriend," she squeaked out as she closed her eyes and lifted her lips up to me, waiting. Her shoulders were thrust back indignantly and I stared down at the curve of her breasts and down to her long legs. She'd grown into a beautiful young woman. A very beautiful young woman that I knew I shouldn't let myself indulge in.

"You're damn right he's not," I growled before bending down and lightly pressing my lips against hers. They were so soft and sweet, and she kissed me back eagerly as her fingers fumbled with my shirt. I grabbed her hands and clasped them in mine as I deepened the kiss, allowing my tongue to enter her mouth and taste the delicate hint of freshly picked strawberries that she'd just eaten. She moaned slightly as I sucked on her tongue and my hands let go of hers and moved up her waist, making their way up to her bra. All thoughts of Cody warning me to stay away from his sister were far from my mind.

"Oh, TJ," she said as she grabbed my hand and moved it up and pressed it against her breast. "Oh, yes."

"Oh, no." I stopped and pulled back. Her eyes blinked open and she looked at me with a slightly bewildered and lost expression. She looked hot and flustered and I loved it, though I kept my grin to myself.

"What are you doing?" She pouted. "Why did you stop?"

"You didn't think it would be this easy, did you?" I said with a smirk, feeling hot and bothered myself. "Nothing happens until I get your decision."

"But, I just can't pretend to be your fiancée, TJ. That's not right." She licked her lips nervously.

"You can't?" I said softly, allowing my fingers to trace the curve of her lips. "Or you won't?"

"I read the contract," she said and swallowed. "What you're asking —it's too much."

"For you or for me?" I asked, my eyes never leaving hers. "What's four weeks, Mila?" I said as I pushed the tip of my finger into her mouth and watched as she sucked it gently. She just stared at me, thinking, and I could see her mind racing. She had no idea what to say or do. I'd beaten her at her own game and she knew it. Now I was ready to take my prize. And I was going to take it whether she became my fake fiancée or not.

One

MILA

SEPTEMBER 19, 2008

DEAR DIARY,

I'm in love. I want to marry TJ Walker. He's Cody's best friend. He has dark brown hair and big green eyes and he's the hottest guy I've ever seen in my life. He stayed over last night and I saw him coming out of the bathroom in only his boxer shorts. I had thoughts I shouldn't have at 15, but I don't care. He gave me a lazy, sexy smile and ruffled my hair like I was some kid. How annoying. He only sees me as a goofy teenager. He doesn't know that I'm ready to date a college man. Even one that's stupid enough to be friends with Cody, but I'll forgive him for that. One day, hopefully soon, I'm going to make him fall in love with me. And when that day comes, I'm going to show him this diary. Perhaps. Until that point, I'll continue to flirt with Harry Jonas, my lab partner. He's kinda cute too. Just not as hot as TJ. Even TJ's name is hot. And Mila Walker sounds a lot better than Mila Jonas. Oh, how I hope to be Mila Walker one day. A girl can only dream.

Mila

XOXO

P.S. Mom, if you're reading this, you are dead to me!!!!!

THURSDAY, TWO WEEKS AGO

His name is TJ Walker. He's 28, hot as can be and he's my brother's best friend. Which means he is off-limits to me. Some may say 28 is too old for my 22 years, but I beg to differ. Guys my age are just way too immature. I need a man, not a boy. And the man I want is TJ Walker. Only, I can never have him.

Not that he wants me. To him, I'm just Cody's little sister. I'm a girl in his eyes. Not a woman. And while I was in high school, I accepted that maybe I was too young for him. But now that I'm out of college and older, I'm willing to do anything to change his mind. At least, I think I am. I mean it's easy to say you're willing to do anything when there is nothing on the table. But who knows what I would do if presented with some real situations?

I'm not exactly a femme fatale. Or at least I haven't been up to now. It doesn't help that TJ and I constantly spar every time we see each other, or that I want to slap him as much as I want to make love to him. Yes, I want to make love to him. If you saw him, you would know why. He's one of the most gorgeous men I've ever seen in my life. He's tall and stocky just like I like them, about 6'2" and 200 pounds of lean muscle. He's got short, silky dark-brown hair and dazzling emerald eyes. He must work out quite a bit because his legs are muscular and his arms are strong, and would be capable of holding me in obnoxious positions for long amounts of time, if you know what I mean.

Yes, I have dirty thoughts, but I've never really been able to act on them. Well, not yet. The only man I want to do all the dirty things I have in my mind to is TJ. I want him to make love to me until I can't even remember my own name. Or his. Though, let's be real, it would be very hard to forget TJ Walker's name, especially when you've been crushing on him for as long as I've been. Don't get me wrong, though, I'm not just waiting around for him to realize he loves me, not anymore, at least. I have a plan that I'm hoping to put into action.

If you haven't figured it out as yet, I'm a realist and a pragmatist, while also being a dreamer. Don't ask how that works. I don't really know. My best friend, Sally, says that I'm an enigma. I tend to agree with her. I don't even understand myself sometimes.

But enough about me, let's get back to TJ. Like I said before, he's hot. Like really, really hot. Tall-dark-and-handsome hot. Or, as Sally would say, take-off-your-pants-and-fuck-me-tonight hot. Of course, I wouldn't say that—well, not out loud I wouldn't. Though, I've had many dreams where I've said that and more to TJ. "Take me now, TJ," being the phrase most often uttered in my dreams. And he always rises to the occasion. If you know what I mean. And it's not just about his looks, or the fact that he's rich. I'm not one of those types of girls. I like TJ because he's a good guy. He helps feed homeless people at Thanksgiving and he's a Big Brother to this kid who is pretty bratty. And I know he's not a psychopath, or at least I hope he's not. I've known him since I was a baby, so I would hope I would have seen the signs.

You may be wondering, if I like TJ so much, why don't I just go after him? Well, for one, he's my brother Cody's best friend and has been for 20 years. So he's known me since I was a little kid with snot in my nose, and I guess that makes him think of me as his little sister. But I sure don't think of him as an older brother. And I'm determined for him to notice me as more than a little girl.

There's just one problem, though. There are parts of him that I don't really like. I mean, I think he's hot and sexy, and I have dreams about him, but in real life, sometimes he's an arrogant asshole who thinks he's God's gift to women, thanks to the many hot women who throw themselves at him daily.

So, yeah. I have a bit of a moral dilemma on my hands. Should I go for it, knowing he's an asshole, or should I leave it alone, because he's an asshole? And to make it perfectly clear, TJ doesn't care who knows that he's a player. That's one of the reasons why Cody told him that if he ever laid a hand on me, he'd find his two front teeth knocked out on the floor. That didn't exactly help my cause when I was younger and openly flirting with TJ.

So now I'm at a crossroads and I'm not really sure what to do. Why is it so important for me to decide now, you ask? Well, he's going to be spending the weekend with me and Cody and the parents at our lake house. It's a tradition in my family to go to the lake house every fall, right before winter hits. And TJ always comes because, as I said before, he's practically a part of the family.

I know, I know—I shouldn't be fantasizing about my brother's best friend like this. I grew up with him, he's an asshole who teased me mercilessly, and I know he's a player, but all I can say is he's hot and I can't help that my body catches fire when I see him. He's all that I can think of every night before I fall asleep, and so I've decided to see if I can take our relationship to the next level. I mean, we did share a special kiss when I was 18. It was hot. But it freaked him out. He was 24, and to him, kissing me was akin to being a pedo. However, I'm no longer 18 and I want him to know that in every way possible. That's why I'm planning on trying to seduce him this weekend. It will be hard with so many people around, but I've come up with a plan.

"That's our bestseller." The sales lady beamed at me as I fingered the sexy underwear. "It's called the Lacy Suspender set. It's guaranteed to get your man all hot and bothered."

"I can see that." I grinned back at her as I played with the soft, flimsy material. "It's very hot and sexy." And it really was. The only worry in my mind was what my parents would think if they saw me cavorting around in this get-up. It was a bit risky to attempt to wear sexy underwear on a family trip, but what option did I have? It wasn't as if TJ and I hung out on the regular. I didn't really see him unless there was a family event he was invited to, and Cody didn't invite me to hang out with him much outside of that.

"Yes, it is." She winked. "But then again, all of our stuff at Agent Provocateur is sexy."

"That's true." I nodded as I looked back down at the barely-there bra and panties with matching suspenders. "How much?"

"Only one hundred and ninety, miss." She continued smiling at me as my stomach dropped. $190? For almost non-existent underwear? I bit my lower lip as I stood there. That would almost deplete my bank account and I knew I couldn't use my parents' credit card. Not here at a lingerie store. Especially because I was only supposed to use it for emergencies, now that I was an adult and out of college. I knew that they wouldn't think that seducing TJ was an emergency. "Will that be cash or credit?" The sales lady's voice was sharp, and I could tell from the look in her eyes that she was worried she'd just wasted the last twenty minutes with a customer who might not be able to pay.

"I'll use my debit card," I said and grabbed my wallet from my bag, my heart beating rapidly. Bye bye, $200, but hello to TJ in my bed.

◆

"SALLY, MY PARENTS ARE going to kill me. Nonno is going to kill me. This might be the last time you talk to me. I think they're going to send me back to Italy."

"First off, why would this be the last time I talk to you? They do have phones in Italy. And secondly, how can they send you back to Italy? You're not from there. And lastly, your nonno is not going to kill you. You're his favorite granddaughter."

"Yeah, I'm his favorite, but when he figures out what I did, he's going to have a heart attack," I muttered as I stared at myself in the mirror. "He's going to wish he was back in Napoli."

"He never lived in Napoli," Sally said matter-of-factly and I groaned loudly.

"You know what I mean. They are going to be upset."

"What exactly did you do?" Sally said impatiently. I could imagine her rolling her blue eyes as she waited to hear about the latest situation I'd gotten myself into.

"I went and bought some sexy underwear, and now I'm kinda broke," I said softly, dreading telling my story.

"Sexy underwear?" Sally's voice was dry. "Not for this weekend with your parents at the lake house?"

"You know who will be there. I need to make my move before it's too late."

"Mila." Sally laughed. "I don't know if this is a good weekend for you to try your Basic Instinct moves."

"I wish I had Basic Instinct moves." I groaned and wondered if I had time to watch the movie before I got my stuff ready for the trip.

"Anyway, why would your nonno know and care about what you bought today?"

"Because I put in a request to get an advance on my next paycheck as soon as I left the mall." I sighed. "And of course, Cody emailed me back asking why and asked if I needed some financial and accounting classes."

"He is the accountant at your parents' business, Mila." Sally laughed. "Who did you think would be looking at your request? And why did you ask for an advance?"

"I have rent due, electricity, cable, car insurance." I sighed. "It all adds up, you know, and I don't have a huge salary."

"You're training to be in acquisitions, right? Didn't you get a raise?" Sally said. "Have they let you make any purchases yet?"

"Yes, I'm in acquisitions now. Dad had me in reception forever, but now he has rotated me into acquisitions, but that still hasn't equaled a pay raise. I'm still on twenty-four thousand a year, as that is what all new graduates start with at the company. Nonno said that Dad doesn't want people to think I'm advancing due to nepotism, but I'm like, 'Come on, Dad, I'm your daughter and you own the company—what do you think people are going to think?' "

"Yeah, twenty-four thousand isn't a lot, but still should be enough, right?"

"I guess." I sighed. "Nonno thinks Dad wants me to move back home, but I told him I'm an adult and Dad will be waiting a long time for me to come back home. I'd rather move to a cheaper place than move back home, with them in my business."

"Or you can move in with me," Sally suggested half-heartedly.

"Thanks, but no thanks," I said and laughed. Sally and I had been best friends since kindergarten, but we were exact opposites. She was a clean-freak and I was messy. She was good with her money and I was spend-happy. We were best friends and loved to hang out, but we didn't live well together. We'd learned that the hard way as roommates our sophomore year in college.

"So, what do you think Cody's going to do?" Sally asked eagerly. She'd had a crush on my brother for years. However, Sally wasn't as bad as me. She hadn't dedicated her life to getting Cody. She was of the mindset that if it worked out, it worked out, and while she was waiting she was going to have fun. And boy did she have fun. Some of the guys she dated almost put TJ to shame. I wasn't sure where she found a continual supply of hotties.

"He's most probably going to question me all weekend." I sighed and collapsed onto my bed. " 'What are you spending your money on, Mila? This is why Mom and Dad don't trust you, Mila. Why don't you let Nonno set you up with a nice Italian boy so you can get married and have kids, Mila?' "

"Nonno still talking about his best friend's grandson?" Sally asked with a laugh.

"Um, yes." I groaned. "His name is Milo and no, I'm not joking. Nonno thinks it's a sign from God. Milo and Mila. I told him hell no."

"And then he told you to watch your language," Sally said with a laugh.

"You know Nonno. 'When I was growing up, girls didn't use bad language,' " I said in a deep voice, imitating my grandfather. " 'They learned how to make pasta from scratch and how to make the best marinara sauce.' "

"Oh, Nonno," Sally said, giggling. "I miss him," she said softly and I felt wistful as I lay back on my bed and spoke to her.

"Me too," I said with a small sigh. "I don't get to see him as often as I'd like to. Maybe we can take him to dinner in a couple of weeks. I know he'd love to see you as well."

"Of course," Sally said. "That sounds great. Hopefully your folks won't have packed you back to the motherland before then."

"Well, you know, if they find a nice Roma boy..." I said, my voice trailing off as I thought about all the times my parents had threatened to ship me off to Italy to get married. Which I thought was pretty hilarious, seeing as my father wasn't even of Italian descent. His ancestors were from England, and Nonno had taken a while to warm up to him when he was wooing my mom as a teenager.

"Haha, imagine you living in Rome?" Sally laughed. "I've got to go, though. Are you going to be okay? Or do you need to talk some more about your sexy underwear and how you're horrible with money?"

"Whatever, Sally." I giggled and sat up. "I'm fine. I'll talk to you later."

"Okay, bye." She laughed. "Try not to buy any whips or anal beads before tomorrow morning."

"Funny—not!" I said and hung up. I looked at the stack of clothes on my bed and then at my suitcase, and groaned. I wasn't sure what I was going to wear and I wasn't sure exactly what activities we'd be doing, but I needed to minimize the amount of clothes I was taking. The pile was high, even for me.

Two

MILA

JULY 14, 2011

DEAR DIARY,

I am going to marry TJ Walker. Yes, I said marry. I am predicting that I, Mila Brookstone, will one day marry TJ Walker. Yes, I'm only 18 and yes, we're not in a relationship, but I know it will happen. How do I know? Because last night was the most magical night of my life. Last night TJ Walker kissed me. Yes, he kissed me. No tongue and not for long, but it was the most perfect kiss I've ever had in my life. Even better than kisses with Channing Tatum. Not that I've kissed him, but I've thought about what sort of kisser he would be and I think that TJ is better. You heard it here first!! I'm going to marry TJ Walker. That is, if he doesn't annoy me too much first.

THURSDAY, ONE WEEK AGO

I stared at my suitcase with a happy smile. I was finally packed. Well, I had two stacks of outfits: one stack was causal-sexy and the other stack was sexy-sexy. I was trying to decide if I should try and go full-out seduction mode on TJ or to try and play it a little bit cooler. Sally advised that I play it cooler because she doesn't want me to embarrass myself if it doesn't work out. Because yes, now she is coming as well. Sally always has an open invite to come and this year she thought she'd be busy with work, but three days ago she found out she has the time off. So now she's coming to the lake house and she is planning on going into cool seduction mode this weekend, only not with TJ—thank God. She's after my brother, Cody. Eww. But who am I to stop her?

My only problem is, if both of us are successful with our seduction plans, what are my parents going to think is going on? We can't just disappear, and there is no way we can have sex at the lake house. The rooms are not soundproof. I mean, I can try and be quiet, but if TJ is as good a lover as he is in my dreams, it's going to be hard. And let's just say that Sally will have a bigger problem than me. I lived with her in college and trust me, she doesn't know what the word quiet means. I giggled as I picked up two different bikinis and tried to decide which one to take with me, when the phone rang. I knew the weather would be slightly cold and the water would be even colder, but I knew my body temperature adjusted pretty quickly to the water.

"Hello, Mila here," I sang into the phone, assuming it was Sally. I looked at the thong bikini and threw it back onto the floor. I wasn't sure why I'd even contemplated taking that. That was not appropriate for a family trip. If my dad saw me in that, I'd be on the first plane out of the country for sure.

"Mila?" The voice was deep and gruff, and tingles ran through my arm to my fingers.

"This is Mila," I said, my voice sounding like a deep croak. "Mila," I said again, almost singing my name, in my nervousness.

"It's TJ." His voice sounded amused. "Auditioning for The Voice or something?"

"No," I laughed, excited to be talking to him. "I'm trying out for The X Factor, actually."

"Oh." He cleared his throat. "I would have thought you would go for The Voice!"

"Why is that?" I said, confused.

"Because they don't see your face at first," he said with a deadpanned voice, and it took a moment for his meaning to sink in.

"You're an asshole." I groaned at him, shaking my head at his diss. That is what I meant about him thinking he was my big brother. It was like he and Cody had sat down one day and discussed the responsibilities and tasks of being my older sibling. And teasing me was the number-one duty.

"You gotta love it." He laughed as if he thought his joke was hilarious.

"Not really."

"Aww, well, sorry to break your heart, but this isn't The X Factor calling."

"Uh huh."

"I was calling because Cody can't pick you up tomorrow. He's stuck at work until early Saturday morning, so he asked if I can pick you and Sally up and drive you up to the lake house."

"Oh, really?" I grinned into the phone, slightly excited that we'd be alone together, but then I remembered that Sally would be with us. "I guess that's fine." I tried to sound nonchalant.

"What time will you be ready?" He cleared his throat. "And an accurate time, please, not an 'I'll try to be ready, but I'll keep you waiting for thirty minutes' sort of thing."

"TJ Walker, shut up." I groaned into the phone. "That was only one time."

"It was one time too many."

"Whatever. I'm sure all your dates keep you waiting as well."

"Yeah, but I know I'm getting something from them that makes it worth it."

I gasped and he laughed into the phone. "So, what time, Milady Sadie?"

"Three o'clock, but I'll check with Sally to make sure she can make that." I ignored his use of the nickname he and Cody had coined for me when we were younger. They had created a rhyme for me that went, "Milady Sadie, went to bathy, and she got a stupid navy. A navy wavy goofy baby, that is our Milady Sadie." It made absolutely no sense, but the nickname Milady Sadie had stuck. I knew better than to get annoyed when they used it anymore. It only fueled their teasing.

"Okay, Milady Sadie. Call me back and let me know."

"You're a child, you know that, TJ?" I couldn't stop myself. "Only a little boy would call me a nickname from when I was a little kid."

"You're still a kid, Mila." His voice was dry.

"No, I'm not." I growled into the phone.

"Oh, yeah. I forgot you're a college graduate now." He laughed. "You're officially in the big girls' club."

"Whatever." I rolled my eyes, even though I knew he couldn't see them.

"Oh, yeah. I may be bringing a friend with me. I spoke to Cody, and your parents don't mind."

"A friend?" I frowned.

"Yeah, her name is Barbie."

"No, it is not." I groaned into the phone and tried to ignore the swell of disappointment that rose up in me as I threw the bikinis down onto the floor. What was the point of me trying to seduce him if he was bringing another girl up?

"Yeah, it is." He laughed. "And she calls me Ken."

"Are you joking? Why is she calling you Ken?"

"I kind of told her my name was Ken when I picked her up at the bar two nights ago."

"Oh, my God," I groaned into the phone, flopped onto the bed and closed my eyes. "Please tell me that is a bad joke. She did not actually believe you?"

"Of course she believed me." He laughed. "So, just let Sally know, I'm Ken for the weekend."

"What are you going to tell my parents?"

"Oh, Cody told me that they couldn't make it. He didn't tell you?"

"No." I sighed. "No one told me anything." I rolled over on my side. "Not my parents and not Cody. So you're telling me that this year the family get-together is going to be me, Sally, Barbie and you?"

"You got it." He laughed. "And Cody will be there Saturday morning."

"Great, that's just great."

"I think your dad wanted to take care of some business stuff and your mom wanted to take your Nonno to get some new sheets or something."

"I'm glad my family let you know what was going on before they told me anything," I said, feeling annoyed. I hated that they never bothered to let me know anything, like I was still some kid or something.

"Don't pout, Mila. You know it doesn't suit you."

"Thanks for nothing." I stuck my tongue out at the phone.

"Anyway, go call Sally and then call me back to confirm the time."

"Yes, sir."

"I like that," he drawled.

"You like what?"

"When you call me sir." He laughed. "I could get used to it."

"I'm sure you could." I paused. "But I guess you'll just have to get Barbie to call you that."

"Don't worry, Mila. You'll have a guy to call sir soon."

"I already have a guy," I lied, slightly annoyed at his comment.

"What?" His voice changed and suddenly became brusque. "What guy?"

"Just a guy I'm dating."

"You never mentioned him before," he said sharply.

"Well, it's a new relationship."

"Hmmm." He paused. "I hope he's not another loser who borrows money from you and doesn't repay it."

"He's going to pay me back," I protested, though we both knew that wasn't true. I couldn't even remember the guy's full name.

"And try not to date another guy who dresses up in women's clothing. That's usually a sign that he's not that interested in you."

"That's not fair," I protested, groaning as he reminded me of Richard, the last guy I'd dated. The one who was more interested in my wardrobe than me.

"Hey, I'm just looking out for you."

"Yeah, sure."

"You don't want to date another loser."

"Do you have someone better for me?" My voice was shrill as he continued teasing me.

"I may." He paused. "I just may."

"I'm going to go call Sally now," I said, changing the subject abruptly, not wanting him to try and hook me up with another guy.

"You do that, Mila." And with that, he hung up.

I sighed and lay back on the bed, frustrated and excited at the same time. This is how it always went with TJ; we had a little flirting, a little bickering, and ultimately it ended up with a whole heap of nothing. And now he was dating some perfect girl called Barbie, who probably gave him head every night, and I was still single—but now having to pretend that I had a boyfriend. I groaned as I closed my eyes and pictured TJ's handsome face in my mind. Ugh, it was so frustrating. I just wanted him to give me a real chance, but I knew it was never going to happen unless I made a go of it. I sat up and grinned as I realized that my parents not coming might not be such a bad thing after all.

Three

MILA

MARCH 18, 2010

DEAR DIARY,

I'm a complete and utter idiot. The laughingstock of the country club. I'm going to kill Sally and I'm going to lock myself in my room for the next ten years. I'm never coming out again. Never. You will not believe what happened to me. I'm so EMBARRASSED!!!! TJ, the love of my life, came home this weekend with Cody. He asked me if I wanted to play tennis with him. Of course I said yes. I called Sally and she told me that he definitely likes me and that he was testing the waters to see if I liked him. I agreed—why else would he ask me to play tennis? I mean, every movie I've seen, the guy only asks the girl if she wants to hang out if he likes her. I mean, yeah he's in college and I'm in high school, but that doesn't mean he couldn't have fallen for me. Anyways, I wore a super short skirt, as per Sally's advice, and I wore a push-up bra and stuffed it with toilet paper and cotton balls. Well, the push-up bra was too loose and the toilet paper fell out of one side of my bra as I was playing. Yes, it fell out onto the court. Yes, I had one double-D boob and one B-cup. No, TJ was not impressed. He started laughing at me in the middle of the game. Like literally stopped moving to point out the toilet paper on the court and then he said, and I quote him verbatim, "Your right boob fell out, dorky. You might want to fix that." I nearly died. I would have died, but I think God was saving me so I could get revenge on Sally first for her bad advice. I'm never listening to her again. Or playing tennis with TJ. Well, maybe I'll play tennis with TJ again if he asks. Which I doubt he will. I don't think he likes me. If he liked me, he wouldn't call me a dork, would he?

Mila

XOXO

P.S. I officially lost the tennis match, if you were wondering. 6-2, 6-2. Pitiful.

FRIDAY, ONE WEEK AGO

"Hey, dorky, where's Sally?" TJ stood outside my front door looking like some hunky model in a TV ad for men's cologne or boxer briefs; very skimpy boxer briefs, I might add.

"She's on her way," I said and ushered him into my apartment, trying not to let him see how eager and happy I was that he was here.

"I thought you said that you'd be ready to leave at three?" He frowned as he stood next to me. His eyes bored into mine with an imperious glance and I made myself stand there, not touching his glorious body.

"I'm ready." I frowned back at him. "It's not my fault that Sally isn't here yet."

"Barbie is going to be upset," he said and pulled out his phone.

"Why?" I cocked my head to the side and studied his face. "Did she get peroxide in her mouth?"

"She's a natural blonde," TJ said with a small smile, his lips curving up at the side, even though I knew he was trying not to laugh.

"Sure she is," I said sweetly. "That's why her pubic hair is darker than the hair on your head."

"You're gross and a brat, you know that, Mila?" He started laughing then. "Is there something you want to tell me?"

"Huh? What?" I said and swallowed hard. Was he going to ask me if I was being bitchy because I was jealous?

"Are you into women now? Is that why you're so familiar with the female anatomy?" He looked me up and down. "I guess that explains why you look so butch today?"

"What?" I screeched and looked down at my outfit. "I don't look butch." But I didn't look particularly feminine, either. I was wearing baggy blue jeans, a big T-shirt and had my hair back in a bun. I certainly wasn't in any seduction-mode outfit, but that was by design. I wanted to look scruffy now, so that when I went into full-on seduction mode in the evening, TJ would be taken by surprise. I had to plan differently, now that I knew I had a Barbie to deal with.

"I'm not a lesbian, asshole." I turned around and walked towards my bedroom. "I told you I'm seeing a guy."

"Oh yeah, you did say something about some putz," he said, following me into my bedroom. "Where is he? Hiding under your bed?"

"He doesn't need to hide under the bed." I turned around and glared at him.

"Oh?" His eyes narrowed and he looked at my unmade bed and then back at me. "Don't you make your bed anymore, Mila? It looks like a mess."

"You're not my dad and yes, I do make my bed. Just not today. I had a late night," I said, which wasn't technically a lie. I did make my bed. Every time I knew my parents were coming over, or when I was having friends over— except for Sally. I didn't bother making my bed every time I knew Sally was coming over. She didn't care that I was messy. Well, at least not now that we didn't live together.

"A late night?"

"Yes, with my man," I said emphatically and fell down on the mattress and closed my eyes, letting out a loud sigh as I rolled around on the disheveled sheets. "We had a really late night. Sorry if I didn't make the bed this morning, but I was worn out," I croaked out, lying like crazy. I had gone to bed late, but not because of any guy. I'd stayed up all night watching episodes of GRΣΣK on Netflix, while simultaneously stalking one of the actors on Instagram. If things weren't going to work out with TJ, they might work out with Scott Michael Foster. He was a decent second option, if I ever had the chance to meet him.

"Hey," I squealed as I felt TJ pulling me up abruptly from the bed. My eyes flew open and I stared at his angry face with an emotion akin to glee. "That hurt," I said as I stood next to him and rubbed my arms.

"Do you think it's appropriate for you to be talking about your casual sex with your unknown man-friend and then to be reliving the memories in your mind while rolling around on your bed?" His green eyes flashed at me. "Do you think your parents would approve of your behavior?"

"Huh?" I said, my jaw dropping. "What are you talking about?"

"I'm talking about the little moans you were making as you wiggled around on the bed just now." He frowned. "I don't want the image of you having casual sex in my mind, thank you very much."

"It's not casual sex," I said with a glare. "We're in a loving relationship."

"Really?" TJ said with a smirk. "A loving relationship? Yet no one in your family has ever heard of this guy?"

"Of course they have." I put my hands on my hips and stared at him.

"No, they haven't," he said with a self-assured smirk. "I asked Cody last night if he had met your boyfriend. And he seemed very confused and he asked your parents and none of them had any clue you were dating anyone, let alone in a loving relationship."

"Whatever, jerk." I turned away, fuming. I should have known he'd ask my parents about my boyfriend. TJ was the sort of guy who knew exactly what he was doing. You could never get the best of him in any situation. He was always ten steps ahead of me, even before I knew to start counting.

"I'm not a jerk. I just wanted to meet this new guy in your life. See if I thought he was going to be a good addition to the family."

"Yeah, right." I rolled my eyes, knowing that everyone was going to be calling me soon to get more information on my paramour. I was surprised Nonno hadn't shown up already and done his "I have Mafioso friends" bit.

"I see I had nothing to worry about." TJ ran his hand through his dark hair. "Your relationship isn't that serious."

"Yet," I said as I released my bun and tossed my long blond hair, which I'd spent a lot of money getting highlighted at my local hairdresser's. I tried not to think of the money I'd spent, especially because Cody hadn't gotten back to me about the advance yet. "You're correct, of course, Troy and I were merely bedroom partners in the beginning, but now it has become more."

"Bedroom partners?" TJ's eyes narrowed again, but he looked unconvinced as he surveyed my face.

"Fuck-buddies, friends with benefits, hook-up pals—you get the drift," I said with a sweet smile as his chin hardened. TJ was starting to look pissed, and I loved it.

"You're telling me you have a fuck-buddy?" he said, his tone edgy, and he stepped towards me again, his brow furrowed as his eyes darkened.

"What's it to you?" I said softly. "Isn't that exactly what Barbie is to you?" I said softly, and he growled and turned away from me.

"I'm not playing these games with you, Mila. Grab your stuff. I'll be in the living room." He stopped at my door and turned back to look at me. "And call Sally. I'm not going to wait around all day for your best friend to show up. We have places to be. And I'm not planning on arriving late. You're the one who confirmed the time with me."

"Well, it's not like anyone will be up waiting for us," I said, annoyed at his tone. "My parents, who still haven't called me, won't be there and Cody's not arriving until tomorrow, right?"

"Barbie and I have plans for the night." He grinned. "I want to make sure they happen and I don't fall asleep as soon as we arrive."

"Well, maybe I can ask Troy to drive Sally and me up," I said, snapping at him. "I'm sure he won't mind."

"Troy?" He lifted an eyebrow.

"My boyfriend."

"So Troy is coming on this trip?" he asked, his right eyebrow still raised. "Cody didn't tell me that."

"It was going to be a surprise," I said churlishly, fiddling with my hair again and wondering where I could get a 'Troy' from at this late notice.

"Am I giving him a ride as well?" he said, his tone annoyed. "And is he chipping in for gas?"

"Is Barbie going to be chipping in for gas?" I said, annoyed. "And no, he's not riding up with us, he's driving his own car up. His Mercedes-Benz sports car, to be exact."

"So, why aren't you riding in his sports car, as well?" TJ asked in that matter-of-fact way that let me know that he wasn't buying in a million years that there was a Troy or that he had a Mercedes-Benz sports car.

"Because..." I stammered, trying to think of a reason. My mind was going blank and I tried not to glare at TJ. He was hot, but sometimes he was just so annoying. It was as if he deliberately tried to taunt me and make me feel like a loser. I wondered if he had any idea of the plans I had for him and the weekend. He wouldn't be looking so cocky and self-assured then. He had no idea that 'little Mila' had grown up. I wasn't some little innocent girl that he could put down and make fun of. I was going to show him exactly how grown up I was now. I was going to show him that I was all adult. That would wipe that smug smile off of his face.

"Because he doesn't have a Benz?" He smirked. "What does he have? A Honda? Hyundai?"

"What's wrong with a Honda? I have a Honda."

"Yeah, you do," he said, smirk still on his face, and I wanted to punch him.

"We can't all afford Range Rovers," I said and then smiled sweetly. "We don't all have rich parents."

"Nice try, Mila. You know I bought the car with my own money."

"Whatever," I said, feeling very much like a little girl again, or at least a petulant teenager.

"So what's going on? Is RoboTron coming? Where's Sally?" TJ looked at his watch and then back at me. "I don't have all day."

"His name is Troy and I already told you that no, he is not coming. Let me call Sally and see where she is." I grabbed my phone and tried to keep my cool.

"Yeah, that would be good. I'd like to get out of here sometime this year."

"Cry me a river," I sang and he laughed.

"Call Sally, dork."

"Hold on." I unlocked my phone and punched in Sally's digits and listened to the phone ringing.

"Wassup," she said happily as she answered the phone.

"I'm here with King TJ and he's wondering where you are," I said and gave TJ a look.

"I'm on the way." She giggled. "I had to make a pit stop."

"Pit stop?"

"Lingerie." She giggled.

"What?" I kept a straight face, but my face was burning. "You too?"

"Yeah, you gave me the idea," she said. "It's going to be game-on this weekend. I'm going to be on Cody like a tornado hitting the Midwest."

"Sally," I groaned, but I couldn't stop myself from laughing. TJ was looking at me with a weird look and I couldn't stop the sly smile from crossing my face. He had absolutely no idea what was going to happen this weekend. I stared into his eyes and wondered what his face would look like when I sauntered into his room in my silky negligee and asked him what he thought of the look. He'd be drooling. I could almost picture the saliva falling from his mouth, like a dog that had seen a big, juicy bone.

"You okay, Mila?" TJ frowned at me.

"Yeah, why?" I blinked at him, feeling like an idiot. I'd totally spaced out.

"Why?" He raised an eyebrow. "You're standing there with a dumb look on your face and I still haven't heard when Sally will be here."

"TJ's in a good mood, isn't he?" Sally said in my ear and laughed.

"Yeah, you know him," I said in a snide tone. "Life of the party."

"Well, we both know that you can change that."

"True." I giggled. "Oh, by the way," I said softly, looking at TJ as I spoke, "Troy said he might be able to make it up there this weekend."

"Who?" Sally said loudly and I quickly lowered the volume of the speaker from the buttons at the side.

"He's just getting his Mercedes-Benz out of the garage."

"Who's getting their Mercedes out of the garage?" Sally sounded confused. "And who the hell is Troy?"

"Yes, they said it was an engine issue. Apparently, he was driving too fast when he went racing the other day," I continued on, with a small smile on my face. TJ was staring at me with a concentrated expression and I just stood there talking like some fool.

"Earth to Mila," Sally said, "I don't know what the hell you're talking about."

"I told Troy that he can sleep in my bed tonight," I said and giggled. "I told him to make sure that he—"

"Oh, is Troy your fake boyfriend?" Sally said, laughing.

"Why yes, I think that is true," I said, trying not to give anything away to TJ.

"You're trying to make TJ jealous? Am I right?" Sally said, acting like Sherlock Holmes. Sally was a district manager for a local cable company and was applying to get her MBA, so she liked to act like she was super intelligent, which she was.

"Yeah, I think that is right," I said and pressed the phone closer to my ear to make sure that TJ really didn't hear anything.

"You're so bad, Mila." She giggled. "Only you would think of a

Troy."

"Yeah, so I think it could get serious with Troy and me," I said with a smile and I saw TJ's eyes narrowing. "I think he is going to ask me to move in with him this weekend."

"No way." Sally screeched and I laughed. She was really playing her role well. "Oh wait," she said sheepishly. "I forgot Troy was made up for a second. I thought you really were going to be moving in with your boyfriend."

"Sally." I tried not to roll my eyes. "So, we'll see you soon?"

"I'll be there in about ten minutes," she said. "See you then."

"See ya," I said and then hung up. "She'll be here in ten minutes," I said to TJ and he just nodded. I watched as he pulled his phone out and made a call.

"Hey, sweet lips," he purred into the phone and this time I did roll my eyes. "My best friend's sister is waiting on her best friend, so we're running a little late. Yeah, Cody's sister." He turned around and looked at me as he listened to whatever Barbie was saying. "She's not dressed up, so don't worry about it." He looked me up and down and I felt my body shivering, as his eyes stayed on my breasts for a little bit longer than was necessary. "No, Barbie. We've never hooked up." He spoke into the phone, but his eyes gazed into mine. "She's my best friend's kid sister and she still acts like she's a teenager. You have nothing to worry about."

I glared at him as he spoke and then pushed past him and headed towards the bathroom, my face a bright red. Kid sister, my ass. And how dare he say I act like a teenager? Who the hell did he think he was? Father Brown or something? I was furious as I slammed the bathroom door and splashed my face with some water. I took a couple of deep breaths and finally calmed myself down. I wasn't sure if I was so angry because he was essentially calling me immature, or if I was angry because he made it seem as if he would never be physically interested in someone like me. Like I was some sort of slob or something. I'd show him—and Barbie—that I, Mila Antonia Brookstone, was not someone to be taken lightly.

Four

MILA

SEPTEMBER 18, 2008

DEAR DIARY,

My life ended today. Officially ended. Like, I cried so many tears that I thought I was going to cause a flood in my room. I was going to be solely responsible for the end of the Earth. Noah wasn't going to be able to build an ark to survive the flood I was going to cause. Why did my life end, you ask? Why? Why? Why? I found out that TJ Walker has a girlfriend. And that, as he said to Cody, she has the 'biggest tits' he's ever seen on a girl. And he knows they are real. Can you believe that? I was shocked. He's there at college playing with girls' boobs and I'm here, basically telling Harry I can't go to Homecoming with him because I'm saving myself for my true love. And my true love isn't even thinking about me. I also hate Cody, too. He was encouraging TJ. He even asked TJ if she was a good fuck. I nearly went and told my mom, but then Cody would know I'd been listening at his door and then maybe he and TJ wouldn't come over so often. Anyway, that's my life now. TJ is going to marry some girl with big boobs and I'm going to be alone for the rest of my life. As long as it lasts, anyway. I swear my tears will be the end for everybody.

Mila

XOXO

P.S. I'm thinking about getting breast implants, but only if TJ doesn't marry his college slut of a girlfriend.

FRIDAY, ONE WEEK AGO

"I'm sorry I was late," Sally said from the back seat as soon as TJ got out of the car to go and get Barbie. "Why did he have such an attitude?" she asked softly, her dark brown eyes curious.

"You know TJ." I rolled my eyes as I looked back at her. "He's as melodramatic as a girl."

"Hey, I take offense to that," Sally said and laughed. She leaned back in the seat and stretched before continuing. "You are not going to believe the outfit I got. It is hot, hot, hot."

"Well, I hope it's not the same outfit that I got." I grinned. "That would be weird."

"I can't believe that you're going to seduce him. With his girlfriend still in the picture," Sally said, her jaw slack as her eyes sparkled. "This is going to be a crazy weekend." She paused and grinned at me. "Notice anything different?"

"Different?" I said, unsure what she was talking about, and then I noticed her long, silky black hair, hanging straight down her back. "Oh, my God, your hair! What did you do to it?"

"I got a keratin treatment." She beamed. "That's why I was really late; don't tell TJ. I mean if he knew I was getting my hair done and shopping, he'd have a fit." She laughed. "Doesn't my hair feel silky?" She leaned forward and I ran my fingers down her locks.

"Wow, yeah," I said, impressed. "You didn't want to be curly this weekend?" Sally had gorgeous curly hair and I was always jealous that I couldn't get my straight hair to have any sort of wave or curl.

"Well, I might go curly if we go skinny-dipping in the lake. Me and Cody." She giggled. "Not you and me."

"Duh." I rolled my eyes and shuddered. "And that's gross, by the way."

"It's totally not gross." She grinned. "I told my parents that we were going to the lake this weekend and my mom just winked at me."

"Oh, funny," I said.

"And let's be real, Cody and I would have such cute kids."

"Sally!" I raised an eyebrow at her. "You're meant to be the reasonable one.

"I am." She giggled. "Well, most of the time." She leaned back and I stared at her caramel complexion affectionately.

"You look like you're glowing," I said. "Makeup, or have you been in the sun?"

"Oh, it's some glow stick I got at Sephora." Her eyes sparkled at me. "I wanted to make sure I looked my best." Her eyes narrowed as she looked me up and down. "I guess you had a change of mind."

"No." I laughed. "A change of plan, but not a change of mind."

"Oh, we're so bad." Sally laughed, her eyes sparkling as she looked at me.

"Would we have it any other way?" I laughed and then she leaned forward.

"No." She laughed again. "I blame it on the Italian blood in both of us."

"Yeah, I would agree." I grinned. "It's the crazy Italiano."

"Yup." She grinned. Sally's father was second-generation Italian and her mother was from Guyana, a country situated on the continent of South America, just south of the Caribbean. She'd gotten the best qualities from both parents and was gorgeous. Men used words like 'exotic' to describe her, but she hated that term. As far as she was concerned, her looks weren't as important as her brains. Though I don't think any of the guys she dated cared about her brains.

"By the way, the Troy idea was epic," Sally said in a low voice and leaned even closer to me and whispered. "It sounded like TJ was pissed."

"Oh, he was so pissed." I grinned. "I just wish that Troy was real."

"About that..." Sally looked sheepish. "I have something to tell you."

"What?" I asked her suspiciously.

"I did something that will make everyone believe that Troy is real." She grinned and my eyes narrowed.

"What did you do?" I asked, but then I hushed her as I saw TJ and Barbie approaching the car. Troy disappeared from my mind and my stomach dropped as I gazed at her. She was beautiful, almost like some picture-perfect image of a Cinderella princess. Why did she have to be so good looking? I was starting to doubt that I could convince TJ to go with me when he had someone like her. Grr, why did he have someone like her?

"Hi," I said with a wide—albeit fake, but still wide—smile to the buxom blonde as she got into the back seat.

"Hi," she said, her face looking sour.

"I'm Mila."

"Like Mila Kunis?" She looked up at me in interest.

"Well, I guess, but I'm just Mila."

"Not Mila Kunis?" Barbie asked me and I shot TJ a look of surprise. Okay, maybe it was more a cross between, 'who is this dumbass?' and 'I'm really trying to be nice here.'

"No, just Mila," I said. "What's your name?"

"Barbie," she said and I watched as she flicked her long blond hair.

"As in Barbie and Ken?" I asked her softly, but she just looked back at me with a dumb expression.

"Hi, I'm Sally, Mila's best friend," Sally spoke up next, her voice seemingly really happy to be meeting peroxide Barbie.

"Mila Kunis' best friend?" Barbie asked her, looking excited, and Sally looked at me with laughing eyes as she shook her head.

"I'm afraid not. I don't know Mila Kunis or any Hollywood stars, to be honest."

"Oh, you just said you're Mila's best friend." Barbie looked confused.

"She's talking about me," I said, a slight attitude in my voice.

"The Mila you just met."

"Oh." Barbie looked at me with a bored expression. "I see."

"I'm not sure you do," I said under my breath as I watched TJ get back into the car, his expression not giving his thoughts away.

"Everyone okay?" he asked with a smile as he looked around, and I looked away from him. I had nothing to say. I didn't want to seem like I had sour grapes, but I had no idea what he saw in Barbie.

"Ken, honey, I thought I was going to be sitting in the front seat with you?" Barbie said in a soft, sweet voice. I turned around to face the window so that no one could see the look on my face. Barbie and Ken, my ass. I bit my lower lip to stop from laughing and then TJ spoke up and I turned around.

"Aww, sorry, babe," he said in a tone I'd never heard before. My jaw almost dropped as I listened to him and then saw Barbie's face looking all soft and sweet. I was feeling confused as I looked at her almost angelic face. What had happened to the sour-faced shrew that had been talking to Sally and me? Barbie was looking like a different person as she batted her big blue eyes at TJ. I bit on my lower lip as I stared at her, all beautiful and flowery, and waited for TJ to ask me to switch seats with his latest paramour.

"But, babe?" She pouted, sucking on her lower lip as she gazed at TJ.

"Aww, next time," TJ said and gave me a quick wink. "Mila isn't the sort of girl who likes to give up the front seat."

"Yeah, I'm not." I looked at Barbie with a small smile and shrug. "I'm sure Mila Kunis doesn't like to give up her seat either, if that helps." I saw Barbie's lips twisting at my words and I turned back around and turned on the radio. "Let's go, James," I said to TJ. "We don't want to be late!"

THE DRIVE UP TO the lake house was pretty quiet. Normally, Sally and I chattered on about what we were going to do, but we were both pretty focused on our own thoughts.

"So, when will Cody arrive?" Sally asked as we pulled off of the exit. We were about ten minutes away from the cabin and I knew everyone was ready for us to arrive.

"He said tomorrow morning. He'll join us for breakfast," TJ answered as he drummed his fingers against the steering wheel. "When will Troy be arriving, Mila?" He looked at me casually and I just smiled sweetly. That jackass knew that there was no Troy arriving.

"He's going to call me tonight and let me know," I answered.

"Who's Troy?" Barbie said, speaking for the first time since we'd left. She'd spent most of the trip playing with her hair and looking at herself in her compact mirror.

"Troy is Mila's boyfriend," Sally spoke up. "And I think he'll be her fiancé soon."

I wanted to groan out loud at Sally's words. I knew she thought she was helping me, but I knew that what she was actually doing was digging me into an even deeper hole.

"You have a boyfriend?" Barbie said, sounding surprised as she looked at me up and down. I knew I didn't look my best, but there was no need for her to be so rude.

"Yes," I said stiffly and looked at TJ, who had a weird smirk on his face. "What's so funny?"

"Nothing," he said and then I felt his hand on my knee for a brief second. "Absolutely nothing."

"Hmm," I said, but didn't get into it further with him.

"So how's business, Richie Rich?" Sally asked TJ, changing the subject.

"As good as it can be in this economy," TJ said, his demeanor changing. "I want to introduce some changes to the company, bring our customer service back to the United States, increase the number of plants we have, change the automation system, and bring in a new marketing company, but Dad is resistant."

"Oh, sad," I said, and Sally also made an 'I'm sorry' noise. I was sure that she, like me, wasn't really sure what he was talking about. "Why won't your dad make the changes?" I said and gazed at him curiously.

"He's a cheapskate." He sighed. "He'd rather save the dollars now. I'm telling him that we need to spend more to make more. That's how business goes. And especially now, we need to expand."

"Yeah, my dad won't listen to me either. I'm trying to convince him to import this new line of rugs from Morocco," I said with a sigh. "What's the point of me working in the buying department if I'm not actually allowed to make any large purchase decisions?"

"I forgot you got moved from being a receptionist," TJ said. "How's the change in department going?"

"Didn't you hear what I just said?" I frowned. "Not great. I still have no real responsibility or real money coming in."

"You just graduated, Mila. Be patient," TJ said with an indulgent smile. "It'll happen. I didn't get to where I am overnight."

"What is it that you do, again?" Barbie asked curiously, and I smiled. If she didn't know what he did, they couldn't be that serious.

"TJ works for Walker Enterprises," I answered for him and turned around to look at Barbie.

"Okay?" Barbie shrugged. The name Walker Enterprises meant nothing to her.

"His dad is Hudson Walker," Sally said. "The Hudson Walker."

"Hudson Walker?" Barbie said and then her eyes lit up. "Hudson Walker, the famous billionaire who dates all those actresses and models?"

"Yes," I said with a smile. "The very same one. He might even have dated Mila Kunis."

"Mila." TJ gave me a look that indicated how annoyed he was, but I didn't care. Let him deal with gold-digging Barbie. She would try to get her clutches into him even deeper now that she knew how well-connected he was.

"Yes, TJ?" I said softly and then squealed as we pulled off Old Harris Road and drove through the woods towards the lake. "Ooh, we're nearly there." I lowered my car window and stuck my head outside and closed my eyes as the cool breeze caressed my face. I took a deep breath and breathed in the air. "Can you guys feel and taste the nature right now?" I sighed in contentment.

"I can't taste anything," Barbie said. I didn't respond.

"You really love the lake house, don't you?" TJ said softly as he pulled off and stopped in front of my family cabin. I turned to look at him and I could see an affectionate look on his face. It was a rare sight; normally, TJ and I spent so much time sparring that we didn't really express any other sort of positive emotion towards each other. I smiled at him, happy in my environment and at my plans for the weekend.

"I do, I feel like it's this magical place. My own private Narnia." I grinned at him and then hopped out of the car. I ran up to the front door and lifted up the big red plant pot and grabbed the front-door key. I opened the door and ran inside, happy to be here, finally. I really did love the lake house. It was the only place that made me feel like I was one with the earth. It was also the only place where TJ and I had once had a moment that had made me feel like maybe, just maybe, there could be something between us. It had only happened once and it had happened so fast that I wasn't sure if I'd imagined it, but the fact that it was even a possibility in my mind was enough, for now.

"Hey, you going to get your own bags or do you expect me to be your man-slave?" TJ shouted into the house as he walked in and looked around the large living room with the massive wood-burning fireplace right in the center.

"I expect you to be my man-slave," I said and walked up to him, my eyes laughing at him. "Just because you're the son of a billionaire doesn't exempt you from your duties."

"Hmm, my duties?" He cocked his head to the side. "What do I get from you in return for fulfilling my duties?"

"You'll see," I said softly and stared into his eyes. "Maybe something wonderful."

"Wonderful?" he said with a small smile and we gazed at each other for a few moments, saying nothing. I moved closer to him and was about to lean in for a kiss when he frowned. "There's nothing you can give me that is good enough for me to become your man-servant."

"Whatever," I said, my heart dropping as I stepped back and walked out of the front door, thanking God I hadn't embarrassed myself by going for a kiss. "I'll get my own bags, lazy-ass."

"I'm not lazy." He grabbed my arm as I walked out and pulled me back to him. His fingers gripped my wrist and I looked at him with an angry, hurt expression. He stared at me for a few seconds and then let go. I turned back around and walked to the Range Rover, my heart thudding. What had just happened there? That had been an awkward moment and I didn't know what it meant.

"Is this where we're staying?" Barbie looked at me with another surly look. I swear I wished the wind would hit her as she was pulling one of those expressions so that her face would stay that way.

"What do you think?" I snapped and looked at Sally, who was trying not to laugh. "We just parked in front of the cabin. I went and got the key and opened the front door. Did you think I was doing it for shits and giggles?"

"I was just asking a question," she said, looking irritated.

"Uh huh, dumbass," I said quietly, but obviously my voice wasn't low enough because she gave me a deadly look.

"Let's grab our bags and choose our rooms," Sally said quickly as she grabbed her small duffel bag. "And maybe you can call Cody, Mila, see what time he plans to arrive."

"Yeah," I said and grabbed my small suitcase. "I'll do that." I walked towards the front door, feeling irritated, annoyed and out of sorts. Maybe this weekend wasn't going to go as well as I'd hoped. I wish I'd known that peroxide Barbie was going to be joining us. I couldn't imagine what TJ saw in her. She had no redeeming qualities, but then maybe the only quality she needed was to lie on her back and keep her mouth shut. A dart of jealousy spread through me as I thought about TJ and Barbie having sex. I tried to shake the thought from my mind, as it made me want to throw up and die at the same time. I didn't want to think about TJ with anyone else. I knew he wasn't a virgin, I knew he wasn't saving himself for me, and I was okay with that. But just the thought of him being with someone like her killed me. Especially after having wanted him for so many years and saving myself for him.

"Wow," Sally said, interrupting my thoughts as we watched TJ bringing in Barbie's suitcase. I could feel my face going red with anger and even more hate and jealousy as I watched them talking and laughing together. "Let's go grab our room."

"Yeah," I said and we walked along the corridor. "I don't know what he sees in her. She has no redeeming qualities."

"Who is she, anyway?" Sally said. "Talk about a bimbo. I didn't think she was his type."

"I don't know." I sighed as we walked into the bedroom and I closed the door behind us and locked it. I fell down onto the bed and groaned. "Do you think I should even go ahead with my plan this weekend? It seems like it would be a waste of time. I don't even know when I'm supposed to try and seduce him if she's here."

"Girl, you have to go ahead with it," Sally said and dropped down on the bed next to me. "Do you think Cody is going to bring someone as well?"

"I don't know." I sighed and turned to face her. "Are we the biggest idiots in the world?"

"Maybe." She grinned, her smile a little sad. "We've been crushing on these guys forever and, well, I just don't know that either of them have even noticed us."

"I know." I chewed on my lower lip. "I feel like, in their eyes, we're always going to be the immature little girls that they remember from high school."

"Yeah," Sally said. "But at least you have a plan. Oh yeah, I wanted to tell you what I did with Troy."

"What do you mean what you did?"

"Well, I—"

BANG BANG.

"Girls, you in there?" TJ interrupted us as he banged on the door.

"Yes," I said and Sally and I just lay on the bed and waited for what he was going to say next.

"I'm hoping you can tell me what room I should give Barbie."

"Isn't she sleeping in your room?" I said cattily.

"No," he said simply and I sat up, my eyes bright.

"No?" I shouted back, grinning down at Sally.

"That's what I said. Mila, can you please come and open the door?" TJ said, his voice annoyed.

"Coming." I jumped off of the bed and ran my hands through my hair, trying to make it a little bit more presentable. I looked at Sally and grinned as I walked towards the door. "How can I help you, TJ?" I asked softly as I opened the door and looked at him with a blank expression.

"Take me to my bed," he said softly with a small smirk on his face.

"What?" My heart started beating fast as I gazed into his devilish green eyes. Was he finally coming on to me? Without me having to wear my sexy suspender get-up? "You want me to what?" I said again, nervously licking my lips. Yes, I wasn't in my right mind. If I were thinking straight, I wouldn't have actually thought TJ was asking me to take him to his bed and ride him like the cowgirl I knew I could be.

"Take me," he leaned forward and said it even softer. His lips were a mere inch from mine and I could see the brown speckles in his green eyes as they danced in glee.

"Now?" I gulped.

"Yes, please," he said and I swallowed hard. "I'm ready to go now."

"Ready to go now?" I said and I jumped as I felt his finger on my cheek, lightly running towards my lips. Oh, my God, I swear I nearly came at his touch.

"Yes, please, Mila." He grinned and stepped back. "I'd like to know where I'm sleeping tonight and so would Barbie."

"Oh?" I said, feeling like a fool as I realized what he was saying. "But you know where to sleep." And then I frowned. "And why aren't you sharing a bed with Barbie?"

"I don't want to be presumptuous," he said as he stepped back, his eyes searching mine. "I'm not sure your parents would appreciate Barbie and me sharing a bed."

"Yeah, most probably not," I said, though I wasn't sure they would care. It was only me they seemed to worry about being proper.

"Okay, that's good," he said softly, bending down to whisper into my ear, "I wouldn't want to keep anyone up too late."

"Huh?" I said, my face burning. "What do you mean?"

"I mean the sounds of the mattress squeaking and the screams of passion and lust."

"I don't need to know about what you and Barbie will be doing," I said with a frown and moved away from him.

"Who said I was talking about Barbie?" he said quietly and I gulped as I felt his hand on my lower back. "I could be talking about any one of us, right?" he continued.

"Uh huh," I said and walked ahead of him, swinging my hips from side to side and hoping I looked sexy. I was going to show TJ Walker that he wasn't the only one who could be a tease. Before this weekend was done, he was going to be begging me to take him in more ways than one.

Five

TJ

FRIDAY, ONE WEEK AGO

I FOLLOWED MILA DOWN the corridor, but my mind was on her lips and her swinging hips. I was letting her get to me and I knew that I had to ignore her innocent flirting. She had no idea what she was doing by flirting with me. She had no idea that she was playing with fire. And that I had promised her brother that I wouldn't let her do that. He knew as well as I did that I would burn her if we were to ever get involved. Not that that stopped the bulge in my pants from hardening. Fuck, she was sexy. I wasn't sure at what point she'd become a woman, but even with her loose jeans and baggy T-shirt, I could see her voluptuous figure. She had perfect-sized breasts, a nice little ass, and long legs that could drive a man wild. And the way she kept flinging her long hair around was driving me crazy. All I could think about was the feel of her hair across my chest and face as she rode me. She needed to stop with her lip-biting and little moans. When she'd fallen on her bed and started going on about her 'boyfriend,' I'd wanted to fall onto the bed next to her and show her how loudly a real man could make her moan. But of course, I'd resisted. I couldn't do that, not to her—but man, did she even know what she'd done to me as she'd rolled around on the bed, messing her sheets up?

"I was thinking that this room would be good for you." Mila's voice interrupted my thoughts. "This is the room you and Cody normally share."

"It has two twin beds," I said, my eyes never leaving her face.

"You want a double bed?" she said, her face tensing as she gazed back at me.

"That would be nice." I nodded, enjoying seeing the rise of a blush in her face. I wondered how red her face would go if I told her the things I wanted to do with her.

"For you and Barbie?" she asked me softly, her tone slightly off.

"Yeah," I said, my mind already gone from Barbie. Mila was right, of course, there was nothing about Barbie that was special. She'd been good the night that I'd met her and she'd given me head without asking for much. We hadn't even fucked and I didn't even care. I wasn't even sure why I'd brought her. Well, that was a lie. I'd brought her because I'd been scared that I wouldn't be able to keep my hands off of Mila if Barbie weren't here. And as much as I wanted to bend her over and hear her crying out my name, I knew that Cody would cut my balls off if I messed with his sister. And not just because he didn't think I was good enough for her. He knew things that Mila didn't. He knew things I was into. Things I was capable of. I understood why he didn't want me with Mila. I even agreed with him. But as she gazed at me with her pouty lips, I wasn't sure I was going to be able to stop what seemed to be the natural course of events between us.

"Hey, TJ, can I talk to you?" Barbie walked into the room, a frown on her face as she gazed at us.

"Yeah, sure," I said and gave her a smile. "Come on in."

"I want to talk to you without Miley."

"It's Mila," Mila said as she rolled her eyes. "I'll be in my room." She gave me a pointed look. "Come and get me if you need me."

"For anything?" I said softly, winking at her as she walked out.

"What do you mean?" she asked suspiciously.

"I was wondering if I could come and get you for anything, as you said 'come and get me if you need me.' "

"Within reason, obviously," she said and played with her blond tresses again.

"Oh, it will be reasonable," I said with a grin. "See you later, Mila."

"Uh huh," she said as she hurried out of the room.

"You're totally playing me, huh?" Barbie said as she closed the door.

"What are you talking about?" I asked her with a weak smile, trying not to show her my impatience. As I looked at her face, I wasn't sure what I'd seen in her the night I'd picked her up.

"Does Mila know what you're up to?" Barbie said as she raised an eyebrow at me.

"What are you talking about?" I asked with a frown, feeling annoyed.

"Does she know why I'm really here?"

"You're not here to make her jealous, if that's what you're thinking."

"I'm not here to fuck you, though, either. Am I?" Her eyes narrowed as she looked down at the bulge in my pants.

"I don't know what you're talking about, Barbie," I said, my brain starting to work in overload. What exactly did Barbie know?

"Yes, you do." She grinned. "You know exactly what I'm talking about. I wonder what Mila would think if she knew. And Cody?" She tilted her head back. "What would they all think if they knew exactly what TJ Walker had up his sleeve?"

"What are you talking about?" I said, but my heart sank, as I knew that this had been a setup. Even the meeting at the bar must have been planned.

"We both know what I'm talking about." She grinned. "So, you going to make the move on Mila, or what?"

"I don't know what you're talking about," I said again as I glared at her.

"She'll be like putty in your hands." She laughed. "And the poor girl has no clue. She's going to think it's all her, when you've had it all planned out."

"I don't know what you're insinuating." I grabbed her wrists and snarled.

"Sure you don't." She licked her lips, like a cat that had just gotten the cream. "You'd better make sure that things don't get complicated for you."

"They won't," I said and pursed my lips. "I'll make sure of that." But as I stood there and thought about what I had planned, I wasn't so sure. Mila was going to complicate things. A lot. And not just because I wanted her in my bed. Not even because I wanted her to be my fake fiancée. No, I had to step very carefully now. I had to make sure that everything went smoothly. And step one of my plan was already in motion.

Six

MILA

JUNE 13, 2009

DEAR DIARY,

Something really weird happened today. TJ asked me what I thought love meant. Like seriously. For a few seconds I thought he was trying to tell me he loved me, but I don't think he was. I think he was trying to talk to me on a deeper level, like I was an adult or something. I said that love is loving someone so much that you think of them before yourself. He then asked if I thought that was truly possible. I said of course. Then he just nodded and said I'd grow up one day. I have no idea what he meant by that. But I think he was saying he doesn't believe in love. That makes me sad. For me and him. I think that's a sign that I'm growing up. Scary, but true. That doesn't mean I wouldn't screw his brains out if I had the chance. Hahaha, I got that term from a book Sally's been reading. I don't really know where it came from. How can you screw someone's brains out? I'm not sure, but maybe one day TJ will teach me. And maybe I can teach him how to fall in love. One can wish!

Mila

XOXO

PRESENT DAY

"So, fun fact, Barbie just barged into the bedroom with TJ and me and demanded to talk to him," I said quietly as I walked back into my bedroom. Sally sat up with a curious expression and a glint in her eye.

"So, what did she want to talk to him about?" she asked eagerly.

"Well, I can't read minds, and she asked me to leave before she started talking, so I have no idea." I shrugged as I sat on the bed next to her. My mind was spinning and all I could think about was TJ asking me if he could come and get me for anything. What did that mean? What was anything? Was he insinuating sex or was he talking about something stupid liking doing his laundry? I could still remember the time he'd come home with Cody and offered to pay me $10 to wash and iron his clothes. The sad part was that I'd accepted his offer gladly. I'd held his shirt to my face like it was some sort of trophy and then I'd sniffed under the armpits and nearly gagged. Maybe that wasn't the smartest idea I'd ever had. TJ may have been the college boy of my dreams, but I wasn't sure he'd known much about deodorant in those days.

"You should have listened outside of the door, duh." Sally said. "Haven't you learned anything from working in corporate America?"

"Um, I was a receptionist and now I'm basically an assistant." I shook my head at her. "I wasn't exactly in the boardroom discussing merger and takeover plans."

"You guys are merging?" Sally asked in a surprised tone.

"I don't really know what's going on. I don't think we're merging with anyone." I bit my lower lip, my head thudding. "I don't know that business is going great. You know how this economy is. I know Dad and Cody have been worried. That's most probably why Cody is working late tonight. I think they were going to go over the books. I mean, don't get me wrong, I'm sure things are fine, but I'm not exactly in the know."

"Oh no, Nonno must be so upset." Sally looked sad.

"Yeah." I bit my lower lip and sighed. "I'm not sure he really knows what's going on." I leaned back on the bed. "That's why I feel guilty about asking for an advance. I'm sure Cody will have something to say about it."

"Yeah," Sally said. "I'll lend you whatever you need. Just pay me back next month."

"You don't have to do that." I shook my head, feeling guilty. I didn't want to borrow from Sally. Nonno had always told me to never lend and never borrow from a friend. And his advice was usually spot on.

"I know that, but I want to," Sally said with a smile. "That's what friends are for."

"You're too kind." I laughed and then moved over on the bed closer to her. 'Do you think I'm making a mistake going after TJ?" I said softly. "Am I a horrible person going after a guy who is kinda seeing someone?"

"Not when that someone is Barbie." Sally shook her head. "And not when the someone you're after is TJ Walker. You've wanted him for years. I don't see anything wrong in you going after him."

"Isn't that going against the girl code?" I made a face. I didn't think I owed Barbie anything, but also didn't want to be one of those shady girls who goes after what she wants without even thinking about the other person.

"Maybe." She shrugged. "Though, it's not like Barbie is honoring any girl code. She's horrible. I don't know what any guy see's in Barbie. She's a bimbo."

"That's what they see and like." I sighed. "Big boobs and pouty lips."

"Ugh, I don't even want to think about her." Sally made a face. "Let's go into the living room. Maybe we can figure out dinner; I'm hungry."

"Yeah, I could eat something as well." I nodded and we headed out into the living room. "I was thinking maybe ribs or something."

"Ribs would be divine." She nodded eagerly. "Ooh and some pulled pork."

"And smoked sausage," I said, my stomach growling. "And banana pudding for dessert."

"Oh, man, remember that banana pudding we got from Magnolia Bakery when we went to New York? It was so good." Sally licked her lips.

"Um, how could I forget?" I said, my mind going back to the drizzly day that had changed my life—well, not really my life. It had changed the way I felt about banana pudding. It had gone from an okay dessert to a 'where have you been all my life' dessert. "That's why I said I want it tonight," I said and I went quiet as I heard footsteps heading towards us.

"I could kiss you all night long." TJ and Barbie walked into the living room with their arms around each other. All happy thoughts of banana pudding fled my mind. I tried not to gag as I saw Barbie's hands in his hair, pulling at the ends of his dark silky tresses. "I could kiss you and touch your hair all night." Barbie almost purred as they stepped next to the fireplace and stood there.

"Yeah, yeah, we heard you the first time," Sally said, giving them a disgusted look.

"Well, don't you have good hearing?" Barbie said as she turned around. She gave me a pitying look and then turned back to TJ. "I'm hungry. Let's go and eat."

"Sure." He nodded, the smile on his lips not quite reaching his eyes. In fact, his eyes looked like he was slightly turned off. I tried to make eye contact with him, but when he finally looked into my eyes, he looked like he was having the time of his life.

"You girls hungry as well?" TJ grinned as he looked at us.

"Is that even a question?" Sally looked at me and laughed.

"Yeah, TJ, was that a real question?" I smiled at him, though I was feeling anything but happy as I watched Barbie running her hands down his back. "Of course we want to eat."

"So I guess this means the romantic dinner you promised me is off." Barbie's voice sounded annoyed and she pouted. "You'll have to make it up to me tonight."

"Of course, baby," he said, his eyes never leaving mine as he grabbed Barbie around the waist and kissed the side of her face. "I'll make it up to you all night long."

"You're a pig." Sally said what I was thinking.

"Well, do you want this pig to feed you or not?" he asked with a raised eyebrow.

"Let's go," I said, wishing I hadn't spent so much money on the lingerie. What had been the point? I wasn't going to have an opportunity to try and seduce him. It wasn't as if I were going to slip into his room, knowing he and Barbie were going to be getting it on. It made me sick just thinking about it.

◆

SALLY AND I SAT in the back of the car on the way to the restaurant. We sat in silence, like two petulant kids whose parents had told them off for something. I stared at the back of TJ's ear, and all I could think about was how much he annoyed me. It was really quite astonishing that I could love him as much as I did, knowing I couldn't stand him so much at the same time. It was how I knew I was really in love with him. No mere crush would have kept my attention for so long. Not for someone like TJ, someone who frustrated me so much that sometimes I just wanted to bang my head against a wall.

"So your dad is Hudson Walker?" Barbie said as her fingers ran up and down TJ's thighs. I wanted to reach forward and slap her hand away from his leg. My heartbeat seemed to be in sync with her fingers because as her fingers got closer to his crotch, my heartbeat increased, and as they slid away, my heartbeat got slower.

"Yes," TJ said, his tone making it clear that he didn't want to talk about his father any further.

"He's really handsome," Barbie said, her voice light and giggly.

"And rich."

"No shit," Sally said from next to me, her tone irritated. Sally really didn't give a shit what Barbie thought about her.

"So, you work for him?" Barbie continued, ignoring Sally.

"Yes," TJ said and the tenseness of his yes spoke volumes. TJ was an atypical son for a handsome, famous, billionaire. While he was handsome and popular, he'd never used his father's name to get ahead. In fact, all he'd ever wanted to do was make his father proud. Ever since I'd known him, he'd been an overachiever—and not because his parents pushed him, either—but because he wanted to prove to his father that he was just as brilliant and capable as him. Yet, his father had never really given him the validation that he needed. I didn't think it was fair. I hated his father. Not because he was mean or rude and not because he didn't love TJ. He loved TJ like a father should love a son, but he never gave him anything extra. He never went above and beyond. He always said the perfunctory congratulations, but he never seemed super proud or overeager. He just assumed that TJ would be intelligent and sporty because he was. And that was the crux of my issue with him. He always compared TJ to himself. IF TJ got an A, he would have gotten an A+. If TJ was second seed on the tennis team, he was first seed. If TJ won a leading role in a school play, he was lead. And it wasn't even as if he were bragging to out-do TJ, that was just his way. TJ's dad had taken his father's business and made it into a multi-billion dollar industry. Hudson Walker was world famous, for his business acumen and for dating the hottest supermodels and actresses in the world. It was his way: he worked hard and played even harder. And somehow TJ had gotten left by the wayside.

"What do you do?" Barbie continued and the air in the car grew tense.

"Let's talk about something else," I said to change the subject. I felt bad for TJ and, while I thought he was a jerk, I didn't want him to have to go into the nitty gritty of his job to someone like her, someone I hoped wouldn't last past the weekend. I didn't like Barbie and it wasn't just because I was jealous. She seemed like the worst kind of gold-digger, and I really hoped that TJ wasn't going to get sucked in by her good looks. I didn't understand why guys could never figure out which girls were the parasitic vultures in the dating world. Did they really not see all the signs or did they just ignore them because the girls were hot?

"Whatever," Barbie said, clearly annoyed that I'd cut her off.

"Whatever," Sally mouthed at me and rolled her eyes and I had to bite my lip to stop from laughing. "So, I sure am hungry," Sally continued and rubbed her stomach. "I wish Troy were here because I know he'd take us all to a nice steak restaurant and pay."

"Sally." I gave her a look and she just grinned back at me. "Troy isn't your sugar daddy."

"But he could be yours."

"You have a sugar daddy?" Barbie turned around and her look was so scornful and shocked that I couldn't stop myself from responding.

"Well, he wants me any way he can have me," I said sweetly. "And as I'm not cheap, he knows he has to work hard."

"Mila's a difficult one to catch," TJ said in an amused tone, and I blushed.

"Not that many have been trying to catch me," I said and immediately regretted my words. I meant to be making myself look more desirable than I was. Not worse.

"You mean this week?" Sally said and giggled. "What about Louis and Damon?"

"What?" I asked, confused. However, my voice was drowned out by TJ.

"Who are Louis and Damon?" he said, his tone slightly annoyed as he glanced at me in the rear-view mirror.

"Mila hasn't told you about Louis and Damon?" Sally said and winked at me.

"And I'm not about to start," I said, cutting her off. I didn't need Sally getting me into any more trouble. Louis and Damon, ugh.

"You can't help it if men just fall in love with you," Sally said. "You're beautiful and smart. Men like that combination. No guy wants a bimbo." She grinned. "Big boobs and no brains is not attractive."

"I guess no boobs and no brains is even worse though," Barbie interrupted and looked back at Sally with narrowed eyes. "I'd hate to be ugly."

"Well, you certainly don't have to worry about that," TJ said and I watched as he squeezed her knee. My body froze as I sat there watching her squeezing his hand. This was the worst kind of torture and I wished that I were anywhere but in this car.

"Just on the inside," Sally said under her breath and caught my eye. I smiled weakly at her joke, but it was hard to rejoice in her humor when Barbie was enjoying TJ's attention in the front of the car, while I sat in the back feeling like a loser.

"I'M STUFFED." SALLY LEANED back into the car seat as we made our way home from dinner. "I literally couldn't eat another thing."

"Not even another bite of that cheesecake?" I laughed as I stifled a yawn.

"Not even another bite." She groaned and then laughed. "Well, maybe another bite, since it would be a shame to waste cheesecake."

"You girls are brave," Barbie said in her teeny-weeny voice.

"Brave?" I asked loudly, the wine from dinner making me lose any inhibitions to talk to her.

"You know that saying, a second on the lips, a year on the hips," she said poignantly as she looked me up and down. "But I suppose you don't care."

"Excuse me?" I said, my voice rising as TJ got into the car.

"Excuse you what, Mila?" he said as he looked at me. I ignored his gaze and shook my head. I was pissed at TJ. He'd basically ignored me all through dinner so that he could whisper sweet nothing's to Barbie. He was so rude.

"I just tell the truth as I see it," Barbie said and turned back to the front with a confident smile.

"What truth?" TJ asked, confused.

"Barbie's just talking about my hips," I said in a huff, still feeling pissed, especially as my jeans were feeling tight after the meal.

"Oh?" he said and looked back at me, his eyes glittering. "What about your hips?"

"That the cheesecake went straight to my hips," I said, feeling embarrassed.

"Well, then you need to eat more cheesecake." TJ winked at me. "Personally, I like a woman with hips—more to hold on to when I'm working my magic."

"TJ," I said, my voice shocked as my face burned red and my stomach flipped in excitement.

"Yes, Mila?" he said, his voice silky smooth. His eyes burned into mine for a few seconds before he looked down my body and stared at my breasts for a few seconds. "I'm just telling you what I like," he said and looked back into my eyes, a huge grin on his face.

"Whatever," I said and looked away from him, though I couldn't stop myself from smiling as I looked out the window. Take that, Barbie! Score 1 to me.

"So, Mila, is that why you have a big ass?" Barbie turned around again and looked at me.

"Is what why I have a big ass?" I repeated after her, glaring at her for making me repeat her offensive words.

"So you can get a man for the night?"

"Excuse me?" I said and my voice rose. I looked at TJ to see if he was going to say anything, but instead he just started the engine and put his car into drive. I shook my head and looked over at Sally, whose jaw was also practically on the ground. "Did you hear what she just said to me?" I said loudly, not caring if I was being rude or making Barbie uncomfortable.

"Yes," TJ answered. "I didn't hear your answer though."

"I wasn't talking to you, Travis James Walker," I said, almost having a hissy fit.

"Oh, okay," he said, his voice clearly amused as he drove. Sally's eyes met mine and we both shook our heads in shock.

"You are not a gentleman, Travis James Walker," I said, saying his full name again, which made him laugh.

"Did I ever say I was?" he answered quickly and I glared at the back of his muscular shoulders. Sometimes I just wanted to hit him. He was so obnoxious. Ugh!

"I didn't mean to offend you, Mila," Barbie said in her fake sweet voice again. "I'm actually jealous of you."

"Jealous of me?" I said in a tone that clearly showed I wasn't buying it.

"I wish I could find a guy to have a one-night stand with me," Barbie said in a pitiful voice, her full pink lips pouting as she gazed back at me with a sad face. "You're really lucky."

"You're telling us you can't find a guy who will have a one-night stand with you?" Sally said in disbelief. I looked at Sally and made a face. I had no idea what game Barbie was playing, but I had a feeling that I was going to end up being the loser.

"That's what I'm saying," Barbie said and I saw her hand on TJ's thigh. "Every guy who meets me wants me for longer than a night. I can't just have a one-night stand because they never want to leave once they've had me once." She looked at me and her blue eyes were like ice as she smirked at me. "That's why you're so lucky, Mila. You can have a man for a night, give them the ride of their life with your big hips and then they walk away and you're both happy. Me, I give them the ride of their life and they want to make me their wife."

"Are you frigging kidding me?" Sally's voice was pissed. "I think you are one of the biggest—"

"Barbie, that was uncalled for," TJ said, interrupting Sally, and I watched as he moved Barbie's hand off of his thigh.

"What?" Barbie sounded breathless. "You know it's true. I'm too pretty for one night. Guys want to make me their trophy. For once I wish I could be average."

"I bet," I said snarkily. "If I had your brain, I'd be wishing for average as well. I wouldn't even aim or hope for genius status. Just average."

"Now, now, girls." TJ's voice was sharp. "Let's play nice or this weekend will not be fun."

"Yeah, I think we already got that phone call," Sally said, sitting back and closing her eyes. "I can't wait for Cody to get here."

"Who's Cody?" Barbie asked and looked back at me with a questioning look, as if she hadn't just dissed me. I couldn't believe that she thought I would answer her.

"Cody is Mila's brother and my best friend, remember?" TJ answered her and it sounded like he was a little bit annoyed. He deserved to be annoyed. There could be nothing that Barbie was providing to him other than sex and I bet it wasn't even good sex. I wanted to scream or tell Sally how annoyed I was, but I knew that I would just sound like a broken record if I kept complaining about Barbie.

"Eh," Barbie said. "So is your dad coming?"

"No," TJ said in an abrupt voice.

"TJ comes up to hang out with my family. His dad has never come," I said, wanting Barbie to know that TJ and I had a long past and would continue to have a long future. "His dad is usually too busy with work."

"You know him?"

"Duh," I said and grinned at Sally. "I've been friends with TJ for years. Of course I know him." I wanted to say more. I wanted to add that Hudson Walker and I were like old pals and that I had him on speed dial, but that was a lie. And I didn't tell lies, at least not in front of the one person who could discredit me in seconds. I wanted to make Barbie jealous of me, but I knew TJ wouldn't appreciate me pretending to be good friends with his dad when I'd barely held five conversations with him in all the years I'd known him.

"Yeah, hmph." She made a weird noise and turned back to the front of the car. "So, what's it like having to follow in the great Hudson Walker's footsteps?" she asked TJ, and my jaw dropped. Barbie really had no filter. I wondered if she was deliberately trying to rile up everyone in the car or if she really had no clue? It wasn't possible for someone to just not understand how rude they were being, was it? I mean, maybe if she was autistic or had Asperger's or was on that spectrum. I knew that people who had Asperger's didn't have the same social cues, but I was pretty confident she didn't fit in that category. Barbie was just a nosey bitch.

"I'm currently driving, so I wouldn't know," TJ said, his tone still slightly off. I poked Sally in the arm gently. I was hoping that Barbie would keep prodding and that TJ would go off on her. That would be epic. That would make the whole torturous evening worth it.

"I mean what's it like working for the man who is—"

"That's his dad," I said, cutting her off, annoyed for TJ. Even though I wanted to see Barbie crash and burn, I didn't want TJ to feel bad. I knew how much he hated questions about his dad, and I wanted to protect him more than I wanted to see her go down in flames. I guess that really was proof that I had deep feelings for him. "Not some random man that you think he should be impressed by because he's famous and rich."

"It's okay, Mila." TJ's eyes glanced at mine for a few seconds in the rear-view mirror before he made a right-hand turn back up the main road to the lake house. "I don't mind answering questions; it comes with the territory."

"Okay," I said and just shrugged.

"Barbie, I don't know what you expect me to say. He's my dad. He's a businessman. I work for his company. I prove myself just like every other employee. Just like Mila has to prove herself as she now works for her family business as well." He pulled up in the driveway and switched the engine off and looked back at me. "Sometimes I wish that I worked somewhere else, that I could do something else. Sometimes I wish that certain expectations weren't set of me, you know?" His eyes bored into mine and it was as if he were talking directly to me and me alone.

"I know what you mean." I nodded and sighed. "Sometimes I feel that way too."

"It can be hard." He nodded. "The path to success isn't an easy one, even if your dad owns the company. Sometimes you just have to show what you're capable of." He ran his hands through his silky hair and his eyes narrowed. "And that's exactly what I'm going to do. I'm going to show what I'm made of and I'm not taking any prisoners."

"Whoa, enough serious talk, baby." Barbie laughed lightly and ran her hand across his face. "Let's go to bed. I want you to show me exactly what you're capable of right now."

"Ugh," Sally said loudly and opened the car door. "Mila and I are going to our room. Thanks for driving, TJ," she said sounding anything but thankful as she jumped out of the car, and I followed suit, slamming the car door behind me as I got out. "I swear I'm going to slap that girl," Sally said as we made our way into the cabin. She's absolutely awful."

"I know," I said softly as we walked to our room. "She really is." We closed the door behind us and I walked over to my bed and sat down and lied back. "This is going to be a long weekend." I sighed.

"Yes, it is, but don't worry. I have a plan." Sally winked at me.

"What plan?" I asked suspiciously.

"I'll tell you in a few minutes." She pulled her top off. "I'm headed to the shower now. I need to wash off this sweat from my body, and I want to deep condition my hair for tomorrow."

"Right now?" I rolled my eyes at her and she grinned.

"No time like the present." She laughed.

"Fine, I'll go in the shower after you and then we can talk. I want to know what you have up your sleeve."

"You'll love it. Trust me." She grinned and I groaned as she made her way to the adjoining bathroom. I had a bad feeling that putting my trust in Sally wasn't going to work out for the best.

◆

I WALKED OUT OF the shower and dried my hair with my big fluffy towel. I was eager to hear what Sally was going to tell me, but as I watched her sleeping, with her mouth slightly ajar, I knew I wasn't going to find out tonight. So instead I grabbed my phone and put on my boots and walked into the living room. I couldn't sleep yet and I felt the urge to speak to my grandfather.

"Hi, Nonno," I said as he picked up. "I hope it's not too late."

"It's never too late for my Mila," he said, his voice gruff. "How is the lake house?"

"Fine," I said, my voice sad.

"What's wrong?"

"Just wish that sometimes I didn't feel so lonely."

"You're there with your friends, no, Mila?" His tone was questioning and I knew he was worried.

"Yea, Sally is here. So is TJ and his girlfriend or whatever. And Cody will be here tomorrow."

"So why do you feel lonely?"

"I don't know." I bit my lower lip and grabbed my coat so that I could head outside.

"Did you and Sally fall out?"

"No, Nonno," I said and quickly zipped up my coat as it was freezing cold outside. I walked down the driveway and headed towards the path that would take me to the lake.

"Some days I just feel like I'm so alone, no matter how many people are around me. I feel like I'm the only one who really knows what's going on inside of me," I said as I headed towards the lake, the one place I knew would bring me some solace.

"You're not alone, Mila. You know you always have me. What's really wrong? Is it TJ?" His voice was astute and I tried not to cry.

"He's never going to want me, is he?"

"If he's the one for you, he will already know. If he's not, it doesn't even matter."

"How did you know that Nonna was the one?" I asked softly as I headed to one of the wooden chaises and sat down.

"You know this story." My nonno's voice became sentimental. "I've been telling you the story since you were a little girl."

"Tell me again," I said and I leaned back and hugged myself as the cool wind hit my face. I looked out at the big, dark lake and then looked up at the night sky and the thousands of shining stars.

"I was working for my uncle who owned a bakery," he said, his voice still sentimental. "I used to deliver the bread to all the people in my village. It was a lot of people."

"I know, Nonno." I laughed. "You were a very hardworking young man."

"And there was one lady—she was the most beautiful girl in the village."

"Auntie Maria."

"Yes." He nodded. "Every boy in the village wanted a kiss from Maria. Every boy, but me."

"Because you were so focused on your job delivering bread."

"I was focused," he said seriously. "And I was saving up for a new bike. Even little boys in Italy wanted fancy, shiny bikes."

"But then you saw Nonna."

"Yes, then I saw your Nonna," he said, his voice full of love. "She was throwing a rock down the street." He laughed. "And it hit my bag and a loaf of bread fell into the street."

"And you were so mad."

"I was so mad until I saw her face and then she put her hands on her hips and she told me that I should be more careful where I was riding."

"And you told her she should be more careful with her girl throws."

"Yes," he laughed. "Who told me to say that? She then threw another rock and it hit my bike. I jumped off of my bike and walked over to her."

"And she asked you if you were going to give her a free loaf of bread to say sorry."

"And I did." He laughed. "I was only fourteen and she was only thirteen, but I knew, I knew as sure as I knew I had two arms and two legs, that your darling Nonna was going to be my wife."

"And she knew right away as well." I sighed as I looked up at the sky. "I miss her."

"So do I," he said, his voice gruff. "Every single day."

"You know what my favorite memory is?" I said softly. "Do you remember that Christmas when TJ came to stay with us and you and Nonna took us out for hot chocolate and Cody was being a spoiled brat and didn't go because he wanted ice cream?"

"Of course."

"Nonna told me she saw you and her in me and TJ," I said softly. "I thought that was a sign that we were meant to be. Nonna knew from the beginning that I had a thing for him and it wasn't awkward talking about it because you two fell in love at such a young age."

"It was a different time, Mila."

"Yeah, I know. Sometimes I wish it wasn't." I sighed. "I hate that he brought that girl, Barbie. I don't even know what he sees in her."

"He's still young, Mila. Men these days don't settle down young. Look at Cody."

"I don't know what Cody's problem is." I sighed. "You know Sally has the hots for him. I don't know how to tell her that he's nothing but a player."

"It's not up to you to get into your brother's business."

"But Sally's my best friend."

"Even more reason why you shouldn't get involved."

"I feel like a bad person."

"Love isn't easy, Mila. It's not all flowers and candy."

"I know that, Nonno."

"Sometimes I wonder if you do." His voice was gentle. "Just because you're feeling jealous doesn't mean you get all depressed and lonely."

"I'm not depressed and lonely," I said and sighed. "I mean, I'm not lonely because I'm jealous," I lied. "Okay, maybe a bit, but I can't help it. I had so many plans for this weekend."

"Life doesn't go according to plans."

"I thought we were fated for each other. Now I wonder if I should give Milo a second chance."

"He's a good boy."

"He's not the boy, though."

"Mia cara," he said with a sigh. "You haven't even given him a chance."

"Do you think Nonna is looking over us?" I said softly. "Do you think she'll give me a sign if I should just give up on TJ?"

"She's always with you. Just as I will always be."

"Don't say that, Nonno. You're not going anywhere."

"How are you feeling?"

"Better," I said and then froze as I heard footsteps. "Hold on, Nonno," I whispered. "I think someone is coming."

"Mila, where are you? You're not in your room?" Nonno's voice sounded alarmed and I bit my lower lip to stop from screaming as I heard a branch snapping. My heart was racing and I sat there in fear, waiting to see who was coming. "Mila?" Nonno's voice rose.

"Nonno, I'm here," I whispered into the phone, covering the mouthpiece with my hand as I looked back and forth in the night sky. It was so dark that I couldn't really see anything and that made it even worse.

"Why are you whispering?" he said. "What is going on?"

"Nonno, I..." I said and my heart stopped as I felt something on my back. "Arrrgghhh. Arrggh!" I screamed and jumped off, dropping my phone on the ground as I started to run.

"Mila, stop." TJ's smooth voice sounded amused as he called out to me and I stopped running, my heart dropping with embarrassment as my face heated up.

"TJ?" I said and I turned around to look back at him. "You scared the shit out of me."

"I didn't mean to." He still sounded amused, though I couldn't make his face out clearly to see the expression in his eyes.

"Uh huh," I said and looked on the ground for my phone. "Nonno," I said as I grabbed the phone up, "are you still there?"

"Mila!" He sounded stern. "You scared me. What is going on? Should I come up and—"

"No, Nonno," I said, feeling guilty. "It was TJ. He snuck up behind me."

"Your TJ." He sounded happy.

"Nonno, you know that isn't true," I said, making sure I didn't say anything that would make TJ suspicious. "I'll call you later, okay?"

"Yes," he said softly. "See? You are not alone, Mila. Not now. Not ever. You'll always have TJ."

"I wish." I sighed and hung up the phone and then jumped as I saw TJ in front of me. "How are you so stealthy?" I groaned. "I didn't even see you walking towards me."

"You were too busy on the phone," he said, his eyes peering down at me. His skin seemed to radiate warmth in the moonlight and I longed to reach up, grab his hair and pull him down to kiss me.

"Yeah, I was."

"Who were you talking to?" he asked, his tone slightly rough. "Troy?"

"No, I was talking to Nonno," I said and tried not to roll my eyes as he brought up Troy. I wished I'd never mentioned him now. It seemed to me that he wasn't going to let it go. I wasn't sure what I was going to say about 'the breakup' that wouldn't make me look like a loser or a liar.

"Good," he said softly and then was quiet. We stood there

standing next to each other and were quiet as we stared out at the lake. It was eerily quiet now and I tried to concentrate on the reflection of the moon in the water instead of the feel of TJ's arm as it rubbed against me gently.

"What are you thinking?" he said softly after a few minutes and I looked over at him. His eyes were bright and curious, and I wondered what he was thinking as we stood there together.

"How strong you look," I said stupidly as I stared at his muscles.

"Thanks for the compliment." He grinned. "That's a first."

"And a last." I laughed.

"Do you know why I'm strong, Mila?"

"No?" I shook my head, not sure where he was going.

"I'm strong so I can carry my lady from my car to the bed. I'm strong so that I can protect her when she's scared, keep her warm when she's cold, love her when she's sad, and fuck her when she's horny." He grinned at my gasp and then flexed his bicep muscles at me. "These guns are about more than looks, Mila. These muscles are to keep my woman happy. These muscles are so I can hold her up when her legs are wrapped around me and her back's against the wall. These muscles are to keep her up when I'm sliding into her with such force that she doesn't think she can stay upright by herself anymore."

"You're gross," I said, my face flushing at his words. All I could think about was what it would feel like to have him pushing me back against the wall and touching me, sliding into me. Ugh, I didn't want to have these feelings.

"You don't really think that," he said with a self-assured grin.

"Yes, I do."

"No, you don't," he said and he lightly touched the side of my face. My skin tingled under his fingertips and all I could think was, "Oh shit, what does he know?"

"I do," I squeaked out and he laughed, a long lazy laugh, his eyes boring into mine with amusement.

"You know how I know you don't think that?" he asked softly

and leaned forward, his lips close to mine as he continued gazing at me.

"How?" I said and I swallowed hard as I felt his breath against me. If I leaned forward, even an inch, we would be kissing. OMG, I could be kissing TJ Walker if I wanted to. My heart was about to jump out of my chest as my brain screamed at me.

"Mila?" I heard Sally's voice calling out into the midnight air and I wanted to groan. Why did she have to choose now to come looking for me?

"I'm here," I shouted back, though my mind was racing in confusion. Was TJ flirting with me? And if he was, why? What about Barbie? Why weren't they back in his bedroom, fucking each other's brains out? Not that I was complaining, of course. The last thing I wanted was for them to be all over each other.

"What are you doing?" She walked towards TJ and me, and I saw her eyes widen as she took us both in. "I was worried about you when I woke up and saw that your bed was empty."

"I just came out to speak to Nonno on the phone and TJ happened upon me," I explained before she jumped to conclusions and said something stupid like, "I'm glad your seduction plan worked already, Mila."

"He happened upon you?" Sally asked, grinning as she yawned. "What's that? Old English or something?"

"Sally, are you sleepwalking?" I asked her, starting to feel a panic in my bones. Oh, God, what was Sally going to let slip?

"No." She moved closer to me. "I woke up and I noticed you weren't there, so I came out to make sure you were okay and not moping."

"I'm fine." I gulped.

"Why would Mila be moping?" TJ decided to join the conversation.

"I'm not moping." I glared at Sally, whose face was looking like she was now realizing what she'd said.

"I gather that," TJ said. "But why would she think you were moping? Moping about what?"

"I think Sally is just sleep-deprived. We should go back to bed."

"No, no." Sally shook her head and faked a big yawn. "You stay here for a few minutes and enjoy the lake. I know you like to be here under the stars and moonlight."

"Sally." I growled at her and she laughed.

"Night guys," she said and turned away. I could hear her singing "Moon River" as she walked away.

"Is everything okay, Mila?" TJ said after a few seconds.

"Yes, of course."

"Are you upset that your Troy couldn't make it up here after all?" he said softly. "I know how badly you wanted to drive in his Lamborghini."

"I never said he had a Lamborghini." I rolled my eyes.

"Well, his sports car, then."

"I'm not sad that Troy couldn't make it," I said and felt proud of myself for not extending the Troy lie any further. "Why are you up so late and outside?"

"I couldn't sleep," he said with a wry grin.

"Even after Barbie wore you out?" I asked, my voice tight as I subtly tried to find out if they had had sex.

"Barbie wore me out with her mouth and that was it." He looked at me and winked. "No need to worry."

"I'm not worrying about anything," I said, trying to figure out how to ask him exactly what he meant. Did he mean she wore him out by talking so much, or something else, like a blowjob? Ugh, I didn't want to know, but I really wanted to know. I felt like I was going to throw up thinking about TJ and Barbie being physical.

"Okay, that's good, then," he said and motioned to the rocking swing a few yards away. "Shall we have a seat?"

"Sure." I nodded and we walked over to the chair swing in silence.

"It's a beautiful night," he said as we sat down, and I looked over at his face. He was staring out at the lake and his face looked thoughtful. My eyes ran over his jaw, so strong and stubborn, and then to his lips and chin.

"Yes, it is," I answered as I looked away from him and back out at the lake. I could see the flickering lights of someone's boat in the distance and I sat back and looked up at the sky. The stars sparkled their radiance to us in the darkness of the night and I let out a small sigh.

"You sound like you have the weight of the world on your shoulders." I could tell from the sound of his voice that he was now looking at me.

"No," I said, but didn't look at him. "I was just thinking of Nonna and wondering if she was looking down at me from Heaven."

"Of course she is," he said as he moved closer to me. "Give me your hand," he said as he grabbed my arm, and his fingers grabbed onto my hand and grabbed my fingers and pointed them up in the air. "Do you see those rings?"

"What rings?" I said, trying to concentrate on the sky and not his touch.

"Look here." He moved even closer and I looked over to see his eyes gazing at me. "Follow the direction that I put your finger in," he said and I concentrated on staring up in the exact spot he was pointing me towards. "Do you see that bright mass of light?"

"Uh huh." I nodded.

"That's Saturn," he said. "And the rings around it are the rings of Saturn."

"Oh," I said and squinted. "I can't really see any rings."

"Yeah, me neither." He laughed. "But if I had my telescope, we'd be able to see."

"Wow, I never thought we'd be able to see the rings of Saturn from Earth," I said, awestruck. "I wish you had your telescope now."

"That's a first." He laughed. "You never hoped for that before."

"Well, you never showed me the rings of Saturn before." I laughed. "All you showed me before was the moon and told me I should go and live there."

"That wasn't me. That was Cody." He laughed. "And I think I

remember you telling him that he should go and join his friends on Mars. And told me to go there as well."

"Yeah, well, I was young." I laughed. "Now that we're older, I wish I'd have a chance to look at Saturn and her rings. Or his rings." I laughed.

"Maybe I'll bring it next year."

"Yeah, that would be cool." I nodded.

"And even if we don't get to view the stars here, we can view them somewhere else."

"Huh?" I turned to look at him. "What are you talking about? Why wouldn't we get to view the stars here?"

"Nothing," he said gruffly and then jumped up. "Want to go for a swim?"

"I don't have on my bathing suit, so no." I shook my head.

"Be adventurous, Mila. Let's skinny-dip."

"Ah, yeah, no." I shook my head again and laughed, though my heart was racing. Should I do it? Should I go skinny-dipping with him? Why would he even ask me to go skinny-dipping if he wasn't interested in me? Was he just trying to shock me? There was no way he was being serious, was he?

"That's what I thought." He laughed as he stood there staring at me with a huge grin. "All talk and no actual game."

"Um, I never talked about going skinny-dipping," I said with a frown. "So that's not exactly true."

"Five years ago you said that you secretly wanted to go skinny-dipping, but you were scared that people would see you, so you'd only go late at night. However, the caveat was that there would have to be one person there with you, so that you wouldn't feel alone and you'd have someone to cover you if someone else happened to come out while you were in the lake."

"How do you remember that?" I asked, looking at him in surprise. "I barely remember saying that."

"Ha." He winked at me. "I never forget when a girl tells me she wants to go skinny-dipping."

"You're a pervert."

"Not quite." He stared at me for a few seconds and my heart stilled as his face turned serious. He opened his mouth and I waited to hear what he was going to say next. It looked like it was something important. "We should go to bed," he said finally and reached out for my hands to pull me up.

"I'm not ready for bed." I shook my head, disappointed. Unless you want me in your bed. Of course I didn't say that out loud, even though I wanted to.

"Mila Kunis, it's time for bed." He grinned at me and I punched him in the arm.

"You're a jerk," I said as I jumped up and then yawned. I ignored the knowing look on his face as he stared at my mouth. "And that Barbie isn't the brightest bulb in the shed, either."

"Now now, Miley, no need to be rude."

"You love it, don't you?" I glared at him. "You won't be loving it if she screams out 'Brad Pitt' or 'Ashton Kutcher' in bed."

"Why would she scream out either of those names?" he said as we walked back towards the cabin.

"Well, she is apparently obsessed with Mila Kunis, so maybe she wishes you were Ashton Kutcher?"

"I think I'm a bit better than him, don't you think?"

"What would I and my big hips know?" I said lightly and he burst out laughing. "It's not funny, TJ." I shook my head at him. "She's horrible."

"I will neither agree nor disagree with your statement," he said softly and I wanted to punch him again. How could he not call her out for being the big bitch that she was? "However, I will say that a girl with a brain and some meat on her bones is worth ten girls with no brains."

"Thanks," I said and I gave him a quick hug as we walked into the cabin. "Night, TJ."

"Night, Mila," he said and gave me a quick peck on the cheek. "Sweet dreams."

I walked towards my room with a smile on my face before I realized that TJ hadn't exactly said what I thought he'd said. He said a girl with a brain and some meat on her bones was worth more than ten girls with no brains, but he hadn't said ten skinny girls with no brains. Did that mean he preferred super-skinny girls with no brains to average girls with brains, or a few-extra-pounds girls with brains or, who am I kidding, more-than-a-few-extra-pounds girls with no brains? I paused at my door and turned around to go back to talk to him and find out. However, I stopped still as I saw that TJ was standing in the same place I'd left him, just staring at me with a weird expression on his face. He hadn't moved since I'd walked away. He'd watched me walking to my room and he was still there.

I could feel my face blushing, and all thoughts of going up to him to ask him if he preferred skinny girls or not went out of my mind. I felt flustered just standing there looking back at him. I didn't know what he was thinking, and part of me was scared to find out. I took a deep breath, trying to build up the courage to go over to him. I wanted to grab his shirt, push him against the wall and kiss him hard. I wanted to press myself into him and tell him that he wasn't going to be sleeping with Barbie tonight; he was going to be sleeping with me.

I stared at his lips as he stood there and watched his chest rising and falling, and my whole body was on high alert with want and need. I wanted so badly to go over to him and take charge. But because I'm all talk and no action, I let my shyness overtake me. I lifted my hand and waved and said, "Night, TJ—sweet dreams of me." I groaned under my breath as I realized what I'd said, and he laughed.

"All night long, Mila. All night long," he said softly and gave me a small wave back. I turned around abruptly and hurried into my room, my skin tingling in happiness. I had no idea what had just happened, but I knew I was going to bed with a smile on my face.

Seven

TJ

MILA CLOSED THE DOOR and I stood there feeling like an idiot. She'd looked at me with such a shocked expression on her face when I'd said I'd be dreaming of her all night long. She probably thought I was joking, just like she probably thought I'd been joking about the skinny-dipping, but I hadn't been joking about either of the two. I knew I was playing with fire and getting myself into potential dangerous territory. I thought about everything I had to do, and I sighed. It wasn't going to be easy. And a part of me didn't want to do any of it, but I knew this was the only way. However, that didn't stop me from walking to Mila's bedroom door. I stood outside the door debating whether I should knock or just go inside and pull her into my arms. That would be the easy way. I'd seen the way she'd been staring at me, with her lips parted and her face a rosy hue. Mila wanted me just as badly as I wanted her. I wanted to take her and make her mine. I couldn't believe that she was letting Barbie get a rise out of her. Barbie, who couldn't even compare in beauty or brains to Mila. Barbie, whom I would have slapped if I weren't a gentleman. I wish that I hadn't brought her, though I knew why she was here. Not that I liked it at all. But it wasn't up to me. Not yet. I just had to bide my time and wait.

My fingers clutched onto the handle and it took everything in me to not open that door. I could almost picture her lying there in the bed, her long blond hair strewn all over the pillow as she hugged the sheets to her body. The bed would be warm and the sheets rumpled as she wiggled around to make herself comfortable. She wouldn't sleep right away. She'd lie awake, listening to the sound of Sally breathing as she slept, and she'd stare out the window and hopefully she'd think of me. She'd wonder if I'd gone back to my room to fuck Barbie. She'd wonder what would have happened if she'd walked towards me just now when she'd turned around. How I'd willed her to come towards me. To give me a real sign that she wanted me. That's all I needed. I needed it to come from her. I needed to know that when I took her and made her mine, it was because she wanted it too.

I knew she wanted me—it would have been difficult to ignore all the signs—but I don't think she knew what she was getting into with me. I wasn't all sunrises and late nights at the lake staring at the stars. I was dark nights with the wolves howling into the wind. I was secrets in corners and dark alleys. I was whips and chains and plush red velvet. I was cuffs and ropes and unspeakable actions that would both turn her on and disgust her.

My hand dropped from the handle and I stepped back. Now was not the time to take her. Now was not the time to make her mine. Not now, not in this way. It would almost be too duplicitous. This was too romantic of a setting. I didn't want to give her the wrong idea. Or the right idea. I stepped back from the door and walked to the bathroom. I needed a cold shower. I needed to focus on the task at hand. Mila could wait another night, even if I didn't want her to. I'd go according to the plan. I'd have her soon. For four weeks. And then she'd see the real me. And I didn't know if that would be the beginning, or the beginning of the end.

Eight

MILA

DECEMBER 19, 2012

DEAR DIARY,

Sometimes I hate my brother. I know that's not a nice thing to say, but he can be such a jerk. I was in the kitchen talking to TJ and I am pretty sure that TJ was going to go in for a kiss and guess who comes into the kitchen and tells me to scat and go to my room—like he owns the kitchen or something? I think he's jealous because TJ and I really get on. He's such a jerk. And selfish. I don't know how Cody and I have the same parents. He's the spawn of the devil. Maybe his real name is Damien and he's the antichrist come to make my life a misery. Hopefully that's not blasphemy! I would ask Nonno, but he would just tell me I need to go to church with him every weekend. And while, I am a Christian, I really don't like going to church every week. I almost feel bad writing that. Like God might strike me down at any moment for saying that sometimes I find church boring. Sigh, now I'm going to go with Nonno on Sunday to make up for some of the sins in this journal entry. See what I mean? Cody ruins everything. Now I'm going to have to see if I can get TJ in that same position by the fridge again. Granted, he might have been reaching for a Coke and not in for a kiss, but a girl can wish, right?

XOXO

Mila

"I'm here." Cody's voice was loud and brash as he burst into the bedroom.

"Cody?" I groaned as I opened my eyes, my brother's grinning, handsome face staring down at me.

"The one and only."

"I was sleeping." I groaned and rolled over in the bed.

"Don't be a brat," he said and ruffled my hair. "Wake up."

"Cody." I rolled over and glared up at him. "Stop."

"Morning, Cody," Sally said and my jaw dropped as she sat up in the bed. Her hair was straight and silky, and her face looked like perfection. I had no idea what was going on, but that was not how Sally normally looked first thing in the morning.

"Hey, Sally." He nodded and gave her a quick smile before turning back to me. "Mila, get up now. I need to talk to you."

"Um. I'm still in bed, jerk face." I rolled over and closed my eyes. "And I'm going back to sleep now."

"Get up and put your clothes on." He pulled the duvet off of my body. "Meet me in the kitchen in ten minutes. Or I'll find another way to get you out of bed."

"You're so rude," I said huffily as I sat up and glared at him. I felt like Cody was even more insufferable as we got older. Shouldn't we have been getting closer? Shouldn't he have been treating me as an adult now and not a kid?

"Ten minutes, Mila," he said as he walked to the door and then looked back to face me. "We need to talk about your salary," he said ominously before walking out of the room.

"Why do I have the feeling that talking about my salary doesn't mean he wants to talk about how much of a pay raise I'm going to get?" I looked at Sally and frowned.

"He didn't even notice how silky my hair is." She made a face. "Or the fact that I'm wearing a strawberry milkshake lipstick that makes my lips a little fuller and shiny."

"Strawberry milkshake lipstick?" I leaned forward and stared at her lips. "I'm not going to lie, Sally, but even I wouldn't have known you had on a strawberry milkshake lipstick. How are we supposed to know that?"

"He would have known if he'd kissed me." She pouted and lay back down on her bed and sighed. "But he didn't even look in my direction, let alone kiss me and try and feel me up."

"No offense, but I'm glad I wasn't here to witness my brother feeling you up. That's not really something I want to see."

"We'd keep it under the covers," she said and I could tell from her tone she was grinning. "I promise you that."

"Why, thanks. That makes me feel better," I said and laughed as I jumped out of the bed. "I'm not showering," I said and looked through my bag of clothes. I have no time to shower if he wants me in the kitchen in ten minutes."

"I wish he wanted me in the kitchen in ten minutes. I wish he were bossing me around." She sighed. "'Sally, in the kitchen in ten minutes and no panties.' "

"Eww, you do remember he's my brother, right?" I groaned as I pulled out my hairbrush and started brushing my hair. If I was going to be looking rough, at least my hair could be looking good. "Do you want to go lie out by the lake this morning?" I asked her. "I can just put on my bikini."

"Yeah, let's do that." She grinned and sat up. "I brought a sexy black bikini that I got at Macy's last weekend."

"Macy's?" I asked, surprised. Sally was a budding fashionista and she never shopped at Macy's.

"Yeah, my grandma sent me a hundred-dollar gift card to use." She made a face. "I was thinking I could get a pair of heels, but they were all so fugly. So I figured what else can I get? None of their jewelry was cute, but I saw this two-piece and tried it on and the top was made for my bust."

"Lucky." I pulled out the bikini that I'd bought at Target. "I can never find swimsuits that fit me well. My boobs are too big, so I always feel like I'm about to pop out."

"You're the lucky one." She stared at my boobs. "I'd die to have 34Cs."

"Um, so would I." I laughed. "I'm 36D."

"Oh, wow." She looked surprised.

"And when I say D, I mean double D." I laughed again and then groaned as I realized I only had about five minutes left to make it to the kitchen before Cody marched back to my room and started acting like some sort of tyrant. He could be so annoying sometimes, but I knew better than to call him out. Especially now, and especially about money. "Close your eyes." I giggled as I pulled my top off and turned around. I quickly pulled my bikini top over my breasts and struggled to pull the material over all of my cleavage. "Argh." I groaned. "This top seemed to be full coverage when I was in the store."

"It looks hot," Sally said as she opened her eyes again. "You should be proud to show off your body. Every guy at the lake will be staring at you."

"Yeah, they will. They'll be trying to catch a glance of nip." I groaned and adjusted my bikini top to cover my breasts fully. "And nip is dirty, not sexy. Only skanks have their nipples showing."

"True." Sally nodded in agreement. "If they can see areola, they are seeing too much."

"Should I change?" I glanced down at my top and frowned. "And look at my belly. Ugh, it's hanging out like I'm pregnant."

"Mila, please." Sally rolled her eyes. "You're far from pregnant."

"Only because I haven't had sex in months." I made a face. "And you know there is no way I could be pregnant."

"That's true." She giggled and then stopped when she saw my face. "Seriously though, you look fine. There are millions of women who wish they had your body."

"Uh huh," I said and then looked at my watch. "Okay, I'll be back to put on the bottoms. I'm sure Cody is in the kitchen waiting for me with a cup of coffee in his hand and a frown on his face."

"Tell him I love him and want him in my bed tonight," Sally said as I made my way out of the room.

"Okay," I said lightly as I walked through the door.

"Don't you dare tell him that, Mila," she shrieked as I closed the door behind me and I just laughed. The corridor was quiet as I walked towards the kitchen. I wondered if Barbie and TJ were up yet. I also wondered what had gone on last night. I didn't think much would have gone on, but I knew TJ had most probably been drunk and seemingly a bit horny based on his comments. Oh my! His comments had kept me up all night. All I'd been able to think about was him holding me up and sliding into me. Even as I walked to the kitchen I could feel my face flushing. Oh, what was TJ doing to me? It was like he knew I'd come here with an agenda and he was trying to one-up me.

"There you are," Cody said as I walked into the kitchen. His face was flushed and angry, and I frowned. Why was he flushed? He'd just gotten here. Was he already working himself up to go off on me?

"Morning, Mila," TJ said, and I looked over by the fridge and saw him standing there with a carton of milk in his hands.

"Morning," I said, looking back at Cody, whose jaw was tense. "You're up early."

"Early to bed, early to raise, makes a man healthy, wealthy and wise," he said with a grin.

"You didn't go to bed early," I said and rolled my eyes. "You making coffee?"

"Cody put it on. It'll be ready in a minute," TJ said, and I saw Cody clenching his fists. What had gone on between them?

"So, what do you want Cody?" I said, walking up to him and glaring. "I thought this was a vacation. I didn't think I needed to deal with my boss on my vacation."

"Funny, Mila," he said, not smiling. "You need to be smarter about how you spend money. I can't believe you seriously called me and asked me for a raise."

"I was joking," I lied.

"No, you weren't." He shook his head and sighed. "What's going on, Mila? Why did you need the money?"

"Do we have to have this conversation in front of TJ?" I said and glared at him. "I like my private business to stay my business."

"I'm like family, Mila," TJ said as he walked over with a mug and handed it to me. "Cody can say anything in front of me."

"Exactly!" Cody said loudly. "Remember you're like her brother." He looked over at TJ, who just walked away.

"Well, he's not my brother and I like my business to stay my business." I made a face. "And I don't want to ruin my trip by talking about money."

"You know the business isn't doing well, Mila," Cody said gruffly. "We need to be careful."

"I didn't know we were doing badly," I said and paused. "Are we in trouble, Cody? Like serious trouble?" I looked up at him and frowned. Why was he acting like the world was going to end? My paycheck wasn't even that high. Certainly not high enough to be causing this much stress.

"We need to be careful." Cody nodded. "Things aren't great right now. Dad is trying to figure out the best plan of action." He sighed.

"But?" I said, my voice timid and slightly scared. Maybe this was more serious than I'd thought.

"But Nonno is challenging him." Cody looked away from him. "Nonno doesn't like Dad's plan."

"What?" I frowned, not believing what I was hearing. "But Nonno lets Dad run the company. He trusts Dad, doesn't he?"

"Nonno has other plans now." Cody sighed. "Look, I can't say much more. I've already said too much. Just make sure you're careful with your money from here on out. I can't be giving you advances on anything, okay? If you're in trouble, let me know." His eyes peered into mine in concern. "You aren't about to get evicted or anything?"

"No." I shook my head. "Nothing like that." I thought about all my bills coming up and I felt my stomach dropping. I was worried, but I didn't want to worry Cody. He already seemed like he had enough on his plate.

"Good." He leaned over and ruffled my hair. "I'm not that flush right now myself. After buying the house and the Beemer."

"Yeah, I understand," I said and bit on my lower lip. I could see TJ staring at me from the corner of the room, and I felt embarrassed. And slightly ashamed. I wondered how he felt knowing that our family business wasn't doing so well and that we were on the way to the poor house while he was the son of a billionaire. I wondered if it made him feel uncomfortable. Was he going to feel like we were going to ask him for money if things went badly?

"Want any breakfast, Mila?" TJ asked softly and I heard Cody inhaling. What was his problem? I glanced at Cody to see what he was annoyed at now, but I saw his face moving to the kitchen door, his eyes alert and a small smile on his face. I looked towards the door and my stomach sank as I saw that it was Barbie who had caught his attention and not Sally. Barbie sauntered into the kitchen in a white tank top, with no bra and short black gym shorts that were practically just underwear.

"Why, hello." Cody grinned as he walked towards Barbie. "I'm Cody. Are you Mila's friend?"

"Mila Kunis is here?" Barbie's eyes lit up as she gave Cody a demure smile.

"Who?" Cody asked, confused, and I wanted to laugh.

"Mila Kunis," Barbie said in a Russian accent and I couldn't stop myself from rolling my eyes.

"Sorry, what?" Cody looked at me. "Did you change your name, Mila?"

"What do you think?" I said and rolled my eyes. "Barbie has a memory problem. Along with other problems."

"Oh?" He raised an eyebrow at me and then looked back at Barbie. "What problems? Any way I can help you?" He moved closer to her and I could see his eyes narrowing in on her nipples. Trust me to have a brother who was a pervert.

"I don't have any problems," Barbie said.

"Other than being too sexy," Cody said and she laughed, her face preening up at him. "I have that problem too, so I know."

"Are you frigging kidding me?" I said loudly and looked over at TJ. "TJ is the one who brought Barbie this weekend. They're dating."

"Practically engaged," Barbie said in a sweet voice and I could see TJ laughing as he stared at me.

"Not even close to engaged," he said as he walked towards me and then gave Barbie a gaze.

"Ugh, I need a massage." Barbie stretched her arms and pushed her breasts out. "Anyone up for providing me some release? I brought some aromatherapy oils with me."

"Not me," I said and I could feel my stomach curling at how obvious she was. I hated calling other girls whores and sluts but, man, Barbie was a slut.

"Sure, I'll help you out." Cody nodded. "We have some loungers out in the back. You can lie face down and I'll get to work, or we can do it on a bed."

"Maybe a bed," Barbie said with a small smile. "I don't want to accidentally flash anyone." She paused and looked at me. "I like to get my massages topless. Feels so freeing."

"I'm going to the lake." I looked at Cody and then at TJ, ignoring Barbie. It seemed to me that she was deliberately trying to flaunt herself in front of me. I knew she wanted to get a rise out of me, but I bet she had no clue how close I was to just slapping her and screaming. And I have never slapped anyone before in my life. "Sally and I need to relax."

"Well, make sure relaxing is all you do." Cody turned to me and his voice was rough. "No shopping and spending money you don't have."

"Yeah, Mila, time to stop the shopping." TJ said, his eyes laughing at me.

"TJ, I swear I'm going to go off," I said to TJ who was barely holding back a grin. I had no idea why he thought any of this was funny. It was far, far from funny. "You tell plastic lady and my brother to stay away from the lake for the next couple of hours, please." I pursed my lips and he nodded, a solemn look on his face.

"What about me?" he asked, his green eyes sparkling.

"What about you?"

"Can I come to the lake as well?" He licked his lips lightly.

"No," I said abruptly and turned away, feeling pissy. I wasn't in the mood to deal with TJ teasing and confusing me. The morning had already gotten off to a bad start and I was still confused about what had happened the previous evening. I still wanted to know why he'd watched me walking to my room and just stood there. I'd had an awful time getting to sleep. I'd been up half the night debating putting on my negligee and going to find him and offering up myself. I just wanted to see how he would respond. My skin had been tingling all night, and when I'd finally fallen asleep, my dreams were filled with TJ's smile and his strong arms pinning me against a wall, holding me up as he fucked me hard.

"I WANTED TO SHOW Cody my new bikini." Sally moaned as we settled into two lounge chairs next to the lake. The sun felt warm on my skin and I closed my eyes as I listened to her complaining that I'd dragged her from the room to the lake without her getting to flirt with Cody.

"He was all up in Barbie's silicone," I mumbled as I settled into the lounger and flexed my toes. "He didn't deserve your presence this morning."

"I can't believe she wore a white T-shirt and no bra. Who does that? Next thing she'll be suggesting a wet T-shirt competition." Sally sounded annoyed.

"You know you'd enter." I laughed as I rolled over and opened an eye to look at her. "By the way, just in case you didn't know, you look hot in that bikini," I said honestly as I gazed at her. The crisp white material of the bikini complemented her honey complexion, and her long black hair hung past her shoulders and to her back, straight and frizz-free. "It's so weird seeing you without your curls," I said as I reached out and touched her hair. "I miss pulling your ringlets."

"As soon as I hit the water, I'll be curly again." She laughed, her eyes crinkling as she gazed at me. "Your face is looking red," she said as she peered down at me. "I think we should put on some sunscreen before we get burned."

"Yeah." I nodded and sat up. "Do you have any?" I asked sheepishly. "I forgot to bring any."

"You were too focused on your sexy underwear." She giggled and I nodded. "You know it." I sighed. "Not that it matters. TJ is driving me crazy. I don't know what he's thinking or feeling. And I don't think I have the nerve to make a move on him."

"Just do it." Sally sighed as she pulled out her sunscreen. "And get on your front. I'll do your back first."

"Just do it. Yeah, right. You know how hard that is. I don't want to be rejected."

"It's obvious that he has the hots for you," Sally said. "The way he looks at you and teases you, and didn't you say he asked you to skinny-dip last night? Who does that? None of my guy friends have ever asked me to skinny-dip."

"He's Cody's best friend. I bet he feels like he's my brother." I sighed.

"Trust me. Your brother and any guy who felt like he was your brother would not want to skinny-dip with you." She laughed and I yelped as she put the cold cream on my back and started rubbing. "Unless he was that freaky guy from that book."

"What book?"

"Flowers in the Attic," she said. "I saw the movie on Lifetime and whoa."

"Whoa what?"

"She hooked up with her brother. And not step-brother, either."

"Eww, that's gross." I made a face into my towel as she rubbed the cream into my shoulders. "Do my lower back as well, please."

"You want me to unhook your bikini?"

"Sure," I said and then laughed as I felt her untie it. "This is the most action I'll be getting all weekend."

"Haha, that's sad." She groaned. "It's just our luck that the same ditzy bitch is after both of our men."

"I know," I said, feeling sorry for myself. "Screw you, Barbie," I shouted into the wind and then lowered my voice, just in case someone could hear me.

"So you really think Cody was into her?" Sally said softly and I could tell from her tone that she was hurt. I wasn't sure how to respond. I wanted to be the positive friend. I wanted to tell her go for him. I wanted to tell her that any man would be happy to have her. I truly wanted to tell her that. I believed it as well. She was great, but I also knew Cody. And he was a player. And he liked big blondes with big boobs. And he didn't care who knew. Or got hurt. And I knew that he would most probably spend a night with Sally if she really pushed it. But I also knew that it would only be a night. If he were really interested in her, I felt like he wouldn't even be entertaining Barbie. He wouldn't be giving her a naked massage on her bed.

"Do you think they're going to have a threesome?" Sally asked, her tone low, and I froze.

"Who?" I said and nearly rolled over, but then remembered my bikini top was undone. "Who?" I said louder, my voice rising.

"Cody, TJ, and Barbie," she said, her voice still low.

"What?" I almost shrieked and she sighed loudly.

"Don't 'what' me. You can't be that shocked. Let's be real. Cody is a player. We both know that. I'm not blind and dumb. And TJ, well, I'm sure TJ is a player too and an undercover freak."

"He's not an undercover freak! Why would you say that?" My voice was indignant, but I knew exactly what she was going to say.

"Come on, Mila. Remember when we found that horse whip and those handcuffs in his backpack, when he was visiting you guys that summer?" she said quickly. Her tone sounded as freaked out and excited as it had that day when we'd been noseying around in Cody's room and looking through both guys' stuff.

"I guess," I said, my legs tingling as I remembered seeing those fuzzy handcuffs.

"And those beads." She giggled. "Remember you put them around your neck and you were trying to figure out how to clasp them because you thought they were a necklace?"

"Ugh, don't remind me." I shuddered.

"And they were anal beads," Sally continued. "TJ is a freak in the bedroom. Who knows what other kinky shit he's into? I'm sure he'd be into a threesome." She laughed. "I mean, I don't think Cody and TJ are going to get it on together, but they'd do whatever two men do to pleasure one girl at the same time."

"One takes the front and one takes the back," I said, like some sort of authority on the subject.

"Say what?" she said and I laughed.

"She sucks off one of them while the other one penetrates her," I said matter-of-factly and then made a retching sound. "But I don't even want to think about that. I do not think they would do that. Especially not with us here as well. I would kill Cody, and I would tell our parents and Nonno, and they would kill him right after I did."

"He'd die two deaths, huh?" Sally laughed and then moved back to her lounger and lay down. "I sure hope you're right. I'd hate to be punked on this trip."

"Yeah, so would I." I sighed and closed my eyes again. The sun felt hot and delicious on my back and I pictured TJ's face in my mind. His lips were so pink and they looked so soft. I wondered how they would feel against mine. I moaned as I felt a trickle of sweat rolling down my back and imagined it was TJ's tongue licking between my shoulder blades.

"What?" Sally asked and I giggled.

"What what?"

"You made a noise," she said. "You okay?"

"I was just thinking about TJ kissing me."

"Oh." She laughed. "Where?"

"What do you mean where?" I giggled. "On my lips."

"Which lips?"

"You're disgusting."

"Hey, don't knock it until you try it," Sally said. "There is nothing like a guy going down on you."

"I was imagining him licking my back, to be fair." I sighed and stretched. "I suppose his tongue could go where it wanted to after that."

"Yeah." She laughed. "Just make sure you get a wax first." Then she groaned. "I can't believe I basically skinned my whole body for Cody and he's not even going to be able to take advantage of that fact."

"Completely hair free?" I asked, impressed.

"Completely." She giggled. "Not even a landing strip."

"I thought you liked landing strips?"

"Yeah, but I don't know if Cody likes that," she said. "I always think it's smarter to go bare first time around and then change it up as the guy makes requests."

"I'm totally not bare." I sighed. "And I'm not even landing-strip ready either."

"Mila, you do not have a jungle going on, do you?"

"A small jungle?" I giggled. "I trimmed, so I'm not the Amazon rainforest or anything, but yeah, I'm a local park."

"Mila." She laughed. "Do you want me to wax you? I know Nair has a home kit we can use."

"No, I do not want you to wax me." I groaned.

"I can," she said. "I mean, what if things get hot and heavy with

TJ and then he gets lost?"

"Lost where?"

"In the jungle." She giggled. "What if the leaves block his view and he can't land the plane on the right spot?"

"He can land the plane on the right spot." I shook my head. "And you're disgusting, by the way."

"I hope he can pilot his tongue to the right spot," she said. "I know some guys who have gotten lost and they were in a desert."

"Hahaha. They just sucked, then."

"Who just sucked, then?" a deep voice said from next to us, and my eyes popped open as my body froze.

"TJ?" I said weakly, wanting to ask him just how much he'd heard. I would die if he'd heard it all. Oh, my God, what if he'd heard us talking about him going down on me?

"The one and only," he said. His lips curved up and he looked at my back. "Need me to rub some more cream onto your back?"

"No," I said and shook my head quickly. I did not need his bare hands on my naked back right now. I was likely to do or say something embarrassing.

"You sure?" He sat on the edge of my lounger and I felt his warm hands on my shoulders, rubbing something.

"What are you doing?" I squeaked, wanting to roll over and push him away, but not wanting to flash myself at him.

"Sally missed a spot," he said as his fingers now started to squeeze my shoulders. "And now I'm giving you a small massage. You feel tense."

"I'm not tense," I said tightly as his fingertips kneaded into my skin. I tried not to moan as I felt my body relaxing. His fingers felt so good on my skin and I could feel my muscles enjoying the pressure of his kneading.

"Sure, you're not," he said. "By the way, someone is here for you, Mila."

"Huh?" I said, not really paying attention as my body loosened up. I wanted to tell him to stop massaging me, but it just felt too good.

"I said, someone is here for you," he said and I felt his hands moving to my upper arms and squeezing. His fingers were so close to the sides of my breasts now and I hoped that he would move them down a little farther.

"What do you mean?"

"I mean that your man is here."

"My what?" My voice rose and I froze. What the hell was he talking about?

"I guess all your dreams are coming true because your man, Troy, is here."

"Troy is here?" I froze. What the hell? I turned over to look at Sally, but she wasn't looking at me.

"Yeah. So you should put your top on and come." His hands abruptly left my shoulders and I felt his fingers on my bikini strap.

"What are you doing?" I said, feeling panicked.

"Tying up your strap, unless you want to walk back topless," he said, his voice rougher. "I'm not sure how Troy would feel about that."

"Uh yeah, thanks," I said, my mind racing. What had Sally done and why hadn't she told me? I was going to kill her. I felt his fingers deftly tying my strap together quickly and I felt peeved that he was able to do it so easily, like he'd had a lot of practice before. He jumped off of the lounger and I rolled over and sat up.

"You ready?" he asked, his eyes intent as they looked at me.

"Yeah." I nodded and then looked down. My boobs were almost popping out because he'd tied the top too tightly. My hands flew to the material and I tried to adjust it so that I didn't have an accidental flashing incident.

"No need to adjust it on my account." He winked at me and I blushed.

"I'm not," I said and stood up. "You wanna come inside with me now?" I looked down at Sally, who was looking up at me with wide eyes.

"I'll lie out for a bit more, if that's okay."

"You don't want to come and say hello to Troy?" I said, my eyes boring into hers.

"Eh, I'll come later." She shrugged and I wanted to shake her.

"Okay, then," I said stiffly and turned to TJ. "Let's go, then."

"Okay, see you in a bit, Sally," TJ said and we walked back to the cabin in silence. My mind was racing as we walked back. Was TJ calling my bluff? Was there anyone really there? I was about to turn to him and tell him he got me good when I saw a man running towards me with a bouquet of flowers. And not just any flowers—it looked like a bouquet of red roses.

"Mila, my darling, there you are," he said as he grabbed me into his arms and spun me around. My heart was thudding as the strange man held me to him. "I missed you, my darling." He set me down on my feet and, before I knew what was happening, he was kissing me on the lips and rubbing my back. I stood there in shock, with TJ staring at me with narrowed eyes, and all I could do was wonder if I'd gone to sleep and woken up in some sort of alternate universe.

Nine

MILA

MAY 18, 2008

DEAR DIARY,

There's this saying that if you pray for something hard enough, you will get it. Or, as Nonno says, everything you wish for can come true, so only wish for something you know you want. I think it's a saying from his village, somewhere on the Amalfi Coast in Italy. Nonno said he will take me and Nonna once I graduate from college. I asked him if Cody will come as well, not because I want Cody to come, but because I want him to bring TJ. Nonno just laughed. Then I went to my bedroom to say a prayer that TJ would get to come. I think it would be romantic if we fell in love in the same country that my grandparents fell in love. It would mean that we were fated to be together and that our relationship would be as perfect as my grandparents'. Sally thinks that's a big wish and prayer, but I figure it can't hurt to try. I'm also praying to stop world hunger and for peace among men, so I'm not being desperately selfish. I'll say another prayer tonight. I'd love to tell my grandchildren the story of how TJ and I fell in love in Positano. I can picture it in my mind already.

Mila

XOXO

"Lunch is ready." Cody walked into the yard and stared at me with Troy for a few seconds and continued without blinking. "Will you go and get Sally, please, Mila?"

"No, why don't you go?" I said with a frown. Wasn't Cody going to even ask me who the guy with his arms around me was?

"Fine," he said gruffly, then he looked at me and frowned. "Who's your friend?"

"This is Mila's boyfriend, Troy," TJ said, responding for me. "He arrived in his Mercedes first thing this morning."

"Yeah, it's a cool car," Troy said and grinned at him. "Much cooler than my Nissan."

"I guess that's why you traded it in, huh?" TJ asked with his eyebrow raised.

"Traded it…?" Troy paused and then grinned. "Yeah, yeah, that's why." He looked at me and took my hand. "Wanna go catch up in the bedroom for a few seconds?"

"I don't think that's necessary," TJ said with a small frown. "So, you like sports cars, Troy?"

"Yeah. I used to drag race in high school. My buddy Pete souped up an old Honda CR-V and we used to take it to the track every Friday."

"I like car racing as well." TJ nodded. "I like to take out my dad's Ferrari and race it."

"Wow, a Ferrari." Troy's jaw dropped. "That's dope."

"Yeah. I drove a Spyder a couple of months ago." He grinned.

"That's cool," Troy said. "I think I'm going to get a Honda CBR and get into some street-bike racing."

"Yeah, I do that too," TJ said. "Though my bike's in the shop. I had a little accident a couple of months ago."

"I didn't know that," I said sharply. "You were in a motorcycle accident?"

"Yeah, no biggie." TJ shrugged. "Just fractured my wrist."

"You fractured your wrist?" I frowned and looked at his arm.

"How did that happen?"

"A truck pulled into my lane and he didn't check his blind spot," TJ said nonchalantly. "It happens. It's the risk you take every time you drive."

"Yeah, but you don't almost die in a car every day, like you do on a bike."

"Bikes are safe," TJ said, his lips thinning.

"No, they aren't," I said stiffly, my heart thudding as my face heated up. I couldn't believe that TJ had been in an accident and I didn't even know. No one had told me—not him, and not even Cody. Did I matter that little? But why would they tell you, Mila? a voice inside of me whispered. What possible reason would you have to know about what's going on in TJ's life? It's not like you're his wife or girlfriend. And, sadly, that was true. I was barely his friend.

"Mila, darling, did you miss me?" Troy asked me, looking at me adoringly. I wanted to ask him what the fuck was going on, but I figured he was some really good actor that Sally had hired to help me make TJ jealous. I kinda wished I'd made up the fake boyfriend for her now. She could have hired someone to try and make Cody jealous. In fact, I was going to tell her that very fact as soon as I got her in a private room. How could she do this to me and not tell me? Ugh! I was so annoyed.

"Of course, my dear," I said to Troy, looking into his sky-blue eyes and trying to smile. I could see both Cody and TJ looking at me and I knew they were trying to figure out what was going on.

"I've been thinking about you all day and night, hoping that I could see you and kiss you all over," Troy said, and I could see Cody's eyes narrowing as he looked over at me. Oh boy, Troy was really laying it on strong and I knew that it was way too strong when I saw Cody at our side.

"So tell me again—who are you, exactly?" he said, looking at Troy properly for the first time.

"I'm Troy, Mila's boyfriend," Troy said confidently, his perfect white teeth looking up at Cody as if he expected that answer to be the solution to any problems that might come up. "Who are you?" Troy's smile faltered as he realized that Cody was now glaring at him.

"I'm Mila's big brother," he said and squared his shoulders. "Her very protective, older, big brother."

"Oh, hi," Troy said, looking at me for help. I nearly started laughing at the absurdity of the situation. Troy, who I'd never seen until ten minutes ago, was looking for me to help him with my brother.

"How long have you been dating Mila?"

"Um, it feels like I've known her all my life," Troy said with a beguiling smile that turned to despair as Cody didn't smile back. "It's been a while," he said weakly and he reached for my hand. I sidestepped to the side of him and stuffed my hand in my pocket. I looked over at TJ and I could see that he was watching everything with an eagle eye and a small smirk on his lips. Jackass!

"Hey hey." Barbie sauntered outside. "What are you two up to?" Barbie looked at Cody and then TJ, and gave what I'm sure she considered was a sweet, sexy smile. "I thought we were going to eat?" She touched Cody on the shoulder and batted her eyelashes. "I was waiting."

"Yeah, we are," Cody said, his eyes lightening as he looked at her. My heart started pounding as I wondered what was going on, but then Barbie walked over to TJ and slapped him on the ass.

"And you, big boy, you need to eat," she said and licked her lips, like some sort of hungry cat that had just seen a bowl of milk and hadn't had anything to drink in days.

"We're coming," TJ said and I couldn't tell if he sounded apathetic or angry. I'm sure he couldn't be happy at the fact that Barbie was now flirting with Cody as well. Unless they shared her. Ugh, I felt sick even thinking about that. Was Sally right? Did Cody and TJ really share women? That was just gross!

"Cody, go and get Sally," TJ said and I saw my brother look over at him, sigh slightly and then head out to the lake to get Sally.

I frowned slightly as I watched my brother just walking away. I heard Troy let out a deep sigh of relief as Cody walked away and he turned to me and whispered, "What's the plan for tonight?"

"What?" I asked, my voice louder than I would have hoped.

"Who are you?" Barbie turned to Troy, looking pleasantly surprised to see another good-looking man in the mix. Maybe she was hoping for a foursome? Ho! I immediately felt guilty about my thoughts and tried to tell myself that she was a perfectly nice girl and that I was just jealous because she had arrived with TJ. Though I knew that what I was feeling stemmed from more than just jealousy. And while I didn't like women to call other women ho's because I felt the term was offensive, I just couldn't stop myself from thinking that about her.

"Hi, I'm Troy. Who are you?" Troy said, his eyes widening in that way that guy's eyes always did when they saw a completely hot chick and got super excited as if they thought they had a chance with her. I glared at him for being so eager and I knew it was irrational to feel so pissed because I didn't know him or really care to.

"Barbie."

"Perfect name for someone like you."

"Oh?" she asked, looking up at him with a questioning look. I started grinning as I thought that perhaps Troy was on my side. Maybe he could see Barbie for what she really was, even if TJ and Cody were both blinded to her true self.

"You're as gorgeous as a doll," he said, practically salivating as he spoke. "And what doll is prettier than Barbie?"

"True." She giggled and pushed her breasts out. "I think I'm going to like you, Troy." She grabbed his arm. "Come inside with me and let me get you a drink."

"Okay," he said eagerly and then paused and looked at me. "Is that okay? We can talk about tonight later."

"Uh huh," I said, feeling pissed. Even my fake boyfriend was leaving me for Barbie. I looked over at TJ to see if he was laughing at me, but his eyes were focused on Barbie, and he looked annoyed.

And that hurt me even more. At least he could have given me a look of compassion. Here I was, standing like some loser, while my 'boyfriend' left me alone.

"See you in a second, my love," Troy cried back at me as he walked into the house, his mind obviously off of me.

"So, I guess Troy is real." TJ walked closer to me and his eyes searched mine. "I owe you an apology."

"Yeah, you do," I said and I felt proud of myself for not technically lying. I didn't confirm that Troy was real, and TJ owed me an apology for many different things, so me saying he owed me an apology wasn't really lying.

"So you find him attractive?" TJ's eyes narrowed.

"What do you think?" I shook my head at him. "That's a stupid question."

"Why is it stupid?" He looked at me with a raised eyebrow.

"Why would I date someone I wasn't attracted to?" I bit down on my lower lip. Okay, I was definitely furthering the lie now. There was no technical glitch getting me out of this lie. I was basically confirming that Troy and I were dating. Ugh, I was going to kill Sally.

"Hold on, Cody is calling me," TJ said as he pulled out his ringing phone. "Hello?" he said as he opened his phone, his eyes not leaving my face. "Okay." He nodded as he spoke and I watched as his tongue darted out of his mouth to moisten his lips. I looked away from his lips and up to his eyes. "Yeah, I can tell Barbie." He paused as he waited for Cody to say something else. "Yeah, I'll keep an eye out." He winked at me then and laughed slightly. "I'll talk to Mila." He nodded at something else that Cody was saying and I wondered what he was agreeing to talk to me about. "Yeah, okay. See you soon," he said and he hung up. "So, Cody and Sally are going to walk to the store."

"The store?" I frowned, though I was slightly happy for Sally as she was getting some alone time with him.

"Not in town, the one on the lake," he said with a smile. "Let's go inside and tell our better halves."

"Yeah," I said weakly and followed him into the house. I watched as he walked to the kitchen and I called out, "I'm going to go to my room. Tell Sally to come and get me when she gets back," I said as I hurried down the corridor. I didn't want TJ to convince me to go to the kitchen with him. I knew that only a hot mess could result from me being in the kitchen with just Troy, Barbie and TJ. And I was not ready to lose it. Not yet, anyways. There was plenty of time left in the weekend for that to happen.

I WALKED INSIDE MY room and sat on the bed, waiting. I was hoping that Sally would come and find me in the bedroom as soon as she got back so that she could tell me what the hell was going on. I had a feeling Cody would bring Troy up and the fact that he'd arrived already. I knew she was most probably feeling bad that she'd caught me unawares. I was feeling pretty pissed off, but I knew I'd forgive her. I just had to figure out exactly what was going on first. Sally wasn't a malicious person and I knew that, under other circumstances, I might have quite enjoyed the fact that she was trying to help me out. Only these circumstances were not the best. Imagine if my fake boyfriend ran off with my nemesis? Ugh, how embarrassing would that be?

I could hear the sounds of laughing from outside the room: deep male laughter, and Barbie's high-pitched squeaking. I wondered if it was Troy or TJ who was amusing her. I felt irritated at the possibility of both. I felt that they were both betraying me in some way that was completely obvious to me, but would have been hard to explain to anyone else. I lie back on the bed and grabbed my phone and texted Sally.

What's the deal with Troy? Why didn't you tell me? I hit send quickly and waited for Sally to respond. I saw the initial dots showing that she was typing and stared at the screen, waiting for her answer. But then the dots disappeared and no response came and I started feeling annoyed. Why wasn't she responding? Ugh! I just wanted to know exactly what she'd told Troy. What was his plan? I turned my phone to my Kindle app and opened it, to try and distract myself from my annoyance. I opened it to the book I was currently reading, a romantic suspense called Sloth by Ella James. It was a real page turner, so I knew it would keep my mind occupied while I waited for Sally to return.

A bang on the door about an hour later woke me up and I realized that I'd fallen asleep.

"Sally, come in," I said groggily as I sat up. I hated having afternoon naps because they always made me feel even more tired than I might have been before.

"It's TJ," he said as he opened the door, and I could see his eyes flying to me in the bed as I stretched my arms. "Late night?" He winked at me.

"Haha," I said and rolled my eyes at him. "You were with me when I went to bed, so obviously you know it wasn't that late."

"I wasn't quite with you." He licked his lips as he walked towards me. "If I'd been with you, it would have been a much later night. And you would have been a lot more tired." He paused for a few seconds and then continued. "From all the working out."

"Really?" You like to play charades at night?" I said, deliberately misunderstanding him. "I know you have to move your arms around a lot, but I don't consider that a workout."

"That's not the sort of workout I was talking about," he said as he sat on the bed next to me. "I was talking about the sort of workout that had you on top of me, bouncing—"

"TJ Walker," I almost screamed as my face went a bright red. "What the hell do you think you're saying? You're so inappropriate."

"I was going to say that you were on top of me, bouncing around as we wrestled on the floor, like we used to do when we were younger."

"We have wrestled twice in our lives." I shook my head, my face still red as I remembered the last time we'd wrestled. It had been all innocent at first as we'd rolled around on the floor, and then he'd pinned my arms up above my head and straddled my waist. Everything had been innocent enough until I'd started wiggling around on the floor against him and then I'd felt something hard against my belly. We'd both frozen for a second and his legs had clenched around me, pushing his hardness against me for a few seconds too long. I had stared up at him, not understanding the funny feelings that had been passing through me and I'd grabbed his back and pulled him closer to me. That had seemed to frighten him and then he had jumped up off of me and pulled me off of the ground roughly, keeping me at arm's length.

"I know. That's a pity, isn't it?" he said, his voice almost purring at me. "I'd love to have you pinned down right now, begging me for your release."

"Begging you for my release?" I laughed. "I could get away from you quite easily." I scoffed at him. "You're not that strong." I looked at his muscles and tried not to imagine how easily he could keep me on the ground.

"That wasn't the sort of release I was talking about," he said softly, running a finger down my cheek and brushing my lips.

"Oh," I gasped as I connected the dots.

"Though I suppose your new man is doing that job now."

"What job?" I asked, frowning, my heart racing. He was sitting too close to me. I couldn't concentrate. I wanted to grab him and pull him towards me. I wanted to touch his chest, squeeze his biceps, suck on his finger—and other things.

"The job of keeping you satisfied."

"Oh," I said, blushing again, and I jumped up. TJ jumped up as well and I took a few steps back. Why was he winding me up? I didn't understand why he was flirting with me if he had Barbie. I wondered what he would do if I took him up on his offer and went a step further. What if I then took charge? Would he be surprised? I knew he saw me as little innocent Mila. How would he feel if I pushed him down on the bed and jumped on top of him? Would he let me take control, or would he roll me over and hold me down and take control?

"So does he?" TJ said, his voice gruff as he took another step towards me. I took another step back; feeling like my body was about to explode.

"Does he what?" I asked, staring at his chest as it moved his shirt back and forth.

"Does he satisfy you in bed?"

"TJ," I gasped, shaking my head as he grabbed my waist and pulled me towards him.

"Mila," he said, mocking me, his eyes darkening as he looked down at me. "I can, you know."

"You can what?" I said, swallowing hard.

"I can satisfy all of your needs." His hands grabbed my ass and he squeezed gently. My body froze as I looked up at him.

"Oh, yeah?" I said softly, finally finding my voice in my shock.

"Yeah." He nodded again, and he moved his face towards mine. "I can satisfy needs you didn't even know you had." He leaned down and blew in my right ear, and I felt a finger sliding between my legs, rubbing me lightly. My whole body thudded and stilled as I felt his finger sliding back out. I was shocked that he'd touched me in such an intimate way that my bikini bottoms grew wet immediately. I waited to see what he was going to do next, but then there was a knock at the door.

"Mila, you in there?" Sally came bounding into the room and I jumped away from TJ. "We're back." She grinned at me, looking happy. "Oh hi, TJ," she said and then smiled at me. "I got us some wine. Let's have some with lunch," she said and walked towards the door, seemingly oblivious to the fact that she had just interrupted something that could have been very hot.

"Saved by the bell," TJ whispered behind me as we walked out of the bedroom, and I felt him tapping my ass lightly. I didn't respond as I walked out, but all I could think about was the heaviness between my legs from where he'd touched me, and the wonder of what would have happened next if we hadn't been interrupted.

◆

"IT'S FUNNY HOW MUCH you love this place," Sally said to me as we grabbed some glasses of wine in the kitchen.

"Why do you say that?" I asked her curiously, looking out the window at the lush green grass and tall trees, wanting to tell her what had just happened with TJ, and wanting to ask her what the hell was going on with Troy but not knowing which one to start with.

"Because you're a city girl, but you love the country." She smiled at me as she took a sip of the red wine she'd just gotten at the grocery store. "Most people either love the city or the country. Not both."

"You know how much I love the city." I grinned at her. "But this is my home. This is the place I come to for tranquility and nature. When I come here, I really feel close to God and humanity. I look out at the blue sky and I listen to the birds and I think, wow. This is so amazing. So beautiful. So perfect. This is what I imagine Heaven is like."

"And that has nothing to do with TJ being here as well?" She grinned and raised an eyebrow at me.

"Whatever." I laughed and took a big gulp of wine and then sighed slightly. "Of course, TJ is a major part of what I love about coming here. I feel especially connected to him when I'm here." I made a face. "And, Sally—oh, my God." I lowered my voice and looked around to make sure nobody was paying attention to us. "I think TJ might be interested. Just now—in the bedroom—he touched me and I think he wanted to take things a step further." She looked back at me excitedly, her brown eyes eager to hear more.

"Oh, my God, he totally loves you," Sally said, her voice rising with her excitement. "I need to tell you what happened with Cody as well on the car ride; but, first finish telling me what happened with you and TJ. How and where did he touch you and what are you going to do next?"

"Wait, I thought you guys were walking?" I said with a small frown.

"He decided to drive instead." She grinned. "Thank God, as I wasn't really looking forward to walking. Now, tell me, what are you going to do about TJ?"

"I'm going to go for it," I said with a grin. "Maybe I do have a real shot, though that could all be in my head and just in my dreams, I suppose."

"What's just in your dreams, dorky?" TJ walked into the kitchen, followed by Cody, and I froze. How much had he heard?

"She was saying that she'd love to be able to go on Chopped, the TV show," Sally said quickly as I stood there in silence, my mouth unable to work as I tried to think of something to say. Thank God that Sally was quick on her feet.

"You?" Cody looked at me with a surprised expression. "Isn't that a cooking show?"

"Yes," I said and frowned at him.

"You want to go on a cooking show?" He laughed and shook his head as he walked to the fridge. "Want a beer, TJ?"

"Yeah, pass me a Blue Moon."

"Blue Moon?" Cody made a face. "Bud Light's where it's at."

"Bud Light?" TJ laughed. "No, thanks."

"So, what are we going to do tonight?" Sally said, her eyes gazing at Cody in a way that told everyone in the room that she was interested. I felt slightly embarrassed for her being so obvious, but I didn't want to hurt her feelings by saying that. And maybe Cody really had given her a sign when they went to the grocery store that he really was interested. Maybe both of us were going to get lucky this weekend.

"Maybe we can shoot some pool at the bar?" Cody said and shrugged. I studied his face to see if I could tell if he was interested in her, but I couldn't read anything from his expression. Was it possible that Cody wasn't reading the signs that Sally was putting out? Was my brother that clueless? And was it possible that Sally was reading his signs incorrectly?

"I don't think anyone wants to drive." TJ shook his head. "And I'm not letting anyone drink and drive."

"Yeah, true," Cody agreed. "What else is there?"

"What is everyone up to?" Barbie walked into the kitchen wearing a skimpy bikini. "Are you guys finally ready to eat?" she said, sounding a bit miffed. My eyes widened as I took in her small waist and big boobs. Her bikini was small and white and her boobs were almost popping out of the top. She must have been cold as well because her nipples were poking out like small pebbles for everyone to see. I watched as she swung her hips towards the fridge, and I could hear Sally gasping along with me as we stared at her naked, perfect, cellulite-free ass. And we saw all of her ass, as she was wearing a thong bottom.

I looked over at Sally and she mouthed the word 'slut' to me and I grinned. Why was Barbie wearing a bikini with a thong bottom, and why did she have to have such a perfect body? Once again I felt slightly insecure in her presence. I looked over to see if TJ was ogling her but noticed that he was staring at me with a peculiar expression on his face. I gazed into his eyes and he raised an eyebrow at me as his lips twisted up at the side. I wanted to ask him what he was thinking, but didn't dare. He was most probably thinking that Sally and I were jealous of Barbie and her perfect body. Though maybe he was also thinking about the inappropriate way he had just touched me and the fact that I hadn't hit his hand away immediately. I blushed as I thought about the feeling of his finger rubbing me briefly and firmly on my bud, awakening all my sexual desires.

"Not yet" Cody said, his voice husky. "We're just trying to decide what to do tonight first?" I looked over at him because his voice sounded strange, but I almost gagged when I saw his tongue practically hanging out of his mouth as he stared at Barbie and her big boobs.

"I have an idea," she said with a small smile as she walked over to him with some grapes in her hand.

"Oh?" Cody said, his eyes moving down to her waist and then back up to her bust as she ate the grapes and jiggled around. My eyes narrowed as I realized that her boobs were brushing against his arm. Ho!

"Why don't we play truth or dare tonight?" she said and we all watched as she sucked another grape into her mouth like some sort of vacuum.

"Truth or dare?" Sally said, her voice pained, the light gone from her eyes. "I don't think so."

"I think it would be fun," Cody said, not even turning to look at Sally. I gazed at her face and I could see that she was hurt, and that made me want to punch him. I was guessing that whatever leeway she'd thought they'd made on the way to the grocery store was now gone.

"Yeah," TJ said and nodded. "So do I. Where's Troy? Let's see if he wants to play as well." He glanced over at me and winked, and I wanted to slap him.

"I think he might be tired," I lied. There was no way I was bringing Troy into this, especially as I didn't really know what he knew or where he'd come from. I really needed to ask Sally what she'd been thinking by inviting him. It had been a good idea but not for the whole weekend. How did she think I'd be able to pull this off? Especially as she'd just sprung the surprise on me.

"I'll go and check," TJ said and he grinned at me. "This is a good way for you to get to know him better. See if he's really the one."

"I never said he was the one," I said, feeling cornered.

"How come you never told me about him?" Cody said, finally breaking his gaze away from Barbie's boobs and looking at me with a frown. "I didn't even know you were dating anyone."

"I don't have to tell you every time I go on a date," I said, glaring at him.

"They need to be vetted, Mila. You know you have questionable taste," he said, sounding very much like the older, bossy brother he's always been. "I don't think Mom and Dad would appreciate you dating someone we don't even know. I know Nonno definitely wouldn't."

"Whatever," I said, feeling like a petulant kid.

"You should be more responsible, Mila," Barbie said and looked at me with pitying eyes. "I know you're desperate, but you shouldn't just date a guy because he asks you out. I know it must be hard to have standards when you don't get asked out much."

"Barbie." TJ's voice was sharp and he frowned as he looked at her.

"I'm just teasing her," Barbie said, looking like a wounded deer. "You know how I love to tease." She looked at me with a sad little face and said, "Please don't take my teasing seriously, Mila. I'm sure you get plenty of men." She gave me an obviously fake smile and walked over to TJ and put her arm through his. "Please don't be mad at me, honey bunny." Her hand caressed his stomach. "Let's get you some food." She then looked around at everyone. "We must all be tired and hungry. We can eat and then decide what to do tonight."

"Sounds like a plan to me," Cody said eagerly, and Sally and I just looked at each other with a frown. We'd gone from exuberant to depressed in five minutes flat, and I wasn't sure what game TJ was playing.

❖

I TRIED TO SIGNAL to Sally to follow me after lunch so that we could talk, but I couldn't tell if she was paying attention to me. I gave her the eye, nodded toward the hallway and started walking. Lunch had been awkward and basically The Barbie Show, so I thought that we needed to come up with a plan to turn things around. I made my way down the hallway and smiled to myself as I heard steps behind me. I turned around to look at Sally and my jaw dropped when I saw that it was TJ.

"Come," he said and grabbed my wrist and pulled me into his bedroom.

"What are you doing?" I said, my tone excited. Was he going to push me down on the bed and have his wicked way with me? And if he did, would I say no, or moan with pleasure that finally the day had come that I'd been waiting for?

"What do you want me to do?" he said and he licked his lips. "You're going to make me do something that I shouldn't."

"What shouldn't you do?" I asked breathlessly, wanting to tell him to just shut up and do it already.

"I want to bend you over and..." He paused as his phone started ringing. I think both of us were annoyed at that point, but a part of me was grateful. I didn't know what was going on; and while a part of me was excited, I was also very confused. TJ grabbed his phone and answered it, his features looking stoic. I took a step back; my heart racing and my brain in overdrive, feeling a bit worried. Yes, I wanted TJ to take me, but I'd had a more romantic setting in mind. I wanted to be made love to, not just fucked.

Ten

T J

"HEY, DAD." I SAID, waiting for him to speak. Mila gave me an awkward smile and started to back out of the room timidly. I reached out and grabbed her arm to stop her and she turned her face to me in surprise. "What's up?" I said into the phone again as my fingers tightened their grip on Mila's wrist.

"How's everything going? According to plan?"

"You could say that," I said as I grinned down at a perplexed Mila. I could feel her pulse racing through my fingers, and I ran my fingers across the soft skin of her hands. It felt smooth to the touch. I wished that I were touching other parts of her body with more than just my fingers to see if every part of her was like finely spun silk.

"TJ, let me go," she whispered, her eyes glaring at me as her nostrils flared. I could tell from the red hue in her face that she was still flustered from our previous conversation. I wondered if her panties were moist and wet with her juices. I'd seen the way she'd parted her legs as we'd talked, as if she were feeling heavy down there. I was glad that she was having the same reaction as me. My cock was hard with need for her. I shifted now since I could feel myself growing harder as I stared at her breasts heaving right next to me. What would she do if I reached over and squeezed her right breast? Would she react if my fingers gently tugged on her nipple? Would she cry out and moan in abandon if I pulled her top up and sucked on her breast? My mouth watered as I stared at her lips, pink and juicy, waiting for my kiss.

"So, what did you want, Dad?" I said, annoyed that he was calling me already. I'd told him I'd update him at the end of the weekend. I already felt like he'd pushed me into a corner. This whole weekend was not what I'd been hoping for.

"How's Barbie?" he asked me softly. I could tell from the tone of his voice that he knew more than I wanted him to know.

"She's fine," I said stiffly, and I could see Mila looking at me curiously. "Not you," I mouthed at her. "Barbie." Her reaction was immediate. I could see the quick glimpse of hurt in her eyes before she masked it with another emotion.

"You didn't tell me that—"

"Dad, I hope you're not spying on me." I was annoyed now and my grip involuntarily tightened on Mila's wrist. "I didn't tell you that Barbie and I—"

"TJ, just get the job done," My dad said. "Don't let anything distract you."

"I'm not," I said and my eyes fell to Mila's breasts again. She looked up at me and with her eyes narrowed, she used her other hand to push against my chest. I was so distracted by her touch that I momentarily loosened my grip and she pulled free of me. She ran to the door quickly, looked back at me for a few seconds and then hurried out.

I shook my head as I stood there. She had more spunk than I'd remembered as a child. She'd always been a precocious and beautiful kid, but she'd always seemed so shy and innocent. It had made me uncomfortable the way she'd gaze at me all doe-eyed and full of love as a teenager. Not that I'd been interested. There were too many college girls. And too many older women to deal with and learn from.

It wasn't until she'd turned 18 and was heading out to college that I'd really noticed her. It had been at the lake house and she'd been wearing a figure-hugging dress and her long blond hair had been hanging down her back, and she'd been laughing and dancing around to something. And I'd looked over at her and she'd given me a long, lazy, carefree smile, her eyes half-closed and her hands in the air as she'd moved slowly and sensually to the song in her head. I can still remember the way that I'd felt when I'd watched her, and later that night when I kissed her, I hadn't been able to stop myself.

I would have tried to move further if it weren't for the innocent look in her eyes and the fact that she is Cody's little sister. And as much as Cody bossed her around and acted like she was a pain in his ass, he loved her more than anything. I wasn't sure if Mila knew how much of his actions towards her were because he was so protective of her. I knew that Cody would have killed me if I'd made a move on his teenage sister. He probably would still kill me if I made a move, but that didn't bother me as much now. Now that I knew that she was older and could make up her own mind. And now that she made me so crazy inside that I just wanted to reach out and grab her and make her mine. No, now was different. There were things I'd risk for the opportunity to be with Mila.

"TJ, are you there? You haven't answered anything I've just asked you." My dad sounded pissed, which was his normal expression outside of the public eye. Pissed or annoyed or angry were the emotions that best described him. Though of course, to the public, he put on a casual, easy, relaxed demeanor. It was better for business for him to just appear as the handsome, nonchalant, happy-go-lucky playboy that the media liked to portray him as.

"I'm here," I said shortly. I heard light giggling from the hall and I walked to the door to look outside. I saw Mila with Troy standing at the corner, whispering about something and Mila was looking up at him with glee in her eyes. The glee that should have been reserved for me. I watched as Troy reached over and ran his fingers through her hair; okay, that might have been an exaggeration. His touch was momentary and it seemed as if he were picking something off of her. My hand clenched on the phone as I stared at them. I could hear my dad still talking, but I wasn't paying attention to what he was saying. I watched as Troy and Mila walked down the hallway past my door and I gave Troy a death stare, though he wasn't paying attention to me. Mila looked up and gave me a coy smile as she passed by, her eyes seemingly mocking me, and I could feel my palm itching to give her a good spanking. That would show her to just walk past me with another man and think she had one up on me. If she only knew the things I was capable of. I watched her hips swaying as they rounded the corner, and I smiled to myself as I thought about the look she'd have on her face if I bent her across my lap and spanked her lightly and then fingered her. I'd roll her over so that I could see her eyes rolling and her lips quivering as I brought her to multiple orgasms with just my fingers.

"TJ, get this done and don't fuck it up," my dad barked into the phone. I hung up, muttering under my breath, "You'd better believe I'm going to fuck it up, Dad." I smiled to myself as I headed to the living room. I was going to fuck it up as hard as I could.

Eleven

MILA
AUGUST 8, 2010

DEAR DIARY,

I know what perfection is. Well, I guess that's not correct. I know what bliss is. True and complete bliss. I was sitting in my room, listening to music on my iPod, feeling quite sorry for myself. TJ and Cody had gone on two double dates and Mom and Dad banned me from watching TV because they said I watch too many reality shows. Whatever! Anyways, there I was, lying on my bed, humming along to Boyz II Men and Coolio, and guess who walked into my room? You got it! My future husband, the wonderful magnificent gorgeous Adonis that is Travis James Walker. He just walked in, sat on my bed, grabbed one of my earphones and put it into his ear. He started grinning as he stared at me and listened to the song. To be honest, I can't even remember what song I'd been listening to. All I can remember is his gorgeous green eyes as they gazed at me and I could see that he'd been working out because his biceps were so buff. I sat up so that my earphones wouldn't break and then all of a sudden we both started rapping to the song that was playing. I didn't even know I knew all the words and I was shocked he knew the words. It was just a perfect moment. We just sat there rapping together and giggling and then we kinda moved back on the bed swaying in time to the beat. I could almost cry it was so perfect. And then Cody had to come and ruin it because that's who he is. The ruiner of all my dreams. Anyways, thought I had to let you know right away. Bliss is rapping to LL Cool J or whoever with TJ Walker on the bed, rubbing shoulders. The only way it could have been better is if he would have kissed me, but then I might just have died.

Mila
XOXO

"I can't believe that I am going to play truth or dare with my sister." Cody looked totally disgusted as we all sat around the campfire that TJ and he had set up just minutes before. "Who persuaded me to do this?"

"The beer did." TJ laughed as he swigged from his bottle.

"And I hope I was a small influence," Barbie said, swaying her hair in the wind as she stood there with a bottle of water in her hand, her breasts bouncing in her hot pink halter top. Once again she was wearing no bra. I wanted to tell her she might as well have kept her bikini on or just gone topless, but I stopped myself. Knowing Barbie as well as I did already, I knew she would go topless in a heartbeat and that would piss me off even more.

"Should we start a collection?" Sally whispered in my ear as she pointed at Barbie.

"I think we're the only ones who would put anything in." I giggled as I whispered back to her. "I think she's allergic to bras."

"You're right." Sally laughed loudly this time. "I think I read about that condition in a medical journal."

"Because you read medical journals all the time." I burst out laughing.

"Hey, I read Cosmo and sometimes they have health tips." She nodded, looking serious.

"Yeah, tips like what should you do if a condom comes off inside of you," I said and I froze as Troy came up to me.

"You're looking pretty tonight." He leaned down and kissed me on the cheek and I could see Sally grinning.

"We still need to talk." I glared at her, moving my face away from Troy.

"Yes, we do." She grinned. "You sly dog, you."

"I'm the sly dog?" I shook my finger at her. "You're trying to get me into trouble."

"I think you do that to yourself." She giggled. "I need to learn from you."

"Learn what from me?" I groaned.

"What are you two talking about?" Troy looked puzzled as he tried to take my hand, and I stepped away from him.

"Where Barbie should carry her rass to," Sally said quickly, and Troy looked confused.

"Huh?" he said and I giggled.

"Sally." I shook my head at her. "Behave."

"I'm trying," she said, her brown eyes boring into mine, looking hurt for a few seconds before looking over at Cody and Barbie.

"What did you say?" Troy said. "I didn't understand."

"It wasn't English," I said. "It's a Caribbean term," I said knowledgeably, feeling like some sort of smarty-pants.

"You're Caribbean?" He looked at Sally in surprise.

"No." She shook her head. "But I have family from Guyana, so I've been there several times, and to Jamaica, Barbados, St. Lucia and Antigua."

"Wow." Troy looked impressed. "I've always wanted to go to the Bahamas to gamble."

"Oh, okay." Sally nodded, looking confused, and I could tell from the look on her face that she thought Troy was annoying as well and she was going to say something. I knew the look well and knew she couldn't stop herself. "You want to go to The Bahamas to gamble, and that's it? Wouldn't Vegas be a better option? I don't know that the Bahamas is known for its casinos." She paused and the look she gave him would have made a smarter man blanch.

"Well, I'm pretty good at blackjack. Last year I won fifty dollars playing Bingo at my grandma's retirement home." He looked proud of himself.

"Uh?" Sally frowned. "Sorry, I don't get the connection between blackjack and Bingo?"

"Well, my grandma's friends told me they thought I'd kill at the blackjack tables with my bingo skills," he said and I had to stop myself from groaning. He was such a dumbass. I wondered where Sally had found him.

"Oh, okay." Sally nodded.

"And I did win fifty bucks," he continued, "so if I keep on winning big, I'll soon be a millionaire."

"I suppose, one one dutty build damn." Sally nodded, rolling her eyes.

"Huh?" Troy looked confused and looked at me. "What's that?"

"Another Guyanese term." I grinned, well versed in the different terms Sally used. "It means that the pennies add up and soon you have a lot of money."

"Oh, I won fifty dollars," he said, looking at Sally, "not pennies."

"It's figurative. Not literal," Sally said and sighed, looking over at Cody. "Hey, you guys ready? I'm ready for some games."

"Let's do it," TJ said and I looked over at him and blushed as he winked at me.

"I know I'm excited," Troy said, hurrying over to the fire and sitting on the ground. He patted the seat next to him and looked over at me, but I looked the other way and hurried to the other side to sit next to Cody.

"So how are we going to do this?" Cody said, drinking his beer and leaning back. My brother looked flushed and handsome, and I could see both Barbie and Sally admiring him. I bit my lower lip as I saw Cody looking back at Barbie. I sure hoped that he wasn't going to do anything to hurt Sally's feelings.

"We'll all write our names on a piece of paper," TJ said. I looked over at him in surprise, not expecting him to be the one in charge of setting up the game of truth or dare. "And we'll all write a few dares and put it into a different hat when people pick dares. When someone picks truth, one person will get to ask them a question."

"What if Mila picks me or I pick Mila?" Cody said, looking over at me in disgust. "I'm not doing any sort of crazy dare with my sister."

"Since when have you cared about crazy?" TJ raised an eyebrow at him. "Back in your frat days..." TJ's voice drifted off and I saw Cody glaring at him.

"You're sick," Cody said, and Sally looked at him curiously.

"What did you do?" she asked him and I stared at him as well, wondering what dirty deeds my brother had gotten up to while he was in college.

"What didn't he do?" TJ laughed and looked at Cody. "I remember a night with four girls, two sets of twin sisters."

"Hey," Cody said, his voice slightly angry, but I couldn't help but notice a proud smile on his face. "They came to me."

"Uh huh," TJ said. "Like those two study-abroad friends from Spain."

"Hey, is it my fault they both wanted me to show them my room?" Cody laughed now. "They both enjoyed my bed."

"Cody!" I shouted at him, my jaw slack. "You hooked up with twin sisters and two friends?"

"What can I say?" He winked at me. "Double the trouble, double the fun."

"You do realize you're boasting about your sick ways to your own sister?" I poked him in the shoulder. "You're supposed to be pretending you're virginal and pure."

"Hahaha." Cody laughed again. "And you would believe that why?"

"Would you like me telling you about all the different guys I hooked up with?" I said to him, feeling miffed.

"What guys?" TJ said, and his eyes narrowed as he looked at me.

"Yeah, what guys?" Cody said, no longer laughing. "You'd

better not have been doing anything Nonno wouldn't be happy with."

"I'm a grown woman. I can do what I want," I said, glaring at him.

"No, you can't," he said and glared back at me.

"You can't tell me what to do."

"Yes, I can," he said with his bossy big-brother tone that I detested. "I'm your brother and I will make sure you stay on the right path if I have to shoot someone."

"Maybe I've already strayed from the right path," I said and I could see both TJ and Cody glaring at me.

"Hey, guys, should we play?" Sally interrupted and tapped Cody on the shoulder. "And if you pick Mila's name or she picks you, you guys can just pick again."

"Fine," Cody said with a huff and then gave Sally a warm smile. "You're looking pretty tonight, Sally."

"Thanks." She practically beamed at him.

"Let's all have a seat," TJ said and I felt him brushing past me. "Oh, sorry," he said and stopped as his hand slid down my back and rested on my ass.

"Sorry for what?" I asked, confused as I looked up at his smoldering gaze.

He bent down and whispered in my ear softly. "Leading you down the wrong path."

"What wrong path?" I asked, my face flushed from his close contact.

"The one that will have you blushing and your brother cussing," he said again lightly and I felt him give my ass a quick slap before he walked away and sat down next to the fire. I stood there feeling confused and turned on, and wondered what he had planned. It definitely seemed like he was coming on to me, even though he was still teasing me and driving me crazy. And even though he was here with Barbie and doing heaven knew what with her. TJ seemed hell-bent on teasing me and I didn't know if he was deliberately playing me to make me feel embarrassed or if he was going to carry through on his word. I knew that in my heart of hearts, I wanted him to follow through on everything he was saying. My ass was still tingling from his touch and I wondered how far he was going to take it. I already knew how far I was willing to go.

"TRUTH OR DARE, MILA?" TJ's voice was smooth as he looked at me.

"I don't know." I looked over at Sally and she shrugged. She didn't know what to tell me to do and I didn't know what to do.

"Come on, sis," Cody said, sounding like he was already half-drunk. "Pick truth. I want to find out all your secrets."

"Dare," I blurted out loudly, feeling panicked. What if he asked me about TJ? How embarrassing would that be? So, everyone, I've had a crush on TJ Walker for years and I came up to the lake house this year with the plan of seducing him. Yeah, that would go down really well. TJ would most probably laugh and say he knew it all along and then Cody would call my parents and get me sent to some convent in Italy or something.

"Okay, pick a name out of the basket," TJ said with a grin. "And then pick the dare out of the dare basket."

"Okay," I said softly, hoping that the dares we'd all written and put in the basket weren't too crazy. I mean, one of my dares was for people to kiss for two minutes, in the hope that I could kiss TJ, or Sally could kiss Cody. I put my hand in the first basket and picked out a piece of paper with a name on it. My heart skipped a beat as I opened it up slowly.

"I hope you picked me, darling," Troy said, his eyes gleaming at me. I ignored his face as I unfolded the paper. He was really getting on my nerves. I wasn't sure what sort of game he thought he was playing. He was paying more attention to Barbie, and I think it was clear to everyone that he thought her almost-naked breasts were far superior to my covered-up ones. Not that I cared. All I could think about was TJ and the way he'd been staring at me all night. My eyes read the paper in front of me and my heart stopped beating for a second. I tried not to grin as I read TJ's name in short, clean black handwriting.

"Who did you get?" Sally asked excitedly. I think she could tell from the sudden change in my demeanor that it was TJ's name in my hand.

"I got TJ," I said with a fake scowl, pretending that I was upset. I looked over at Sally and she winked at me and made an 'ohlala' movement with her mouth.

"Ooh," Cody said with a laugh. "I hope you guys get my dare. You'll have to go and get more beer from the grocery store."

"That's not a dare." I rolled my eyes at him as I put my hand in the dare basket and pulled out a piece of paper. I was hoping it wasn't something too crazy and absurd. I would be happy with a kiss. Maybe even a French kiss. Maybe even being handcuffed together. That would actually even be kind of exciting. I unfolded the new piece of paper and I could feel my skin burning as I read it. I felt a sudden surge of excitement and shame. This could not be right, could it? Who would have made a dare like this? I just didn't understand why someone would write this as a dare. Then I looked at Barbie and I realized she would die for the chance to do what she'd written.

"Read it aloud, Mila," TJ said, staring at me with a weird look on his face. I stared into his eyes for a few seconds and swallowed hard. He looked way too serious, way too sexy, and way too out-of-my league. I'd be happy with the kiss, but I wasn't sure I was ready to go completely naked.

"I'm not doing this," I said, my face red as I wondered if I'd shaved recently and if my boobs would look saggy in the moonlight. Saggy, wet boobs were not the same as boobs pushed up in tight lingerie as I lay on the bed with my hair hanging in my face.

"You have to," Cody said as he swigged from his beer. I wanted to slap him. If he knew what the dare was, he wouldn't be saying that. No siree.

"No, I don't."

"Stop being a baby," he said with a laugh and I glared at him as he gave me a mocking look. I'd show my big brother that he couldn't just keep talking to me like a little baby.

"Fine. I'll do it." I shook my head at him and then looked at TJ. "Get up and get ready to take your clothes off, TJ, we're going skinny-dipping in the lake."

"Oh hell no, you're not." Cody's demeanor changed right away as he jumped up and put his beer down. Sally, Barbie, and Troy looked over at him with surprised looks on their faces. They were likely surprised at how quickly his mood had changed, but they had no idea that this was how Cody always acted with me. I felt sorry for his kids. He was going to be a tyrant.

"Yes, we are." I walked over to TJ and grabbed his arm. "Let's go."

"TJ, you cannot skinny-dip with my sister." Cody looked at him and sounded pissed.

"I'll take her to the lake, but I'll make sure she's safe," TJ said. "After all, a dare is a dare. Plus it's dark, so no one will see us."

"I don't want you seeing my sister naked." Cody was starting to sound even more pissed off and I could see his face turning red as he glared at his best friend.

"I'll close my eyes." TJ shrugged and then looked at me. "I don't particularly want to do this myself," he said and I saw him look me up and down. "Let's go and get this done with," he said and grabbed my arm and led me down to the lake.

We walked quickly and I could feel my heart racing. Were we really going to do this? Was TJ really only doing it because it was a dare? My answer came swiftly as we stopped by some chairs next to the lake and I watched him pulling his shirt off and turning to me with a grin as he dropped it to the ground.

"Get your bra and your panties off, baby, it's time for me to get you wet." He bent down and splashed some water on my legs, his green eyes shooting promises of deeds unknown as he stared up at me and then stood back up. "What are you waiting for?" he said as he started to unbutton his pants.

"What are you doing?" I asked stupidly as I gazed at his chest, my eyes devouring his abs and his muscular pecs. We had gone from 0-100 in two seconds flat and my brain was sending warning signals all through my body. I wasn't sure if I was feeling panicked about going skinny-dipping or if I was feeling panicked because I had an almost-naked TJ standing a mere inch from me.

"Like what you see?" he said as he flexed his pecs and moved them back and forth. My eyes were mesmerized by the movement and I wanted to reach out and touch his chest to see what it felt like when he moved them back and forth.

"TJ," I squeaked as he grabbed my hand and put my fingers on his right pec and ran them down his chest on the way to the top of his pants. I wasn't sure if he had ESP or what, but the feeling of his chest moving was quite enjoyable. "TJ," I squeaked again as he held my hand firmly and pressed it against the top of his pants. "What are you doing?"

"I want you to make me wet as well," he said, his lips close to mine. "It's only fair," he said again, and I could feel his breath on my lips as I felt something underneath his pants twitching. He laughed at the look on my face and then pulled away, leaving me standing there breathless, just staring at him. "Last one in is a dork," he shouted and pulled his pants and boxer shorts down swiftly before running into the lake. I stared at his naked ass as he ran and all I could think was, Oh, my God, I'm about to skinny-dip with TJ Walker, and his ass is tan, when highlighted by the moon. How did he have a tan ass? My hands flew to my top and I pulled it off without even thinking. I needed to get into that water with him. I wasn't sure if he was testing me, but I didn't care. This was like all my dreams come true plus 100. I wasn't going to let anything get in the way of some possible sexy time with him.

"You coming?" TJ said, shouting from the water as I stood there in my bra. "If you don't get in here in twenty seconds, I'll come and get you."

"Come and get me, then," I said giddily, already feeling like I was having an out-of-body experience. I froze as I saw him coming towards me, his body gloriously naked and drenched in water as he approached me. My jaw fell as I stared at his manhood: strong, thick, and majestic. I swallowed hard as he came closer and closer and I could feel my throat becoming drier and drier. I couldn't move and I felt like a statue as he stopped in front of me, towering over me, his dark hair slick on his head as drops fell from his face onto my shoulders.

"I'm here," he said and I felt his wet hand on my back, touching my bra strap.

"I'm ready," I said softly and I felt him unclasping my bra. We both stood there in silence as my bra fell to the ground.

"Those are the words I've been waiting for," he said with a smirk, his fingers lightly running across my collarbone and then down the valley between my breasts. I gasped as his fingers ran down to my stomach and played in my belly button before continuing down to my shorts. He didn't even pause as he undid the button on my shorts and then slid the zipper down. I grabbed his hand then, feeling panicked at what I was about to do, and my finger accidentally grazed his hardness. I felt and heard his sharp intake of breath at my touch, and his fingers stilled.

"You're never going to forget tonight, Mila," he said as he whispered into my ear. "Now take off your panties and join me in the lake before I do something everyone on the lake will be talking about in the morning." He took hold of my fingers lightly and brushed them against his cock again. This time the touch was deliberate and sensual, both of us knowing what we were doing. I took a hold of him and ran my fingers down the length of him, barely able to breathe and I could see his eyes darkening.

"Join me in the lake," he said, his right hand reaching up to caress my right breast. His fingers were cold against my skin and I shivered slightly as he grabbed my breast and rubbed his palm against my nipple. I moaned involuntarily and he grunted, squeezing my breast even more tightly and pinching my nipple before stepping back and releasing his hold on me. "Join me in the lake. You can leave on your panties or take them off," he said gruffly. "Whichever one you decide will let me know what you want to do next."

"What about Barbie?" I said breathlessly.

"What about Troy?" he said and raised an eyebrow before shrugging and walking back into the lake slowly and confidently. I stood there for about ten seconds before I pulled my panties down and followed him into the water. It was freezing cold against my body and I yelped as I surged down into the water, letting it cover me completely, so that I could get acclimated to the cold water quicker. I felt his strong hands grabbing me and pulling me out of the water and his face looked down at me with a stern look.

"What are you doing, Mila?" he said with a frown as he held me.

"I was just getting my body adjusted to the temperature," I said, glaring at him and then gasping as I felt his fingers sliding down my waist and in between my legs, rubbing me gently in my most private of spots.

"What are you doing?" I gasped, pushing against his shoulders as my breasts brushed against his chest.

"Checking to see if you were wearing any underwear," he said, his fingers still lingering between my legs and rubbing on my clit.

"Well, you know the answer now," I said, feeling turned on as I grabbed his arm and pulled it back.

"Yes, I do," he said as he finally removed his fingers and then grabbed me around the waist and pulled me closer to him, so that my body was now pushed up against his as the water splashed over us.

"So now what?" I said, my voice squeaking as I felt his hardness moving against my stomach. I wasn't even sure how he was still hard as I thought men grew flaccid in cold water.

"Now you tell me that you want me more than you want Troy,"

he said, his hands falling to my ass and squeezing.

"No, you tell me you want me more than you want Barbie," I said and I felt myself losing my balance and moving my legs up around his waist.

"Was there any ever any doubt?" he said as he bent down to kiss me. "Right now, I want to fuck you more than I've ever wanted to fuck anyone else before."

Twelve

TJ

DAMN! I KNEW FROM the look on Mila's face that she didn't appreciate my last words. She didn't want to hear how badly I wanted to fuck her. She didn't want to hear how her bud had quivered against my fingers as I'd rubbed her. How I'd felt her releasing her juices against me even though we were in the water. Her breasts felt soft and hard as they pressed into my chest and her legs were wrapped around me tightly as if she were scared she was going to drown. Fuck. How badly I just wanted to drive my hardness into her and make her mine. It would be so easy. I was so close to her opening and she was ready for me. I could feel it in the way her pussy had been pulsing as I'd rubbed her clit. She wanted me inside of her, even if she didn't know it. One shift of my body to the right, one movement of her right leg up just a little higher, and I'd be inside of her, making her mine.

But I knew that now was not the time to be playing with fire. Everything was too complicated. I needed to play it cool. Especially as Cody was here. He was going to be trouble and I didn't know what to do. He was my best friend, but even his wishes couldn't stop me from doing what I was going to do.

"TJ." Mila gasped against my mouth as her lips kissed me back hesitantly. I could tell that she didn't really know what was going on but that she was willing to give me whatever I wanted.

"Mila," I said, teasing her and tugging on her lower lip with my teeth. She moaned and shifted her position against me and I could feel my cock twitching to be inside of her. My hand moved up to her breasts and squeezed gently, my fingers rubbing against her cold and hard nipples, doing things that I wanted my lips to be doing.

"Oh TJ," she cried out and pulled away from me, her eyes wide with passion and shock.

"Sorry, I got a bit carried away," I said, treading water next to her, my body missing the closeness of hers in the cold water.

"You seem to be doing a lot of that today," she said, her lips still slightly parted. My cock grew harder as I thought about her sucking me and taking me deep into her mouth. I looked away from her mouth then. I wasn't sure I'd be able to resist fucking her if I continued thinking about her moans and her groans as I fucked her into oblivion.

"I'm going for a swim," she said, her eyes looking slightly anxious as I stared at her. She could probably see in my face that I was feeling confused. Maybe I even looked gruff. Maybe I was scaring her, looking like some wolf in the night that wanted to eat her. She drifted onto her back and floated away from me. I watched as her breasts glistened through the water. She looked like a nymph that was tempting me. Staring at her made me think of Shakespeare and poetry. The moon made her body glow enticingly and I could feel myself stilling as I watched her. She was such a work of art; a beauty to behold that was both innocent and tempting at the same time.

"Above the lake a mist was lifting; through milky clouds across the sky, the ruddy mood was softly drifting, when water drew the friar's eye." I whispered the words to Alexander Pushkin's poem,

The Water-Nymph to myself as I watched her, moving in the water. I felt surprisingly at ease, as if the moment were magical. And then something inside me stirred; my loins grew tense and aching. The wolf was awakened. And I was ready to take what was mine.

I paused then, trying to think about more than just my carnal thoughts. I felt more for her than just sex. I could feel it in my bones, in the way my heart raced as I gazed at her graceful movements in the water. I found myself staring at her face as she stopped floating and started treading water to me. I immediately swam over to her, my strokes fast as I ached to get to her quickly.

"Enjoy your swim?" I said lightly, stopping a couple of inches away from her. Though I wanted to touch her, I didn't want her to think I was all about sex. I wanted her to like me for me. I wanted her to want me, not just because I was attractive and rich. And I wanted her to know that my interest in her wasn't just about sex—even though I wanted to fuck her into oblivion. Things were going to get complicated and I didn't want the start of everything to be ruled by our sexual attraction to each other.

"The water feels good." She nodded, her eyes gazing into mine wonderingly. She looked disappointed, and I had to hide a smile. She wanted me to move closer to her and take her into my arms. I knew it as well as I knew that my name was TJ Walker.

"It's not too cold tonight." I nodded and tried to ignore the slight parting of her lips. Her eyes looked huge in her face as she stared at me and her blond hair was slicked back.

"Do you want to race?" she asked me finally, and I laughed.

"You know I always beat you. Are you sure you want to go down that road again?"

"You don't always beat me." She glared at me and her expression reminded me of when she was a child and got annoyed when Cody or I teased her, which we had done a lot.

"I don't think you've ever won any race that we've been in," I said and raised an eyebrow at her. I found myself moving closer to her, as I just couldn't stop myself.

"Whatever," she said, her breathing slightly faster as our bodies lightly touched. "I'll beat you now."

"Where do you want to race to?" I said, never one to turn down a challenge when pressed.

"We'll race out to that buoy." She nodded her head to a lighted buoy in the far distance. "And then back to shore."

"You really want to take on that distance?" I asked her in surprise. By my calculations it would be at least half a mile there and back to shore.

"Yeah, you got a problem with that?" she said, her brown eyes glittering at me, as if to say, don't call me out for your problems.

"Nope," I said, ignoring the desire to kiss her. "Let's do it."

"Okay," she said. "On your mark, get set, go." She screamed and I felt a huge splash of water in my face as she swam off, kicking through the water with all of her might.

I swam behind her at a leisurely pace. I knew I could beat her, but I wasn't swimming to win. I wanted to make sure that she didn't get a cramp in the water or run into trouble. That was more important to me than winning the race. I picked up my pace slightly when I realized that she was still going strong as she made it to the buoy in what I thought must have been record time. I felt a wave of appreciation for her and I was impressed at how quickly she was swimming. Mila was really in this race to win it. I picked up my pace slightly as she did a flip and started swimming back towards the shore.

"Sucker." She grinned as she saw me still swimming to the buoy and I was just about to answer when she put her head back down so she could front crawl as quickly as possible back to shore. I laughed as I flipped and I started to do the breaststroke as I made my way back. I could keep my head above water and continue to watch her as I swam. I found myself catching up to her quickly and I knew I could either let her win or take over. A part of me wanted to win so that I could watch her huffing and puffing and fuming about how I'd cheated, but I didn't. It didn't feel important to win this. Not now. Not with everything I had planned. I'd be winning plenty pretty soon. I might as well give her this. I slowed down my pace and watched as she made it to the shore and jumped up in excitement, a huge smile on her face as she jumped up and down. My loins froze and my cock swelled as I watched her breasts bouncing up and down. Damn, she was sexy.

"I beat you." She squealed at me as I swam up to her. She immediately stopped jumping and made her way back farther into the water as she became self-conscious.

"You cheated," I said with a half-smile, finding it hard to ignore the feelings of want that were coursing through my body as she swam over to me.

"No, I didn't." She giggled. "I beat you fair and square. You just suck."

"I'll show you who sucks," I said, frowning at her. "Let's race again."

"No," she said, her eyes bright as she licked her lips. "I already won."

"Then beat me again," I said directly to her lips as I stared at the tip of her tongue. My cock twitched as I watched her tongue darting back and forth. I could already feel her tongue on me, licking up and down my shaft before she sucked on my balls. I groaned as I grew harder.

"What did you say?" She frowned and her eyes narrowed as she looked at me.

"I said, beat me again." I moved closer to her and touched her lips softly.

"I'm too tired to race again." She shook her head and some sprinkles of water fell from her face to mine.

"Then wrap your legs around me." I grabbed her hands and pulled her up against me.

"TJ." She gasped as her breasts crushed against my chest.

"Wrap your legs around me," I said, knowing that I would pick them up and guide them around my waist if she didn't.

"What are you doing?" she said as she complied. I felt her legs wrap around my waist and I held her closer to me. I pulled her down slightly so that she could feel my hardness pushing into her. I wanted her to feel what she was doing to me. How hard she had made me. I wanted her to know just how patient I was being for her.

"TJ," she moaned. "What are you going to do?" Her lips trembled as my hands ran up and down her back.

"I'm not going to fuck you," I said as my fingers slid down between her legs. I leaned forward and kissed her hard, pushing my tongue into her mouth and kissing her passionately. She kissed me back just as hard, her breathing labored, and I could feel her heart racing next to mine. She kissed me with abandon, no longer trying to pretend that she didn't want this as well. I rubbed my fingers against her clit and she moaned against my lips. Her legs shifted and I slid two fingers inside of her and then sucked on her tongue. Each time I pulled my fingers out of her, I sucked on her tongue harder and I could feel her body shaking next to me. Her pussy was tight and my cock was jealous that my fingers were getting all of the action. She moved her ass back and forth as my fingers entered her. I could feel that she was close to orgasm as her pussy lips tightened on me.

"TJ," she cried out as I felt a warm gush on my fingers as she clenched for a few seconds and then her body grew more relaxed against me. I kissed her hard for a few more seconds and then pulled away slightly. Her eyes looked up at me lazily and full of lust. My heart expanded for a few seconds as she looked up at me with trust.

"Enjoyed yourself?" I said with a smirk and I could see her blushing slightly.

"I, uh, ..." She looked at my lips and paused.

"Congrats." I winked at her.

"Congrats for what?"

"For winning the race," I said. "That was your prize." I lifted my fingers out of the water and sucked them slowly. Even though they were wet from the water, I still thought I could taste her juices. Though that might have been wishful thinking. "And this is my prize," I said as I continued to suck my fingers. Her eyes widened and I could see the shock on her face as she watched me.

"You're disgusting," she said, and I could see her watching me diligently.

"What can I say? You taste good." I licked my lips and then sucked on my lower lip for a few seconds. "I wish you could taste yourself," I drawled. "But maybe next time."

"There will be no next time." She blushed, though she didn't move away.

"Oh, there will be a next time." I laughed and reached out and grabbed her breast and played with her nipple. "Only next time, we'll both be coming."

"I didn't come," she said and looked away. I could tell she was embarrassed. Though I wanted to tell her not to be. I wanted to tell her that she would have a lot more intense situations to be embarrassed about if she continued to go down this road with me.

"Okay," I said and I shrugged. "Let's go back to shore," I said. "The others will be wondering what happened to us."

"Okay," she said, sounding disappointed. I swam away from her and headed back to shore. I reached the shore a good eight strokes before her and I stood and waited for her to get out of the water. "So we're going back now?" She walked towards me, her head held high and I swallowed hard as I stared at her naked body.

"Not yet." I shook my head and led her over to one of the lounge chairs.

"Oh?" she said, looking at me curiously.

"I have some unfinished business," I said and pushed her down on the chair. "Lie back."

"What?" She blinked up at me. "Why?"

"Just lie back." I pushed her shoulder down and laughed at the confusion on her face.

"TJ?" she said hesitantly as I knelt down and spread her legs. I leaned forward and licked all the drops of water off of her pussy. "TJ, what are you doing?" She moaned and I could feel her legs trembling.

"You said you didn't come," I said, my voice deep, even to my ears. "That means you didn't get your prize," I said and looked up at her. "We can't go back until you get your prize."

"You can't..." she mumbled, her face looking nervous.

"Oh, but I can," I said and bent back down and immediately pushed my tongue inside of her. I felt her gush of orgasm as soon as I entered her, but I didn't stop. I couldn't wait to lap up her juices as she lay there, her body bucking. I sucked on her clit for a few seconds and then kissed my way up her body, sucking on both of her nipples before positioning my body on hers and resting on my elbows. I let my cock rest between her legs and I felt her legs shifting slightly. I leaned down and kissed her and she kissed me back, moaning into my mouth. I rubbed the tip of my cock against her clit and next to her entrance and it took everything in me to not enter her.

"Oh, TJ." She groaned, reaching her arms up around me.

"Yes, Mila?" I said softly, waiting for her to ask me to fuck her.

"TJ." She moaned again, her eyes gazing into mine deeply, searching for something. My cock paused as I lay on top of her. I was seconds away from entering her. Seconds away from filling her up and making her mine. She shifted again and the tip of me entered her and she moaned again—a deep, long, aching sound—and she reached up and ran her hands through my hair, playing with my tresses softly. "Make love to me, TJ," she whispered into the night, and I froze. I jumped up off of her and stood upright, bending down only to help her up.

"That's Troy's job," I said, my voice cracking as I turned my back on her and walked over to my clothes. "I don't make love. I only fuck and when I say fuck, I mean hard." I said harshly. I couldn't even look at her as we pulled our clothes back on. I don't think she knew it, but my words probably hurt me more than they had hurt her.

Thirteen

MILA

OCTOBER 28, 2011

DEAR DIARY,

I saw a dirty movie yesterday. Not on purpose. I was just flipping channels and this French film came on and this lady was doing stuff with this man. And then he was watching her do something to herself. It was so awkward to watch. And then, of course, TJ walks in and catches me. He stared at the TV and then at me and then at the TV again and just laughed. I turned the TV off right away, but he just grinned and turned the movie back on. "There's no shame in pleasuring yourself, Mila," he said softly and I thought I was going to die of embarrassment. He walked away then and I dismissed it from my mind, but last night I had a dirty dream and all I could think about was TJ guiding me and teaching me how to pleasure myself. I'm not sure what that means—if it's wishful dreaming or if I'm some sort of pervert now. I'm not going to tell anyone about the dream, not even Sally. How am I supposed to tell her that TJ is in my dreams doing things to me that make my body feel so strange and good? I just hope that one day, those feelings happen in real life as well. I think TJ has a magic touch.

Mila

XOXO

"Sally, are you awake?" I whispered to her for what must have been the tenth time that morning. I wasn't sure why she was in such a deep sleep. Maybe she'd had too much to drink, but she had already been gone from the fire when TJ and I had gotten back from our skinny-dip. Cody, Troy and Barbie had all been laughing and drinking when we'd gotten back and they hadn't even seem concerned that we'd been gone for so long. Barbie had kinda looked at me with narrowed eyes when we'd gotten back, but not for long, and Cody had essentially ignored me, which had been surprising for how crazily he'd been acting before we'd left. "Sally," I said louder this time as I noticed her rolling onto her back.

"Ugh," she said as she lazily opened one eye and looked at me.

"Are you awake?" I grinned over at her.

"No." She moaned and closed her eye again and rolled over.

"Sally, wake up." I groaned. "We need to talk."

"I'm sleeping," she said and pulled the blanket over her head.

I leaned over, pulled the blanket down and said loudly, "TJ and I fucked last night."

"What?" she said, her eyes popping open as she rolled over to look at me in shock. "You did not," she said, her jaw open as she stared at me, her eyes searching mine. "How was it? Was he good?"

"It was amazing." I laughed. "And no, we didn't actually fuck. Well, at least not really."

"What do you mean not really?" she asked with a frown as she yawned. "You either did or you didn't. There is no such thing as kinda fucking." Then she sat up straight and her brown eyes widened in excitement. "Unless you let him do anal." She raised an eyebrow at me. "Is that what you did? Oh, my God, Mila, I can't believe you let—"

"Sally." I rolled my eyes at her and laughed. "He finger-fucked me. No anal."

"Oh snap," she said, though she still looked shocked. "I knew something crazy would go down. Wow."

"Wow, indeed." I fell back against my pillows. "And then he went down on me."

"What?" she said loudly. "He did both?"

"Yup." I nodded and grinned at her. "I came both times." I writhed in memory. "I wanted him to fuck me." I sighed. "So badly. I thought he was going to. He was right there." I bit my lower lip and stared at Sally. "It felt so good."

"So why didn't he?" Sally looked confused.

"He said something about Troy." I groaned. "I guess he felt bad because he thinks Troy is my man."

"Hmm." Sally frowned again. "You think so?"

"Yeah." I nodded. "He said, 'Let Troy make love to you. I only fuck.' "

"Hmm," Sally said again. "He didn't care about Troy when he was fingering you or eating you out, though?"

"Yeah, who knows." I sighed. "Also, why didn't you tell me your plan?"

"What plan?" Sally looked confused.

"Your plan to hire Troy," I said softly. "I mean, it was a good idea, but it would have been nice if you would have told me before. Also, he seems to be paying more attention to Barbie."

"What are you talking about?" Sally frowned and we both froze as we heard two loud screams. "What's that?" she said as we scrambled out of bed and to the door. I opened it quickly and we heard another scream. We looked at each other and frowned, both of us frozen to the spot.

"Yes, yes." Barbie's voice floated through the air and we both stood there, our jaws dropping as she screamed again. This time we both realized that these weren't bloodcurdling screams of fear, but screams of pleasure. "Fuck me harder." Barbie screamed again and I felt my body freezing, my heart sinking to my stomach. I rushed down the corridor and towards the bathroom as I could feel myself feeling sick. TJ hadn't refused to fuck me because of Troy. He'd refused because he wanted to be with Barbie. What sort of sick game were they playing?

"Fuck me, big boy." Barbie's screams and shouting were getting louder and I could feel myself growing faint. I just wanted a hole to open up and swallow me whole. "I'm coming," she cried out and her moans matched the banging of someone's fist against the wall. I looked around to look at Sally, whose face looked crushed for me as she hurried towards me.

"You okay?" she said with trepidation, knowing I was far from okay.

"I will be," I said softly, still feeling very sick as I gazed at her.

"You two okay?" TJ's voice bounded down the corridor as he walked towards us from the kitchen.

"TJ?" I asked him, confused as I listened to the sound of Barbie still moaning.

"The one and only." He grinned as he stopped next to us. He cocked his head and frowned as he listened to Barbie moaning. I looked over at Sally and we both looked at each other in confusion. If TJ wasn't with Barbie, who was? My heart sank as I thought about Troy. What a loser he was going to make me look like. He was supposed to be my 'boyfriend,' but here he was with Barbie, fucking her early in the morning for all to hear.

"Barbie woke us up," Sally said weakly as we all three stood there.

"Yeah." TJ looked annoyed. "I guess she's not very loyal."

"I'm sorry about Troy." I bit my lower lip as I stared at him, but felt like this was some sort of karma. TJ and I had messed around and now our other halves were messing around as well.

"Sorry for what?" TJ asked, looking at me curiously.

"You know," I said and nodded towards the direction of the sound.

"Troy went out early this morning," TJ said matter-of-factly. "He wanted to do some shopping at the mall, he said. Maybe he went to go and get you a ring or something."

"Oh," I said, my face heating up as I realized what that meant. I ignored his comment about the ring and looked at Sally, her face looking pale and distraught. All of a sudden the door down the hallway opened and Barbie came walking out, her hair a mess and her body wrapped in a white sheet.

"Morning," she said to TJ and rubbed his chest. I watched as he nodded at her and then as her sheet dropped down slightly. "I hope I didn't wake you up," she said only to him, pouting her lips at him.

"I've been up since early," he said, his voice not betraying his true thoughts.

"I wouldn't have minded being woken up," she said and her sheet dropped even lower, exposing her naked breasts to everyone. She had no shame and I could feel myself tensing up. Then we heard more footsteps as Cody walked into the hallway.

"There you are." He grinned down the hallway as he spoke to Barbie. "Go and get me my coffee, woman."

"I was just seeing if TJ was okay," Barbie said with a shrug and pulled the sheet up again. "Go back to bed. I'll see you in a few minutes."

"Fine." He grinned and I turned to him with a frown, thoroughly disappointed in him. "Morning, bro," he called out to TJ and winked at him. Then he looked at me, winked, then at Sally, and I could see a slight look of shame on his face before he headed back into his room.

"I'd better go and get his coffee," Barbie said with a purr. "I think he needs it before round two." She walked back down the corridor and I turned to TJ. "You're okay with your girl hooking up with Cody?"

"She's not my girl," he said, his eyes boring into mine. "It wouldn't be the first time Cody has taken my leftovers." He shrugged and then continued. "Looks like you're part of the only happy couple on this trip." He looked at my lips and then flicked his tongue for a few seconds. "You okay?" He turned to Sally with a small frown and she nodded, though I could see her eyes were red.

"Excuse me," she squeaked out and hurried to the bedroom.

"I need to go with Sally," I said as I made to follow her, but TJ grabbed my arm and stopped me.

"Just answer me this question first," he said with a straight face.

"Sure." I nodded, unsure of what he was going to ask.

"When you played with yourself last night, was it my face or Troy's that you imagined on top of you?" His eyes darkened as he gazed down at me and he pushed me back into the wall, pressing himself into me before he lowered his head and whispered into my ear. "Was it my cock or Troy's that you imagined sliding into you, making you wet?" he muttered as I felt his hardness pushing into me. I swallowed hard as we stood there, and I was about to answer when I heard Troy walking back into the house and shouting, "Honey, I'm home."

Fourteen

T J

I STEPPED BACK FROM Mila and I could see her face reddening as she looked down the corridor. Troy came bounding through the hallway with a huge smile on his face and a big bouquet of flowers. "There you are, darling," he said with a huge grin as he spied Mila.

"Hey," she said weakly and I could see her looking at me. I ignored her face as I knew I would break out laughing.

"I missed you this morning," he said as he stopped in front of us. "I wish we could have shared the bed last night," he said and gave her a light kiss on the lips. I wanted to smack him then but instead kept a neutral expression on my face.

"So what are the two of you going to do today?" I asked them with a congenial smile. "Planning on going for a ride in the Mercedes?" I looked at Mila and smiled widely. "Oh, wait, I don't remember seeing the Benz in the driveway." I frowned and looked at Troy. "What car did you bring?"

"What Mercedes Benz?" Troy looked confused.

"The one you like to drive up the highway." Mila gave him a look. "The convertible," she prodded. "I told TJ about it. I didn't know you wanted to keep it a secret."

"I, uh, yeah." Troy gave me a look and it was all I could do to stop from laughing. I couldn't believe that Mila was carrying on with this charade. I hadn't been prepared for the fact that she'd play along with it so long. I'd thought she would lose it when Troy showed up out of nowhere. The Troy she'd made up in her mind. The Troy I'd hired, whose real name was Mike. I wasn't sure what she was thinking. Did she really think that Troy was real? Was she crazy? I bit my lower lip to stop from laughing. My best guess was that she thought that Sally, her crazy best friend, had hired Troy and they hadn't had a chance to talk about it. I was going to enjoy staring at Mila's face when she found out the truth. I wasn't sure what she'd say when she realized I knew that Troy didn't exist. She'd be pissed. Maybe she'd shout at me. Maybe she'd smack me. Maybe she'd hold me tight and wrestle me to the ground and sit on me, pinning me down to the ground in her eagerness. I almost groaned at the thought. That was wishful thinking on my side. I wanted her to take her frustration out on me physically. I'd love to feel her dominating me, taking control, making me beg her to let me loose. I'd go along with it because I knew that after she made me beg, I would be making her beg. And I wouldn't be showing mercy.

"So what are your plans for the future?" I asked, my face serious as I stared at the two of them. "I hope your intentions are pure," I said as I stared at Troy, one eyebrow raised.

"I, uh," Troy stammered again and swallowed hard. He looked over at Mila and I watched as he stared at her body. "I was hoping I could take you to dinner tonight, just you and me," he said softly and I froze. What the hell was he playing at? Was he seriously trying to take out Mila? My Mila!

"Um, where did you want to go, honey?" Mila said, her expressive face looking surprised as she gazed back at Troy. I wanted to grab her and pull her into my arms and tell her to stop acting. I knew that Troy was a fake.

"Maybe seafood?" Troy said with a small smile. "I heard the lobster and crabs around here are good."

"Yeah." Mila nodded. "The lobster is amazing."

"Do you really think that's a good idea?" I said, interrupting their conversation but talking only to Mila.

"Why not?" Mila said pursing her lips.

"Because I had plans for us for tonight," I said and waved my fingers at her. I watched as she blushed and glared at me. "I thought we could do something." I licked my lips slowly and then stepped back. "I wouldn't mind trying some of that dessert you gave me last night."

"What dessert?" Troy asked. "I'd like some too."

"She only made enough for me." I gave him a death stare. "There's only enough for me to eat."

"We can always share," Troy said with a smile, and I froze as I heard Mila giggling.

"Yeah, what do you think of that, TJ?" Mila gave me a petulant look.

"I don't share my dessert." I stared into Mila's eyes. "Ever."

"I see," Mila said and I watched as she licked her lips nervously.

"Good," I said and tapped my fingers against the wall. "In fact, I'm feeling pretty hungry right now." I stretched and looked at her. "There's a growling in my stomach," I said softly. "A yearning in my belly. For seconds."

"That must have been some dessert," Troy said, looking like he was starting to feel hungry himself. I was going to have to take care of the Troy situation myself if Mila continued to go along with this farce. Troy was starting to get a bit too into the role and he was starting to act as if he really had a shot at dating Mila. I'd hit him so hard if he even thought about getting any of Mila's cookies.

"It was," I said. "Though I think Mila enjoyed my eating her dessert as much as I enjoyed eating it." I grinned as I stared into his eyes. "There's something so enjoyable about giving and receiving pleasure, don't you think?"

"I guess." Troy looked at me in confusion and back at Mila. "What did you make, brownies?"

"No," Mila squeaked out.

"Yeah, tell your boyfriend, Troy, what it was you served me last night, Mila," I said and let my hand fall right down the back of her butt softly. She jumped slightly at my touch and I tried to hold back a grin as I felt her trembling slightly.

"Something I'll never be serving you again," she said tightly, her face furious as she glared at me. "What time shall we go to dinner, Troy?" She turned to him and it was my turn to become furious. Mila was not acting in the way I had thought she would. All of her words and actions were out-of-line and not what I'd been expecting. It annoyed me that she wasn't playing along. She was supposed to be like putty in my hands. She had been like putty in my hands the night before. Shit, she'd been like putty to my tongue as well. I grinned as I remembered the taste of her and how she'd moaned and cried out when I'd made her come. When I fucked her, I planned on going slow. I was going to make her beg for it, and when she asked why, I was going to remind her of this moment and her dismissive tone towards me. That would show her that I meant business. I could feel myself growing hard just thinking about it... Her legs flipped in the air, her ass off of the mattress, her eyes rolling in her head in ecstasy and anticipation as she waited for her release.

"T.J." Mila's voice was soft as she spoke and I blinked down at her.

"Yes?" I said and then frowned. Troy was gone. "Where's Troy?" I looked around.

"He just said bye." She blinked at me. "He needed to go to the restroom."

"I see."

"What do you think you're playing at?" She hissed lightly as her voice lowered. "How dare you mention to my boyfriend that I gave you dessert last night?"

"Would you rather I have showed him the dessert you gave me?"

I said, flicking my tongue against my lips, and she gasped.

"You really are a pig."

"You really have no sense of humor," I responded and grabbed her hands and pulled her towards me. "You're not really going to dinner with Troy tonight, are you?"

"Yes! Why shouldn't I?" She tried to extricate herself from my embrace, so I turned and pushed her back against the wall.

"Why shouldn't you?" I asked, my voice low as I pushed my hardness into her stomach.

"TJ." She moaned, her lips slightly parted. "I'm sorry about Barbie, but you can't use me to try and make her jealous."

"Barbie?" I laughed. "The girl who just slept with your brother? Do you really think we have anything going on?"

"You're the one who brought her here and insinuated that..." Her voice trailed off. "Well, you know."

"I'm single, Mila." My lips brushed her cheek and moved closer to her mouth. "Very single."

"What do you want from me?" she asked, her light brown eyes looking more confused than I'd ever seen them before.

"It's funny that you should ask that," I said, pretending to be nonchalant. This was the moment I'd been waiting for all weekend.

"Oh?" she said, eyes growing even wider.

"I have something for you to read," I said and stepped back. This was important now. She had to understand what she was getting into.

"Read?" She wrinkled her nose. "Like a book?"

"No." I shook my head. "Like a contract."

"Contract?"

"Yes." I nodded my head. "Come to my room with me now. We need to talk in private."

"I told Troy I'd bring him some coffee," she said and shook her head. "Maybe later."

"Yeah." It took everything in me not to shake her for bringing up Troy again. I ran my hand up to her breast and rubbed my palm against her nipple instead. Her face reddened and I could feel her nipple growing hard as she adjusted her position against the wall. "You go and talk to him, and then you come and find me later." I leaned forward and kissed her hard on the lips and stuck my tongue into her mouth as I pinched her nipple hard and pushed myself into her even harder. She moaned slightly against my lips and I felt her hand on my back. It was then that I moved away from her. All I had wanted was to remind her of how badly she wanted me as well.

"I'll see you later," I said and walked to my room, slowly and confidently, knowing she was watching me as I walked away. She was probably wondering why I hadn't tried to take things further again. She was probably feeling disappointed. I grinned as I opened my door and then walked into the room. I pulled out my phone and waited for my dad to answer.

"What's the news, son?" he asked me abruptly and I felt a jolt of annoyance at his tone.

"It'll happen this weekend, Dad. It'll definitely happen this weekend," I said and then hung up and put my phone down on the dresser. I pulled off my clothes and then walked into the bathroom. And then turned on the shower and made sure the water was cold. I stepped in and closed my eyes, willing my body not to react to the freezing cold water that rained down on me. I stood there taking my cold shower with nerves of steel and all I could think about was Mila and what was about to happen. Everything was about to change, and all I could hope was that everything went according to plan. If one thing went wrong, my whole life would be ruined.

Fifteen

MILA

JUNE 5, 2008

DEAR DIARY,

Today I found out that TJ is a millionaire. Yes, a millionaire. And yes, he himself is a millionaire. Not just his dad. His grandparents left him a whole bunch of money or something. Could life be any more unfair? He's hot. He's sexy. And he's a millionaire. What chance do I have now?

Depressed and moping.

Mila

XOXO

P.S. I would love him even if he were poor and ugly.

"Hey, it's me." I opened the door to the bedroom and walked in. "You okay?"

"What do you think?" Sally looked up at me with red eyes, her face tinged with tears as she gave me a sorrowful look. "I just want to go home."

"He's a jerk. I'm sorry." I walked over to her bed and sat down and rubbed her shoulder. "I don't know how he could have slept with Barbie."

"He's a pig and she's a whore." Sally looked bitter. "I mean, I'm not surprised. Her breasts have been out all weekend. I wouldn't be shocked if all three guys have hooked up with her this weekend."

"You think so?" I bit my lower lip as my stomach churned. "That would seem really messed up."

"It's not like these guys are saints." Sally's eyes were angry. "I'm sure they don't mind sharing."

"I don't think TJ would do that," I said, my voice weak. "Though, who knows about Troy. You know him better than I do."

"I know who better?" Sally's eyes darted back to mine.

"Troy."

"I don't know Troy from Adam." Sally sat up slightly and shook her head. "Though he has been checking out Barbie's ass too."

"Where did you find him?" I sighed, trying to keep my cool. I was pissed that Sally hadn't even done any research on Troy before she'd hired him.

"Find who?" Sally's voice was abrupt and she was starting to look like I was feeling: frustrated and angry.

"Troy," I almost shouted. "Where did you find him and why didn't you tell me what you were doing before he showed up?"

"What I was doing?" She blinked. "I didn't find Troy anywhere." Her eyes widened. "Are you saying you didn't hire him?"

"No, I didn't hire him. Are you saying you didn't hire him?" My jaw dropped open and my heart started beating slowly.

"I didn't hire him." She shook her head slowly.

"Oh, my God," I said with a whisper. "You're not joking, are you? Because if you are, this isn't funny."

"Mila, I did not hire Troy. I have never seen that man before in my life."

"So why did you say you'd done something for me? To go along with the Troy thing?" I said weakly, hoping she was about to burst out laughing and say, "Gotcha."

"I created a fake Facebook profile for Troy." She smiled weakly and shrugged. "I was going to tell you to friend him and then we could change the status to 'in a relationship'."

"A Facebook profile?" I licked my lips nervously. "That was it?"

"That was it." She chewed on her lower lip. "I didn't even think of hiring anyone. I thought that the idea was ingenious, though. I was shocked you did it."

"Yeah, well, we were both shocked." I sighed. "Because I didn't do it."

"So, then who?" she said and we just stared at each other in silence. I felt my stomach twisting in shame as I realized that there really could only be one other person who had hired Troy. Someone who was most probably laughing at me right now for pretending that Troy and I were something that we weren't. "Oh boy," Sally said, her brown eyes looking shocked. "Not TJ?"

"Who else could it be?" I groaned. "No one else knows about him because he didn't really exist."

"Wow," Sally said, her lips twisting up as she gazed at me. "What's his game?"

"What do you mean?" I frowned.

"I mean, why did he hire Troy? And why did he bring Barbie? And why is he hitting on you and trying to get you into bed?"

"Maybe he's on some weird power trip and doesn't want Cody to know."

"Hmm." Sally frowned as I said Cody's name again. "I guess. I mean, are we sure Cody doesn't know? I mean, why would he sleep with Barbie if he thought she was TJ's girl?"

"Yeah, that I don't know." I shook my head. "But one thing I do know is that Cody would not be cool with TJ going down on me and fingering me in the lake."

"I wish Cody would finger me in the lake," Sally said and plopped down on the bed. "Sorry." She made a face at me as I shook my head in disgust. "I know he's your brother, but gosh darn it, I want him so badly. I don't understand why he won't make a move on me."

"Do you even want him now knowing he's been with skanky?"

"Would you still want TJ if you found out he'd been with skanky?" she asked poignantly.

"Maybe he has already," I said, feeling sick to my stomach just thinking about it. "Do you think he has?"

"Honestly?" Sally asked as she gazed up at me.

"Yeah, honestly."

"No." She shook her head. "That skank only wishes that TJ would have slept with her."

"You really think so?"

"Yeah." She sighed deeply. "He has standards, unlike your jerk of a brother."

"He is a jerk." I nodded. "Wait until I tell Nonno about what he did."

"You're going to tell, Nonno?" Sally said in surprise. "You talk to him about sex stuff?"

"It's not my sex stuff." I laughed. "And yes, I tell him everything. He's my best friend, aside from you."

"Do you want to call him now?" she asked, a dim smile on her face.

"You want me to?"

"I think we could both use some advice from him right now."

"Yeah." I nodded. "That's true." I groaned. "Wait until he hears this." I grabbed my phone from my pocket and pressed the buttons to call his number. I listened impatiently to his phone ringing and a smile burst out on my face as he answered. "Hey, Nonno."

"How are you, mia cara?" he said softly. "Feeling better?"

"Kinda." I sighed.

"What happened?" He sounded gruff. "Do I need to come to the lake?"

"No, you don't have to come to the lake, but Sally and I need your advice."

"Sally is with you?" His voice softened. He loved Sally. He thought she was a good best friend to me. He told me that I was lucky to have her as a best friend and that I should treasure her friendship. I tried to remember his advice when she made me mad.

"Yes, we need your advice, Nonno." I pressed Speaker on the phone so that Sally could hear what he was saying as well.

"What has happened?" He sounded worried.

"Cody slept with that plastic girl I was telling you about."

"The one who TJ took with him?" Nonno sounded confused.

"Yes."

"I thought she was with TJ? Why would she sleep with Cody?"

"You tell us." I sighed. "Sally is here, Nonno. She is heartbroken. What should she do?"

"Are there really any decisions to be made?" Nonno said softly and I knew what he was saying, but it was not something I wanted to say to Sally myself. How could I be the one to break her heart? How could I tell her that her hopes and dreams were wasted on my brother? He was the definition of a playboy. He was the sort of guy who I'd never be friends with if he weren't in my family.

"Do you think he likes me, Nonno?" Sally asked, her voice weak as she spoke. I couldn't look at her then. My normally confident friend was so worried and hopeful at the same time. I didn't know what she expected Nonno to say. I didn't know what I expected Nonno to say.

"Sally, my dear. Love is an emotion that is overpowering in its simplicity," Nonno said softly. "Until the heart is ready to accept that someone else is in charge of their life and soul, one will never be ready to settle down."

"So you're saying Cody isn't ready to accept love?" Sally said, sighing deeply.

"Cody isn't ready to tie his shoelaces," Nonno said lightly, and I couldn't stop myself from laughing. I was pleased to see that Sally had started laughing as well.

"Nonno, I need your advice as well." I groaned. "I told TJ that I was dating this guy called Troy."

"Who is Troy?" he asked suspiciously.

"He doesn't exist." I paused. "But now he kinda does."

"What do you mean, this man kinda exists now?"

"I told TJ I was dating this guy Troy and a 'Troy' showed up and pretended to be my boyfriend. And I thought Sally hired him to help me out, but she didn't. And now I'm pretty sure it was TJ and I'm just so embarrassed. I don't even know what to do."

"I think you need to speak to TJ," Nonno said in an amused tone.

"It's not funny," I wailed. "I need your advice. Should I say something to him or just pretend I don't know what he did?"

"Mila, ignorance is never the answer," Nonno said, and Sally nodded.

"I feel like an idiot. He's going to think I'm a liar."

"You did lie, mia cara."

"Nonno," I wailed again and gave Sally a look.

"Maybe you and Sally need to have a talk about what you really want and maybe you both need to talk to your young men and see if they want the same thing."

"Yeah, that's going to happen," I said sarcastically. "Thanks, Nonno, I've got to go now."

"Don't be upset with me, dear. I'm just giving you the best advice that I can."

"I know," I said and sighed. "I love you, Nonno. I'll call you when I get back."

"I love you too," he said and then I hung up and looked at Sally.

"So that wasn't a big help," I said as I flounced back on the bed next to her.

"Yeah, it was." She looked at me, her eyes gazing into mine sorrowfully. "Cody's not ready for love, and TJ is playing the same games you're playing."

"I'm not playing..." I stopped talking and made a face. "Okay, I'm playing games, but only because I'm scared to put myself out there. I don't know what TJ wants."

"You know he wants you." She raised an eyebrow at me. "He's obviously sexually attracted to you. He wants you."

"Yeah, he wants some sex from me. Woohoo." I rolled my eyes. "I'm sure you could hook up with Cody as well, if you wanted. I want him to want more from me than just sex."

"So tell him that."

"Are you joking?" I looked at her. "Would you tell Cody that?"

"Hell no." Sally laughed slightly. "Fine. Don't tell TJ you want his babies."

"Yeah, or the fact that I've saved myself for him."

"Yeah, or that fact." She shook her head. "You're crazy—you know that, right?"

"Yes." I nodded and hugged myself. "But even if it doesn't go anywhere with TJ, I still want him to be my first. I'm a romantic like that."

"Uh huh," Sally said. "TJ doesn't look like the sort of guy who's going to make love to you the first time you're together."

"Sally!" I blushed.

"What? She giggled. "He looks like he's going to pound the shit out of you and have you begging for more."

"Sally." I shook my head at her as my body tingled.

"What?" She grinned. "He'll be flipping you over, bending you over, having you touch the tips of your toes while he—"

Knock knock.

"Mila, you in there?" TJ's deep voice interrupted Sally talking and we both froze. "Mila?" TJ knocked again and then opened the door. "Am I interrupting something?" he asked as he looked at us lying on the bed together.

"No." I glared up at him, annoyed that he looked so handsome and so cocky at the same time. "What do you want?"

"To talk to you." He winked at me. "Unless you're otherwise engaged."

"What do you want to talk about?" I sat up, feeling my heart racing. If he made some sort of sexual innuendo, I was going to scream.

"Stuff." He shrugged, his eyes crinkling. "Can't we just have a conversation together? We're adults now. Friends, even. Can't friends just talk?"

"Yes, they can," Sally said, answering for me, and pushed me out of the bed. "Go and talk to the man, Mila. I want my bed to myself."

"You sure?" I looked over at her. "You going to be okay?"

"I'll be fine." She nodded, putting a brave face on.

"Okay." I jumped off of the bed and looked at TJ. "We can talk." I walked towards him and he smiled at me gently.

"Good." He stepped back into the hallway. "I'll see you later, Sally."

"See you guys," she said and gave me a small smile and a wink before I headed out of the room.

"SO, WHAT DID YOU want to talk about?" I crossed my arms and looked at TJ as we walked down the corridor.

"Not much," he said, looking amused.

"Just come out with it, TJ. I know you hired Troy."

"Troy—your boyfriend?" TJ looked shocked. "How could I hire your boyfriend? The man that you love?"

"You know I do not love Troy." I glared at him as we walked into the living room.

"How am I supposed to know that?" He raised an eyebrow at me.

"Last night wouldn't have happened," I said, my face red.

"What happened last night that wouldn't have happened?" he said with a grin, as he licked his lips.

"You know," I said, staring at the tip of his tongue and remembering how it had felt the night before.

"I know what?" he said.

"You know." I shook my head.

"Are you talking about how I made you come with my fingers

when we were in the lake or how I made you come with my tongue when we were out of the lake?" he said with a huge grin as his green eyes sparkled.

"You're a dog."

"Not a pig?" he said. "Have I gone up in the world or come down?"

"Travis James Walker! What do you want? And why did you hire Troy?"

"I did it for you." He smiled sweetly. "You said you wanted your Troy to be here this weekend and I was pretty sure there wasn't a real Troy, so I figured a different Troy would do."

"You made me lie to you."

"I made you lie to me?" His eyes crinkled. "Or you just continued on with your lie?"

"You're twisting things." I sighed. "I wasn't intending to continue the lie." I looked away from him, feeling slightly embarrassed.

"So let me ask you a question." TJ's voice was serious and I could feel my heart slowing as I gazed into his eyes. I wasn't used to a serious TJ.

"Sure," I said, trying to smile but failing.

"What do you think of me?" he asked, his eyes not leaving mine.

"What do you mean?" I frowned.

"What do you think of me?" he asked again. This time his lips looked thin and I wondered where he was going.

"Are you asking me if I think of you?" I asked, wondering if this was some sort of trick question.

"No, Mila." He let out a sigh and turned away from me. "Just forget it." I could hear the exhaustion and frustration in his voice, and I knew that I needed to think of his feelings more than my own pride and embarrassment. For some reason, this was really important to him.

"Wait," I said and grabbed his shoulder. "I'll tell you." I bit down on my lower lip and I could feel my stomach curdling. I had no idea what I was going to say to him. I had no idea how honest I was going to be with him.

"It's fine," he said as he turned to look at me. "It doesn't matter."

"It does matter," I said and searched his face. I knew that for some reason what I was about to say really mattered to him, but I just didn't understand why.

"Okay." His lips pursed and we stood there in silence, just looking at each other.

"So can I ask you one question before I say what I think of you?" I asked softly.

"I want to know what you think of me because I think that perhaps you're the only person in the world whose opinion matters to me," he said before I could even ask him the question.

"How did you know what I was going to say?" I blinked up at him.

"Because that's the same question that I would have asked." He gave me a half-smile. "And you know what, I'll answer that question for you. Mila. I think you are like the birds in the morning: chirpy, bright, colorful, full of life and wondrous. The birds remind us that we are alive, they make us happy, they sing their hearts out with nary a worry and they deliver us gifts of love and joy without asking for a thing back."

"You really think I'm like that?" I asked him with a laugh. "I don't know how many people think I'm delivering gifts of love and joy in the morning. I think Cody would beg to differ with you."

"Cody wouldn't know a gift of love if it hit him in the face." TJ grinned. "He's your brother. Most brothers don't see what the rest of the world sees in their sisters"

"Or their sisters' best friends," I said and I felt a pang of pain for Sally. Cody had ripped her heart out and didn't even seem to care.

"Cody is a fool." TJ made a face. "I'm sorry for Sally."

"It's fine." I pursed my lips. "She deserves better than him. I'm sorry for you."

"Why are you sorry for me?" He frowned.

"Because of Barbie?"

"Ha." He shook his head. "Barbie was never mine and I never

wanted her to be. She was my Troy."

"She was your Troy?"

"Are you trying to make me forget the question I asked you?" TJ said with a small smile. "Do you want to go by the lake?"

"We can go by the lake." I nodded. "But I wasn't trying to change the subject." I looked at him thoughtfully. I wasn't sure why TJ wanted to know what I thought of him. I didn't know why it was so important to him. His mood seemed different, more intense and less teasing. We walked outside and took the path to the lake and I listened to the birds whistling as I tried to think of what to say. I grabbed his sleeve to stop him before we got to the deck chairs and looked up into his face. "So, TJ Walker. You wanted to know what I think of you?"

"Yes." He nodded. "I do."

"I think you're handsome," I said with a smile, but instead of grinning back at me or making some smart quip, he just stared back at me intently. "I think you're fun. I think you're a good friend to Cody." I paused, my heart racing as I wondered how honest to be with him. "I think you're pretty sexy." My voice almost sounded like a croak, I was so nervous.

"You think I'm sexy," he said, finally smiling.

"Yeah," I said and nodded, my face burning. "I think you're a bit of a jerk, but underneath it all, you're a really nice guy."

"What if I'm not a really nice guy underneath it all?" He stepped closer to me. "What if I'm a wolf in sheep's clothing?"

"Are you?"

"What do you think?"

"I think you're a good guy," I said and swallowed hard as he grabbed my hands. "I think you're the sort of guy I'd like to get to know better."

"Even better than you got to know me last night?" he asked softly, his voice deep and gruff.

"Yes." I nodded, staring up into his eyes.

"Show me, then."

"Show you what?"

"That you want to get to know me better."

"How?" I said, wondering what he expected me to do. He shrugged in response and we just stood here staring at each other. I wanted him to kiss me. I wanted him to pull me into his arms. I wanted to feel his hands on my skin, his tongue on my tongue, his cock inside of me. I felt feverish as I stood there waiting for what he was going to do next. I could barely breathe, my anticipation was so high.

"Mila," he said, my name a lullaby on his lips.

"Yes," I breathed out, ready to say yes. Yes, TJ, I want you. Yes, TJ, you can take me. Yes, I will take my clothes off. Yes, I will let you make love to me. Yes, I will do anything you want me to do in this instant. Yes, yes, yes.

"I'm going to go inside now," he said softly, and my heart sank. "I'm going to go inside, but tonight I'll be waiting."

"Waiting for what?" I breathed out.

"Waiting for you to show me exactly what you think of me and exactly what you want." He leaned forward and pressed his lips against mine for a few seconds and then stepped back. "The next step is all yours, Mila. The next step is all yours."

◆

I COULD HEAR EVERY creek in the floorboards as I made my way to TJ's room. The house was eerily quiet and I wondered if everyone was ready to leave the next day. I'd not really seen anyone else all day: only Sally and TJ earlier in the morning. Cody, Barbie and even Troy had all been inconspicuous. Not that I really cared. I hadn't wanted to see any of them. Not Cody, not Barbie and definitely not Troy. I was worried that he really thought he had a chance with me now, and I didn't want to have to explain that I'd only been flirting with him because TJ had been there. I mean, even I knew that that had been immature, and a part of me was worried that I'd gotten Troy's hopes up. I didn't want to be responsible for hurting anyone else's feelings.

I stopped outside of TJ's bedroom and my hand froze on his doorknob. I shivered slightly in my negligee as I debated going back to my room and forgetting about going through with my plan. I was about to turn back around and head back to my room when I thought of what TJ had said to me earlier, that the next step was mine. I knew he'd meant it as well. He wasn't going to make another move unless I showed him I really wanted it. And I did want it. I mean, wasn't that why I'd bought the negligee in the first place? Wasn't that why I'd essentially been begging Cody for an advance? I didn't really know what was going on with Cody and Barbie, I didn't know what was going on with Troy, I didn't know what TJ and Barbie were up to, and I also didn't care. I'd been waiting too many years for this moment. I'd been wanting TJ to be mine for a long time. And even though, this was just a midnight clandestine affair, it didn't mean that it wasn't special, in some sort of way. Granted, it wasn't the flowers and candy moonlight serenade I'd pictured in my dreams, but it was a start. All I really wanted was a start. I knocked on the door and then opened it quickly.

"I thought you were never going to come," TJ said, his eyes alert as I walked into the room. He was sitting on top of his bed in a pair of long linen white pants and no shirt. His chest was tan and cut with a light sprinkling of hair across his pecs.

"You thought I wouldn't?" I said with a coy smile as I closed the door behind me. He jumped off of the bed and walked towards me.

"No." He grinned. "I knew you'd come." His eyes looked me over and I could feel every hair on my body standing on edge as he took in my appearance. I wondered if he thought my negligee was sexy. I didn't have to wonder long as he looked back up at me with lust-filled eyes. "I just didn't know you'd be looking this hot." His eyes fell to my breasts and I could see them narrowing as he stared at my nipples, which were visible through the see-through lace. "You walked down the corridor like this?" He looked back into my eyes and took a step closer.

"Yes." I nodded. "I did."

"Without worry that Cody or Troy would see you?"

"I didn't care," I said confidently, though I'd been scared out of my mind.

"Interesting," he said with a small smile as his fingers touched the button on my negligee and played with the lace. He lifted it up slightly and touched the front of my panties. He grinned as he stared at me, his fingers moving up to touch my stomach lightly.

"What are you thinking?" I asked softly as his fingers moved back and forth on my stomach. My body was trembling slightly and I reached out to touch his chest.

"I'm thinking about how sexy you are," he muttered as his fingers fell to my panties again and he slipped them between my legs. "I'm thinking about how wet you are for me, even though you just entered my room." His lips fell next to my ear and he nibbled on my earlobe as he rubbed me through my panties. My legs parted slightly and I moaned at the feeling of his fingers rubbing me gently.

"You like that, don't you?" I said, almost purring at him. My fingers ran down his back and I moved in to kiss him. My body was on fire and the room was spinning around me as I gave in to the feelings that were surging through me. For some reason, I no longer felt self-conscious. Maybe it was because we'd spoken earlier and I knew he felt something for me too. I wasn't sure why, but I was ready for TJ and whatever he wanted to do to me.

"Is that even a question?" he asked as he lifted me up and pushed me back against the wall.

"TJ." I moaned as I felt his hands squeezing my breasts. He leaned down and started kissing me hard. I kissed him back, relishing the feel of his tongue in my mouth. "Ooh." I moaned as I felt his tongue slipping into my mouth. I ran my hand through his hair and almost screamed as he started sucking on my tongue and rubbing my clit at the same time. I wasn't sure where he'd learned that trick, but it was dynamite. I felt like I was going to explode as he built my body up to a frenzy.

"I want to take that sexy piece of silk off of your body," he muttered as he stopped kissing me.

"It's lace," I said back stupidly, and he laughed, his eyes looking wild as he stared at me.

"I don't care what it is," he said and I felt his arms going around my back. "Hold on to my back and wrap your legs around me tighter," he commanded me as he stepped back.

"Where are we going?" I asked eagerly.

"Not far." He grinned and carried me over to his bed and dropped me down. "Lie flat," he said and I did as he said. He leaned down and pushed my negligee up with his fingers and then I felt his tongue on my stomach, licking a trail to my belly button. I closed my eyes and gripped the sheets as I felt his lips and tongue on my already feverish skin.

"Oh," I cried out as I felt his teeth on the top of my panties.

"You didn't think they were going to stay on, did you?" His voice was gruff and held a hint of amusement. I opened my eyes and looked back down at him. His eyes glanced up at me and he winked before he pulled my panties off with his teeth slowly. I felt his nose rubbing against my pussy slightly as he pulled them down and I gasped as I felt his tongue darting out and flicking my clit for a few seconds before continuing down my legs. He growled as he pulled my panties off of my feet and then I felt his hands pushing my legs apart and he kissed back up my thighs. I reached down and grabbed his hair and closed my eyes again, wanting to concentrate on all the feelings running through me.

"You taste like sun-kissed nights on the beach," he said as he kissed back up my stomach. I flicked an eye open and looked at him lazily, slightly saddened that he hadn't gone down on me right away. My legs were shaking and I was so wet, waiting to feel him on me in my most intimate of spots. "Put your arms up," he said and he pulled my negligee off. "I love having you naked again," he said as he threw my negligee to the ground. I felt his lips on my right breast, his teeth tugging on my nipple as he sucked. My body shuddered as his lips moved over to my left breast and I felt his fingers moving down between my legs.

"TJ." I moaned, shifting on the bed, not knowing how much longer I could take the teasing, even though it had just begun.

"Hold on, doll." His voice was smooth as he slipped a finger inside of me at the same time he bit down on my left nipple.

"Ahhh," I screamed out, and TJ laughed and nibbled on my nipple even harder. His finger moved inside of me quickly and I felt him adding another finger to my wetness. I could feel my lips closing in on his fingers as he moved them in and out of me with urgency, and then he slowed his movement. I cried out again, wanting him to pick up his pace. He was driving me crazy.

"Shh," TJ said as he stopped sucking on my nipple long enough to look up at me. "You know how noise carries in this house. You don't want to wake anyone up."

"I don't care," I cried out, my mind on nothing but TJ's fingers and the pleasure he was giving me.

"Really?" His green eyes pierced mine as he bent down and took my nipple in his mouth again, his eyes not leaving mine.

"Really." I nodded and groaned as he started sucking and tugging again. His tongue flicked against my nipple as he continued to finger me and I felt my body bucking as I felt his thumb massaging my clit at the same time. The pleasure was almost too intense. My body couldn't stand it: the flick of his tongue on my tender nipple as his lips suckled, the feel of his fingers gliding inside of me, exploring my hidden depths, as his thumb rubbed gently against my clit, bringing me to the brink of ecstasy. "TJ," I cried out again, moaning his name loudly as he increased the pressure of his thumb.

"Mila." He said my name lightly as his lips moved from my breast and back up to my mouth. "I'm going to fuck you," he whispered feverishly against my lips as he kissed me. I kissed him back eagerly, not even caring that his words were crude. In that moment, they didn't feel crude. They felt sexy, apt, spot on. I wanted him to fuck me.

"TJ." I groaned, blinking up at him as I felt my body shuddering under him as he brought me to another orgasm with just his fingers. "TJ," I screamed as his fingers moved faster and his thumb started tapping against my clit.

"Say my name." He growled against my lips, his eyes peering down into mine. "Say my name as you come and then get ready for an even bigger orgasm."

"Oh TJ," I screamed out and his lips crashed down on mine harder as I came underneath him. I kissed him back fervently, enjoying the taste of him as his tongue consumed me. He moved his hand from between my legs and I wrapped my legs around him, wanting to feel his hardness against me. I reached down and slipped my hand down the back of his pants and touched his tight ass.

"Mila." He grunted against me as my fingers slipped around the front of his pants, trying to get a feel of his cock.

"Your turn now, TJ," I said with a smile as I pushed him off of me. I pushed him down on the bed and sat up.

"Mila?" His eyes narrowed as he gazed at me getting up onto my knees.

"Shh, TJ." I winked at him and pushed him down onto the mattress. "I only want to hear you saying my name if you're screaming it out in passion."

"Oh yeah?" he said with a grin.

"Yeah." I leaned down to kiss him and then kissed down his chest. His skin felt soft to the touch and tasted like sandalwood and musk. I buried my nose into his chest and just breathed him for a few seconds before kissing him again. I could feel his heart beating fast as I made my way down his chest to his abs. My fingers ran across his abs and I let my fingernails dig into his skin as I admired his perfect body. I reached the top of his pants and I heard TJ take a sharp intake of breath as my fingers ran down the front bulge of his pants lightly. I felt his hardness twitch beneath me and I tightened my fingers over his cock. It was my turn to breathe in deeply then. Boy, was he big.

"Mila," He groaned out as I started to pull his pants down.

"Yes, TJ?" I looked up at him and paused.

"You know what's going to happen if you take my pants down, right?"

"I knew what was going to happen when I decided to come to your room tonight," I said with a sly smile and continued to pull his pants off. I pulled them down his thick, strong thighs and calves, pulled them off of his feet, and threw them to the ground. I just sat there for a second and looked over his body, letting my eyes enjoy the view before running my fingers up his muscular legs. I couldn't quite believe that I was here with TJ, finally. And soon he would be mine.

"Mila." He groaned again as I took his cock in my hands and ran my fingers up and down his shaft. "Mila." He grunted and I saw him closing his eyes. I smiled to myself as I leaned down and took him into my mouth. He groaned when he felt my tongue running along his shaft as I sucked on the tip of his cock and tried to take him as deeply as I could into my mouth. "Mila." He groaned again. This time the sound was more guttural and I knew that I had him where I wanted him. I closed my eyes and sucked him gently, moving my mouth up and down as I played with his balls. I could feel his hands in my hair, tugging on the strands as I bobbed up and down and increased the intensity of my sucking. He didn't want me to stop and I didn't want to stop. I enjoyed having him in my mouth. I moved and kneeled beside him so that I had easier access. I loved the feeling of power as I sucked him and I loved the salty taste of his skin and I moaned as I felt his fingers lazily playing with my breasts.

"Mila." He groaned as I took him even deeper into my throat. I opened my eyes and looked up at him, his eyes staring down at me with an intense look. "Fuck." He grunted and I felt him pushing me up and onto my back. "I need to be inside of you." He growled as he peered down at me, holding my arms above my head.

"I wasn't done."

"I don't want the first time I come with you to be in your mouth," he muttered, his eyes moving to my jiggling breasts. He positioned himself on top of me and I felt his hardness between my legs. I moaned as I felt him hard and hot against me.

"TJ."

"I'm going to take you now, Mila." He growled as he kissed my lips and tugged on my lower lip for a few seconds as his right hand played with my nipple. "I'm going to fuck you and I'm going to come inside of you. I'm going to—"

"There's something I have to tell you." I moaned as I felt the tip of him at my entrance. I widened my legs as my pussy trembled, waiting to feel him inside of me.

"What?" He grunted, his lips kissing down my neck.

"I'm not on the pill," I said softly. He paused, his eyes looking back at me with a darkened expression.

"You're not?" He groaned, the tip of him moving inside of me slightly. I could feel his cock right there and I could feel myself growing wetter, knowing that he was already partially inside of me.

"No." I shook my head and grabbed his head, pulling him down to kiss him, to let him know I still wanted him to continue. "Do you have a condom?"

"Yes." He groaned against my lips, his cock twitching inside of me. "I don't suppose you'd be cool with me just pulling out?" His grinned as he kissed me again. "I'm joking," he said again as I actually considered his request. I couldn't believe that I was actually considering having sex with him without any sort of protection, but that was how much he'd taken over my mind.

"I don't mind," I said, widening my legs even more. "I just want to feel you inside of me."

"Oh, you'll be feeling all of me." He growled and then he reached down and starting playing with my clit with the head of his cock. "You're so wet for me, Mila."

"TJ." I moaned. "Please."

"You want me, don't you?" He positioned his cock between my legs again and I felt the tip of him inside of me again. "You want me to fuck you."

"Yes." I moaned.

"I have to put on a rubber." He groaned, but I felt him pushing his cock inside of me a little bit more.

"Oh my." I squealed as I felt my walls expanding. "TJ," I said as I held him to me. "Please."

"Oh, Mila." He groaned as he slid inside of me a bit more. "I'm not going to fuck you without a rubber." He continued his gradual thrust inside of me.

"TJ." I scratched his back, needing to feel all of him inside of me.

"Mila, fuck." He growled and he moved again, this time pushing harder, his cock moving inside of me deeper until it wouldn't go any farther. "Mila?" he said, his eyes widening in shock. "Are you a virgin?" he asked, his voice sounding incredulous as his cock stopped still inside of me. I was about to answer when the door came bursting open.

"What the fuck is going on in here?" Cody's voice was loud as he turned on the light switch, and as I looked over at his red and angry face, I wasn't sure who wanted the earth to open up and swallow them up first. "TJ? Mila?" he shouted as he slammed the door behind him.

"Cody." TJ pulled out of me swiftly and grabbed the sheet and covered me before he stood up, in all his naked glory. I lay there, trembling, staring at his naked ass, and all I could think about was how much I missed having his body next to mine.

"What the fuck is going on, TJ? Are you in bed with my sister?" Cody's voice was furious and I shivered as I stared at him.

"Yes, but we have something to tell you," TJ said softly. "We wanted to wait, but I suppose that this is as good a time as ever."

"What's that? You wanted to tell me you're sleeping with my

sister? How long has this been going on?"

"We're engaged, Cody," TJ said simply and I froze in the bed. What was he talking about?

"What?" Cody's eyes narrowed as he looked at me and then back at TJ. He looked as shocked and incredulous as I felt.

"Yes." TJ nodded and looked back at me with a warm smile. "We're engaged and we just wanted to celebrate the occasion. I didn't mean to disrespect you, Cody. You know I would never do that."

"Yeah." Cody still looked annoyed, but not as pissed. "You two were loud as shit. I could hear moans." He shuddered. "Keep it down."

"Sorry, bro," TJ said. "We were going to wait to tell your parents and Nonno before we told anyone else."

"Yeah," Cody said and then frowned. "I didn't even know you guys were dating. What about Troy?"

"Cody." I made a face at him. "Not now, please."

"Mila." He looked annoyed, but then shook his head. "You're in such big trouble." He sighed and then looked at TJ. "Though, I suppose this can be helpful with what we were talking about last week."

"Not now, Cody." TJ shook his head, his voice loud and insistent.

"Yeah." Cody shrugged and headed back to the door. "I'll see you two lovebirds in the morning. Please try and keep it down, and might I suggest locking the door."

"Will do, bro." TJ laughed and followed him to the door. I watched Cody walking out of the room and then as TJ locked the door and headed back to the bed. I stared at him and I couldn't keep my eyes off of his erection. I knew I should be asking him about the lie he'd just told, but all my body was thinking about was finally losing my virginity to TJ Walker and having him inside of me.

"We need to talk," TJ said as he sat on the bed.

"Oh?" I said, disappointment hitting me. "Can we talk afterwards?"

"Afterwards?" TJ looked down at me with a smirk.

"TJ." I moaned and sat up, letting the sheet fall down so he could see my naked breasts. "I want you."

"Oh?" He pulled the rest of the sheet away from me. "Do you?" he said as he moved up next to me, running his fingers down my right breast.

"Yes." I moaned and pulled him down next to me.

"You want this?" he said as his fingers parted my legs and he slipped a finger inside of me.

"No." I shook my head and reached down to his cock.

"Oh, you want this?" he muttered as he removed his finger and positioned his cock back at my trembling entrance. He pushed the tip of his cock inside of me again and I moaned and nodded. "You want me to fuck you, Mila?" he said as he kissed my lips. "Or do you want me to make love to you?"

"TJ." I groaned. I just wanted him to stop talking.

"Did you want the love-making to happen before or after you told me you were a virgin? Or before or after we talk about what just happened with your brother?"

"After?" I tried, grinning up at him, but he just laughed, pulled away from me and sat up. "TJ?" I pouted. "Please."

"Please nothing," he said and kissed my cheek. "We need to talk before we do anything." He pulled me into his arms and kissed my forehead. "Don't get me wrong. I want you very much, Mila, but there are some things we need to talk about first."

"What things?" I moaned, not wanting to talk.

"Things like how you're going to be my fiancée for the next four weeks."

"What?" I said with a frown. "Why?"

"I'll explain that later. It will be mutually beneficial of course."

"Oh?" I licked my lips, wondering what was going on. "How?"

"For one, you'll enjoy multiple orgasms every night." He winked at me as he kissed down my body again and parted my legs. "I think you need a release before we talk."

"But I want to make love." I moaned as I felt the tip of his tongue on my clit.

"You'll just have to enjoy another orgasm from my mouth for

tonight." He grinned up at me. "I'll let you come again, and then we can talk about the arrangement I want us to make."

"We can just talk now." I moaned and then promptly shut up as I felt his tongue sliding inside of me to do all the things he hadn't let his cock do.

Sixteen

MILA

AUGUST 5, 2009

DEAR DIARY,

TJ got a new car. A sports car. It's red and has a top that goes up. This morning he drove up in his car and got out and he looked like an actor. My heart almost popped out of my chest, if such a thing is possible. He looked so sexy, and when he walked into the house, he gave me a smile that went straight to my heart and my stomach. In that moment, I knew I would do anything to make TJ Walker mine. And I mean just about anything.

Mila

XOXO

The touch of TJ's warm hands on my naked ass the next morning woke me up. I opened one lazy eye and stared at his face that was grinning down at me with an evil look.

"What're you doing?" I yawned as I opened the other eye.

"Touching you," he said matter-of-factly, his hand squeezing my ass-cheek again.

"I like you touching me." I grinned at him, leaned up and kissed him. His green eyes flashed down at me in surprise. "I'm not a withering little buttercup." I winked at him.

"I never said you were." He deepened the kiss and held me close to him.

"You looked surprised that I kissed you."

"I was surprised that you told me that you like me touching you," he said, his fingers trailing up my back. "Normally you're combative in the mornings."

"I'm not combative." I moved my mouth to his shoulder and bit down into his skin.

"Really?" He laughed. "You can say that with a straight face?"

"You were able to tell Cody you were my fiancé with a straight face," I said.

"Touché." He laughed. "So, are you ready to hear my proposition?"

"You were serious about that?" I said, feeling my toes curling as he ran his fingers between my legs. I moaned softly as he slipped a finger inside of me.

"How are you so wet already?" He groaned as he buried his face in my neck and kissed down my skin. His finger continued to move back and forth, and I groaned.

"The same reason that you're so hard," I muttered, feeling myself close to an orgasm already.

"I want you to pretend to be my fiancée for four weeks," he said as he continued to touch me.

"Why?" I said, gasping for air as he slipped a second finger inside of me.

"I'm doing it for two reasons. One is to make it so Cody doesn't kill both of us for thinking we're just hooking up right under his nose. The second is more personal. It's for me. You know I work for my dad, right? He's trying to get me a seat on the board of directors, but they won't approve me unless they think I'm a family man. Which is ironic considering who my dad is." He sighed and looked down into my eyes, his features intense as he paused. He watched my face as my body trembled beneath him. "I like watching you come," he said softly and his thumb started rubbing my clit as I felt myself coming.

"You're a bad boy." I gasped as my body buckled from the swift movement of his fingers and thumb.

"That's not a lie," he said and collapsed back down next to me. I watched as he moved two fingers to his mouth and started sucking.

"TJ!" I blushed as I watched him sucking my juices off of his fingers.

"What can I say?" He grinned and licked his lips. "I'm a bad boy who likes to do bad-boy things."

"So, tell me more about this board of directors thing?" I asked him seriously, wanting to get back to the matter at hand. My face was burning from embarrassment and pleasure. I couldn't quite believe I was here, and I didn't want to think about it too much.

"They are voting in four weeks," he said with a smile. "If they buy my act as a man in love, looking to get married and have kids, they will probably approve my seat on the board. Once that happens, we can break up or whatever. They won't be able to remove me."

"Isn't that a lie, though?" I frowned.

"The investors love me." He shrugged. "It's the board that's acting like dicks. I don't care if I have to tell a small lie to get my rightful position on the board. It is my dad's company, after all."

"He can't just give you a seat?"

"It doesn't work like that." He shook his head. "There will be a vote."

"Oh, I see." I bit my lower lip. "So you want me to pretend to be your fiancée for four weeks?"

"Maybe a little over four weeks." He nodded. "Just until I get my seat on the board. It will help me. And also it will help you, too."

"How will it help me?"

"Cody won't think you're a slut." He laughed and I shook my head at him. "And he won't kill me."

"Uh huh." I rolled my eyes.

"Plus, it will be fun." He grinned. "It doesn't have to be in name only."

"What do you mean?"

"We can have all the perks of being engaged." He grinned and ran his finger across my collarbone. "You can stay with me. I'll give you a credit card and a weekly allowance."

"Stay with you? Credit card?" My eyebrows rose.

"Of course you'll stay with me." His voice was adamant. "In my bed. And we'll make sweet love every morning and every night."

"You didn't even sleep with me last night," I said, still feeling hurt.

"I didn't want to make love last night." His eyes bore into mine. "I wanted to fuck you. Hard. Without a rubber." He paused. "And I wasn't about to let that happen."

"Why not?" I squeaked out.

"Because you're a virgin." He spoke softer now. "I'm not going to let your first time be like that. Plus, we need to take better precautions. You need to go on the pill."

"Why? You have condoms."

"When I take you, I want you to feel all of me," he muttered. "My skin next to your skin."

"Aren't there condoms that feel like real skin?" I asked softly.

"No," he said and smirked. "There is no lambskin that will feel as good and as raw as my skin next to you as I fill you up."

"I see." I swallowed hard, barely believing I was having this conversation.

"So, will you do it? Will you be my fake fiancée?" TJ asked with a wide smile.

"I don't know." I shook my head and sat up. I needed to get out of the room and take everything in. I needed to talk to Sally. I was already so confused about so many things. I didn't know which way was up right now. "I need to go and shower."

"We can shower together."

"No." I shook my head. "I need to shower alone."

"Aw." He pouted. "I could make it worth your while."

"T.J." I groaned. "Stop tempting me."

"Why? You tempt me every time you look at me with those innocent come-fuck-me eyes."

"How can innocent eyes say come fuck me?" I asked with a small smile.

"Shh." He laughed. "Stop the sass before I change my mind and have my wicked way with you right now."

"Why don't you?" I said and let my sheet fall down. I stood up and got out of the bed, my naked body shivering in the cool air.

"You tease." He groaned and got out of the bed as well. His body looked strong and magnificent as he stood there in front of me. I made the mistake of looking down and I saw his erection pointing directly at me, proud and hard. I waited for him to pull me into his arms eagerly. I was more than ready for him to take me. In fact, I was feeling as if I should just push him down on the bed and jump on top of him. That would shock him for sure.

"Put your negligee on and go back to your room before we don't leave this room for the next four hours." He bent down and picked up my nightgown and handed it to me. I took it from him, disappointed.

"So you want me to leave?"

"I don't want you to leave, but I do want your answer." He sighed. "You need to understand what's going on between us. I like you, Mila. I want you. Badly. But we need to be on the same page about everything."

"We are," I said as I slipped the negligee back on.

"No, we're not." He grimaced. "I didn't even know you were a virgin. And I don't know if you really know who I am, either. This engagement isn't just about business. I want to get to know you better. I want to do things with you that aren't PG or even in the bedroom. I'm going to take you to new heights, Mila."

"I want you to."

"I know." He frowned. "That's what scares me."

"THERE YOU ARE." SALLY'S jaw dropped as I snuck back into the room and closed the door behind me. "Oh shit, did you sleep with TJ?"

"Yes and no." I made a face and hurried over to my bed. "Sally, I don't know if I'm still a virgin."

"What?" She made a face. "Is he that small?"

"Small?" I was confused for a second and then started laughing. "No silly. He's not small at all." My eyes gleamed as I thought back to his large, thick manhood.

"So how do you not know?"

"He put it in, but Cody walked in and then he pulled out and we stopped."

"Oh snap." Sally's eyes widened and she sat up. "Cody walked in on TJ on top of you?"

"Yup." I giggled nervously. "It was so embarrassing and I thought the earth was going to open up and swallow me."

"So what happened when Cody left? I take it Cody didn't kill either of you."

"Nothing happened." I sighed. "We didn't have sex. TJ told Cody we were engaged, but he wouldn't sleep with me."

"Whoa—what? Engaged?" Sally jumped out of her bed and came over to mine. "What is going on?"

"It's not real. He doesn't love me or anything. He didn't declare his undying love. It's so he can get a seat on the board at his dad's company or something." I paused. "But he does want to sleep with me. And he said we would do other stuff, like kinky stuff."

"Say what?" Sally's brown eyes looked like she couldn't take in anything else. "What did you say? And what do you mean kinky stuff? Oh, my gosh, what is going on here?"

"I don't know, like sex stuff?" I shrugged. "He would want me to live with him, he said."

"Live with him?" Sally looked suspicious. "Why?"

"Just to make it look real to the board."

"How is the board going to know you're living with him?"

"I don't know." I shrugged. "And honestly, I'm not sure I care. This is everything I've been waiting for, Sally."

"I don't know, Mila." She looked worried. "This all seems to have come out of nowhere. Just a couple of days ago, you still hated each other. Shit, you were pretending you had a fake boyfriend."

"Things are different now. TJ has the hots for me too."

"Yeah, but a lot of guys have the hots for you, Mila." She sighed. "It just seems fishy."

"It's not," I said, though I wasn't too sure of that fact.

Knock knock.

"Hello," I said and looked towards the door.

"Hey, you." TJ walked in and gave me a look, no smile on his face. "Hi, Sally."

"TJ," she said with a deep, unfriendly voice.

"I wanted to give this to you, Mila. To look over." He walked over to me with a brown envelope in his hands.

"What is it?" I frowned as I took it from him.

"A contract," he said simply. "Read it. We'll discuss it later."

"Okay," I said and watched as he walked back out of the room. He closed the door gently and I looked back at Sally, who was frowning. "What?" I exclaimed.

"He just happened to have a contract with him?" She raised an eyebrow at me. "Doesn't that seem very suspicious?"

"I don't know, Sally." I sighed and held the envelope close to me. "I mean, what does he get out of it?"

"I don't know." She shrugged. "I mean, just be careful. You've had the hots for him for a long time. I don't want you to get caught up in something you don't really know anything about."

"I know TJ. He's been Cody's best friend for years."

"And I thought I knew Cody." She shrugged. "I've been your best friend for years."

"I'm sorry about Cody, Sally." I reached out and patted her on the back. "He's a jerk."

"It is what it is." She shrugged and took a deep breath. "Hey, I'm sorry for being a party-pooper, I'm excited for what's going on with you and TJ. I just don't want you to get hurt."

"I don't want to get hurt either."

"And you know what?"

"What?"

"You're still a virgin." She grinned. "The tip doesn't count."

"It was more than the tip." I laughed.

"If his tongue didn't count, one motion of his cock sure doesn't." She laughed. "Though, don't quote me on that. I'm not an expert on these things."

"Okay, I won't." I laughed and looked down at the envelope in my hands. "Should I open it now?"

"Duh." She laughed and then stood up. "Though you should put more clothes on first. I feel like you're trying to seduce me."

"You wish." I laughed and jumped up. "I'm going to shower and change, and then we can read it."

"I can't wait," she said, a twinkle back in her eye. "I just hope it's not all whips and chains and dark dungeons. I'm not sure I'll be able to look at him the same way again."

"Sally." I just shook my head as I made my way to the shower, but I couldn't stop myself from trembling. It hadn't occurred to me that TJ's kink was anything more than regular kink, but maybe that was why he had a contract. Maybe he really did have another side I knew nothing about. I closed the bathroom door behind me and closed my eyes as I grinned to myself. This weekend had gone even better than planned, and I knew I was ready for TJ—whips, chains, dungeons and all.

Seventeen

T J

I WALKED OUT IN the rain a few hours after I'd given her the contract because I couldn't stop myself from wondering what she was thinking, and worrying if Sally was trying to convince her not to go ahead with it. I was also still pent up from not having fucked her. I'd been shocked when I'd found out she was a virgin. I still felt tense about the fact that she wanted me to take her virginity. Tense and proud. I wanted her badly, but I also wanted to stop myself from doing something that I shouldn't. I had been about to cross the line. I'd been inside of her. My mind had been so foggy, but I hadn't wanted to continue. I hadn't wanted to take her. Not then, not like that. I had to make sure I didn't cross the line.

Though, I had to admit to myself that I could barely see the line anymore. It had become blurred in my mind. I was becoming caught up in my own trap. I was worried that I was going to give Mila four weeks, but she was going to try and hold me to more. I didn't know which way was up anymore. All I knew was that she was the guiding light in my sky. She was the beacon calling me home. And home was where I wanted to be.

The only problem was, I knew that once she entered my reality and found out who I really was, the dream she had of me would end. And, oh Lord, I didn't know if I was ready for that. I knew that I needed to be myself with her. I needed to show her the side of me that I'd kept hidden. And that meant taking a risk. Step one had started last night. In the lake. She'd had no choice but to succumb. I knew as soon as I'd touched her that it would give me the upper hand, but at that point, I didn't care. My body craved her too much. I needed her as badly as I needed air.

I headed towards the lake, even though I knew I shouldn't. I should wait for her to come to me. I should wait for her answer. I knew that I should, but I wasn't going to.

She sat there, with her feet in the water, not doing a thing, and all I could think was that this woman had changed my life. She'd changed the very universe I lived in—not by her actions or words, but with the curl of her lips as she smiled and the light in her eyes when she gazed upon mine.

"TJ?" she said as she glanced back, her voice like a Beethoven symphony to my ears.

"Yes, Mila," I said, walking towards her, my feet knowing the path to her body, while my heart still searched for the path to her soul.

"I didn't hear you come out," she said, standing up and turning towards me. Her hair fell forward as she bent down to brush something off her leg.

"I guess there are many things you didn't hear," I said and paused as I stared at her face, trying to memorize every inch for the time I wouldn't be with her.

"What else didn't I hear?" She frowned at me, looking confused.

You didn't hear the sound of my heart breaking when I lied to you, I thought as I stood there. I stared at her, my heart wanting to tell her all the things in my head, but I knew I couldn't. You didn't hear the feeling of shame that fell to my stomach when I asked you to pretend to be my fiancée. You didn't hear the excitement in my veins as I thought about waking you up every morning with my own special alarm clock.

"TJ," she said again and stepped forward. "What else didn't I hear?"

"You didn't hear the sound of your clothes coming off when I told you to get naked." I touched her shoulder, not able to resist touching her.

"You didn't ask me to get naked." She blushed then, a delicious pink-red hue that reminded me of her innocence. The feeling both delighted and destroyed me.

"That's because I don't ask, I tell," I said gruffly and my eyes narrowed as I stared at her. "Take your clothes off and get naked." I stared into her eyes, a fire burning in my soul as I commanded her to give herself to me completely. Once again, I could feel my world shifting as she stood there considering her next action. I knew what she was going to do. I knew, and I wasn't going to stop her. That was the magic of the situation. I was changing her life, just as much as she was changing mine. The only difference was I knew she would hate me once she found out.

Then I laughed and put my hand on hers. I had to laugh to let her know that while I wanted her, I wasn't going to let it consume me. I wasn't going to let my want for her body make me act irrationally. I needed to get her answer first.

"Have you made your decision?" I asked softly.

"I don't know what to do." She bit her lower lip and shook her head. "What should I do, TJ?"

"I can't make your decision for you, Mila." My voice was deep; some might say husky, as I looked down into her wide eyes. She was gazing at me with a question in her big brown eyes and her lips were slightly parted. "What's your answer?" I said abruptly, needing to know so badly that it was killing me inside to not know.

"Why are you doing this really?" she asked me softly as she stepped towards me, licking her lips nervously. Her long blond hair hung around her shoulders and small runaway wisps blew into her eyes. I leaned over and moved them gently behind her ear. She blushed at my touch and I made sure to let my fingers linger on her cheek for a few seconds. I could feel the heat emanating off of her skin onto my fingertips.

"I want you to experience the happiness, the joy, the goodness that you deserve." My voice sounded too serious and I wasn't altogether sure why I'd chosen those exact words. I myself wasn't really sure why I was here, with her, about to do something I knew I shouldn't do.

"I wish I could control what happens next," she said, her voice breathless. I gazed down into her eyes and my heart stopped as I saw the emotion there. She was letting me in, baring her soul to me in a naked, vulnerable way. Her eyes reminded me of a young, innocent doe I'd seen in the woods one year when I'd gone deer hunting with a friend's family. I'd felt guilty then and I felt guilty now as well.

"There's not much that is going to happen next." I sounded harsher than I'd intended. I didn't know how to tell her that I was mad at myself and not at her. She wouldn't understand the inner turmoil I was in. "We're going to kiss and then you're going to dump that loser of a 'boyfriend'." I put my hands on her waist and stilled them from going higher.

"He's not my boyfriend," she squeaked out as she closed her eyes and lifted her lips up to me, waiting. Her shoulders were thrust back indignantly and I stared down at the curve of her breasts and down to her long legs. She'd grown into a beautiful young woman. A very beautiful young woman that I knew I shouldn't let myself indulge in.

"You're damn right he's not," I growled before bending down and lightly pressing my lips against hers. They were so soft and sweet and she kissed me back eagerly as her fingers fumbled with my shirt. I grabbed her hands and clasped them in mine as I deepened the kiss, allowing my tongue to enter her mouth and taste the delicate hint of freshly picked strawberries that she'd just eaten.

She moaned slightly as I sucked on her tongue and my hands moved up her waist, making their way up to her bra. All thoughts of Cody warning me to stay away from his sister were far from my mind.

"Oh, TJ," she said as she grabbed my hand and moved it up and pressed it against her breast. "Oh, yes."

"Oh, no." I stopped and pulled back. Her eyes blinked open and she looked at me with a slightly bewildered and lost expression. She looked hot and flustered and I loved it, though I kept my grin to myself.

"What are you doing?" She pouted. "Why did you stop?"

"You didn't think it would be this easy, did you?" I said with a smirk, feeling hot and bothered myself. "Nothing happens until I get your decision."

"But, I just can't pretend to be your fiancée, TJ. That's not right." She licked her lips nervously.

"You can't?" I said softly, allowing my fingers to trace the curve of her lips. "Or you won't?"

"I read the contract," she said and swallowed. "What you're asking—it's too much."

"For you or for me?" I asked, my eyes never leaving hers. "What's four weeks, Mila?" I said as I pushed the tip of my finger into her mouth and watched as she sucked it gently. She just stared at me, thinking, and I could see her mind racing. She had no idea what to say or do. I'd beaten her at her own game and she knew it. Now I was ready to take my prize. And I was going to take it whether she became my fake fiancée or not. I knew that for a fact as she nibbled on my finger. She'd driven me to the brink. I needed to have her now. I didn't care about anything else in that moment.

"TJ, what you asked, well–"

My lips crushed down on hers to stop her from speaking as my hand crept over her breast. My other hand moved down to her shorts to unzip them. I was going to take her in the lake. It would be fitting. And then, before I was about to fuck her, I would make her answer me and tell me yes. She'd say yes and then I would take her, in the water, in the most primal fashion. And we would become one.

"Hey, Mila." Sally's voice was heading towards us and I froze. "We're getting ready to leave. You ready?"

I swore under my breath and stepped away from Mila as Sally came into focus. Her eyes narrowed at me as she stared at the two of us, and I knew that she knew what was in the contract.

"Let's go, Mila," she said, and I could tell she wanted to say something else. "Cody wants to tell you something before he leaves."

"Okay." She nodded and gave me a small smile as she headed towards her friend. "We have to go now, TJ."

"I'm going to get your answer sooner rather than later, Mila," I whispered as she walked past me. "And when I do, you're not going to know what hit you."

Eighteen

MILA

FEBRUARY 14, 2010

DEAR DIARY,

Nonno made me promise today that I would marry for love and not for money. I told him that of course I wouldn't marry for money. I think he was worried because Sally and I were talking about the cars we wanted to drive when we were older. I'd love a Range Rover, black, sports edition. Nonno said to me that he hopes I plan to work hard for it. I nodded, of course, but I think he heard me giggling to Sally telling her that TJ might buy me one when we start dating. I don't know if Nonno was upset that I wanted to date TJ or that I wanted TJ to buy me a car. Which I really don't want him to buy. I was just joking. I can buy my own car. One day. If I ever make enough money.

Mila

XOXO

"Did you talk to TJ about the contract?" Sally mouthed to me in the back seat.

"No," I mouthed back, my eyes on the front seat to make sure TJ and Barbie weren't paying attention to us.

"I can't believe that he expects you to sign that," she whispered and I nodded. "Who does he think he is?" She shook her head. "He thinks he's some sort of god."

"Sally." I widened my eyes at her and put my finger to my lips. "Shh."

"What's going on back there?" TJ looked directly at me.

"Nothing," I said innocently, staring back into his mesmerizing eyes, wondering what he was thinking.

"I see," he said and turned back to the front to concentrate on his driving.

"I'm surprised you didn't drive back with Cody," Sally said, looking at Barbie.

"Why would I do that?" Barbie looked back with a smirk.

"Because you slept with him." Sally gave her a venomous look.

"So?" Barbie said and she put her hand on TJ's thigh. "I like men."

"Cut it out, Barbie," TJ snapped and removed her hand from his thigh. "Mila knows we aren't dating. Though I'm pretty sure you didn't care what she thought when you hooked up with my best friend."

"You never cared who I hooked up with before." She purred and looked back at me, her eyes narrowed. "Not even when we talked about me becoming a Walker."

"What?" Sally's voice was loud.

"Oops." Barbie smiled and then shot a look at TJ. "We weren't talking seriously." She looked back at me. "I would never marry or think about marrying TJ. Way too many skeletons in his closet."

"And what's stuck in yours? Dicks that fell off from touching you?" Sally snapped back and I giggled.

"I'll have to check when I get home and see if Cody's dick is in there," Barbie said as she fluffed her blond hair and gave us both a narrow smile. "I wouldn't be surprised, seeing as it was in everything else of mine this weekend."

"Enough." TJ's voice was cutting. "Let's all just listen to some music and go home."

"Yes, boss," Barbie said in a sweet tone. "Whatever you say, big boy." She ran her fingers all the way up his thigh and I saw her grab his package, giggle and then sit back. I felt the blood going straight to my face. I was going to slap her. If I ever saw her again, I would beat her down. She was such a bitch.

"BYE," I SAID AS I jumped out of the car. I didn't even bother looking at TJ; I was still so pissed that he'd let Barbie touch his junk without saying a thing. Even though it had only been for a second, I still felt he should have said something. I walked to the back of the car and waited for TJ to open the trunk so that I could get my bag.

"Bye? That's it?" TJ said as he got out of the car and walked to the trunk and stood next to me.

"Well, if you'd dropped Barbie off before me, that wouldn't be it." I looked away from him. "But no, you dropped off Sally, and then decided to drop me off next."

"I'm not sleeping with Barbie, Mila."

"Let me get my bag." I glared at the back of his car.

"Mila, look at me." He grabbed my face and pointed it towards him. "I dropped you off before Barbie because I need to talk to Barbie. I want to make sure she's not trying to play Cody."

"Oh?" I looked up at him, my heart softening.

"Really." He nodded. "I couldn't really do it at the house with Cody there and I couldn't do it in the car with you and Sally, and I don't really want to see her again after today."

"I guess I can understand why." I grinned at him now.

"Good." He leaned down and kissed me. "I'm going to call you tonight."

"Okay." I nodded.

"Have you made your decision yet?" His eyes searched mine.

"No." I shook my head. "I need to think about the contract."

"What about it?"

"It gives you a lot of power over me and my every decision," I said, with a frown.

"I like to be in control," he said, his eyes not leaving mine.

"It's only four weeks. What does it matter?"

"Is it going to be a problem?"

"There are some parts I have problems with." I nodded.

"Mark them up and we'll discuss them." He kissed me again. "I'll call you tonight, dorky."

"Don't call me dorky." I glared at him, but I couldn't stop myself from smiling as I watched him driving away. I walked to my apartment and dumped my bags on the ground and then opened my purse again to reread his contract. I grabbed a pen from my table and sat down on the couch to read through the contract.

I looked at the first page and my heart thudded for a few seconds when I read that the contract was between "Travis James also known as TJ Walker and Mila Brookstone." I bit down on the pen and thought about what Sally had said, wondering why TJ had just happened to be carrying a contract around with him that had both of our names on it. That meant that he'd been planning this for a while. And I'd had no clue. Absolutely no clue. I wasn't sure if I should be happy about that or not.

My eyes scanned the contract until I got to the nitty gritty.

"The contract between TJ Walker and Mila Brookstone will last for the maximum duration of a year, not to exceed three hundred and sixty-five days. The minimum length of time for the contract is forty-five days," I said out loud, wondering why it didn't say four weeks like TJ had said, not that that was a huge deal to me. It was the next part that I was more concerned about.

"TJ Walker shall have full knowledge and access to all of Mila Brookstone's legal documents, bank accounts, social media accounts and phone records for the duration of the arrangement." I repeated that twice and then grabbed my phone. I needed to speak to Sally again. I called her number and waited for her to answer.

"You're home?" she said, answering right away. "Alone?"

"He dropped me off first. He said he wanted to talk to Barbie."

"Ugh, don't talk to me about that bitch." Sally started pissed off, and I knew I had to cut her off before we got into a long bitch session about Cody and Barbie. I felt bad for her, but I didn't want to keep talking about my brother.

"TJ said he's going to call me later to go over the contract. He wants me to mark up the stuff I have issues with."

"So the whole contract, then?" Sally sounded indignant. "He sounds like a control freak and just a freak."

"Sally!" I admonished. "We don't know that."

"Mila. He wants to control your life in and out of the bedroom. I mean, he wants you to start doing yoga with him and he wants you to designate a day to tantric sex techniques—like, what the fuck?"

"That's better than whips and dungeons, though." I laughed, though I was also puzzled about the whole tantric sex day thing as well.

"He's building up to that," Sally said. "Look, I know you've loved him forever, but I feel like this guy is trying to get you caught up in something crazy."

"What do you mean crazy?"

"I mean crazy, twisted, Nine and a Half Weeks type of shit."

"That wasn't that twisted." I laughed. "Don't blow things out of proportion."

"Mila, you know his contract is crazy. Isn't that why you called me? I thought this contract was for him to convince the board of directors that he's not a playboy and that he wants to settle down? Why does he need all this extra shit?"

"That is the point of the arrangement. But I guess he wants to experiment as well."

"Is this really what you want, Mila?" Sally's voice softened. "I know you've wanted him forever, but is this really what you want?"

"Things can change. Maybe he'll want to make the engagement real," I said hopefully.

"Are you sure you would want that?"

"I don't know." I sighed and then jumped up. "Look, Sally, I want to go and have a bath. I'll call you later."

"Call me after you talk to TJ," she said. "I want to know exactly what he says and what gets stricken off of the contract."

"Yes, ma'am," I said and hung up quickly. I looked down at the contract again and flipped the pages until I stared at the paragraph that had given me the most pause. The part of the contract that had stood out the most was that I had to trust him, even if I felt my life was in danger. Why would I think my life was in danger? That scared me more than it thrilled me. Trusting him with my life was something I did implicitly, but to have it in a contract made me wonder if there was something about him that I couldn't trust.

I didn't care if he was into a little role-play or something—that could be hot—but what if he wanted to choke me or something? I wasn't sure that I was down for that. Why would a contract state that I was to trust him in all endeavors?

I walked into the bathroom and started running a bath and took a deep breath. I looked into the mirror and studied my face, not altogether displeased at my reflection. I looked confused and pretty—or, as Cody would put it—pretty confused. I leaned forward and studied my eyes and lips. Did I look like someone who had just had a crazy weekend? Did I look like someone who was contemplating signing a contract to be TJ's fake fiancée even though I really had no idea what I was signing? I wasn't even sure if I cared. I turned back to the bath and put my hand in it to test the water to make sure that the temperature was perfect. I grimaced as the cold water touched my skin, and sighed. I turned the faucets off and walked back to the living room. The water tank was out of hot water. I'd have to wait twenty minutes and try and run the bath again.

Beep beep. I looked down at my phone and froze when I saw TJ's name on the screen. He'd sent me a text message. I grabbed my phone and tapped the screen so I could read what he'd written.

I miss you already.

Sure you do.

I do. Did you think about the contract?

You have a one-track mind.

Why do I think you're not talking about sex.

How did Barbie take the talk?

How do you think?

She pushed her boobs in your face.

Are you psychic?

Funny! Not!

Did you make up your mind about the contract?

You said we could go through it first.

Can I call you now?

I was about to have a bath.

Can I come over then? :)

You wish.

Yes, I do.

Call me.

Ring ring.

"That was fast," I said as I answered the phone with a smile on my face.

"You did ask me to call."

"Well, if we're going to be technical about it, I only said that after you asked if you could call me," I said, feeling light-headed.

"What's bothering you about the contract?" he asked me, changing the subject.

"You're really interested in me agreeing to this contract, aren't you?"

"What do you think, Mila?"

"I want to know why you had a contract with my name on it already."

"What do you think, Mila?"

"I want to know if this is a plan you've had for a while?"

"What do you think, Mila?"

"I think if you don't stop saying that, I'm going to scream."

"I'd love to hear you scream." His voice deepened. "I'd love to hear you screaming out my name as I—"

"Yeah, yeah, TJ." I rolled my eyes into the phone, though I couldn't stop myself from shivering slightly at his words. "You want me in your bed. You want to make me come. You want me to make you come." I paused and took a breath, but he interrupted before I could continue.

"It seems like you know me inside and out." His voice was smooth and I wondered what he was thinking.

"No, I don't. That's why I want to discuss the contract with you. Why exactly do you need access to all my personal information?"

"So I can make sure you're not cheating on me."

"How can I cheat on you if the relationship is a farce?"

"The engagement is a farce. The relationship won't be."

"Oh." I bit my lower lip and mumbled. "So I'll be your girlfriend?"

"No." He sighed. "Not exactly."

"Okay. So I'm just meant to let you have power of attorney over everything in my life. I'd think you were after my money if I had any and you weren't a millionaire." I laughed.

"I'm not after your money, Mila." He sounded amused. "Your body, yes. Your money, no."

"What does the clause mean that I need to trust you?" I said softly. "Even if trusting you means I'm scared for my life."

"Is that what's bothering you the most?" he said, the words sounding smooth and light as if what I'd just brought up was of no significance to anything.

"Yeah, that's bothering me. What exactly would you be doing that would have me scared for my life?"

"It's a general contract, Mila. I just want to know that you're giving everything to me and not holding anything back."

"What would I be holding back?" I frowned into the phone. "And you didn't really answer my question."

"For this to work, I need to know that you will give me the benefit of the doubt. I don't want to control you. I don't want to dictate your everyday life to you. I just want to know that you'll be open to suggestions of different things."

"What different things?"

"You'll see."

"I don't want to see. I want to know."

"There are some things you can't know right now, Mila."

"What can I know?" I sighed.

"You can know that I want you very much. You can know that this engagement will benefit both of us. You can know that I will not do anything that will hurt you."

"But you'll put me in harm's way? Possibly?"

"I would never put you in harm's way." He sighed. "Though you might always think that."

"You're scaring me, TJ. I don't understand what you're asking. How can I say yes to something I don't really understand?"

"You can say yes if you can answer to these three things," he said softly. "If you want to help me. If you want to make love to me. If you want to be taken into a world of passion and excitement that you never knew existed before."

"When would I have to move in with you?"

"If you say yes—now, tonight," he said, and I wasn't sure if he was joking.

"Tonight? I haven't even packed."

"You won't be needing clothes, so that doesn't matter."

"TJ! What?"

"I'm joking, Mila." He laughed. "I'm not having you move in with me so you can be my sex slave, if that's what you're worried about."

"I'm not worried about that," I said softly. "If anything, you'll be my sex slave."

"If you say yes, we can get you on the pill tomorrow."

"You're so eager for me to get on the pill."

"It's safer. There may be times and situations where a condom won't be the easiest thing to remember or put on," he said softly, and I froze.

"What does that mean?"

"It means exactly what I said it means." His voice lowered. "Can I come over?"

"Come over for what?"

"To discuss the contract further."

"You're not really answering any of my questions, TJ." I sighed. "I don't see the point of you coming over, just to further ignore me."

"Have dinner with me tomorrow," he said in a deep, sexy drawl. "Have dinner with me and let me take you on a date. I won't ask you about the contract or your decision unless you ask me to talk about it."

"I don't know." I sighed and rubbed my forehead. I wasn't sure it was a good idea to go and see him before I'd made up my mind. And I wanted to make up my mind when I was in a rational state instead of in the throes of want for him.

"Just dinner, Mila. That's it. No hanky-panky."

"I don't believe that you can have dinner with no hanky-panky."

"I mean, I can't promise I'll stop you from feeling me up." He laughed.

"You wish."

"Yes, I do." He laughed again. "So what's your answer?"

"Fine, yes," I said with a smile. "I'll have dinner with you."

"She said yes!" he exclaimed excitedly.

"To dinner, nothing else."

"I've never had a lady take so long to answer my marriage proposal before."

"How many women have you proposed to?" I asked, slightly jealous.

"For real? None. For fake? One," he said seriously. "Only you, Mila."

"Uh huh," I said and shook my head at myself as I felt butterflies in my stomach. This isn't a real engagement, dumbass, so stop thinking that it is, I lectured myself silently as I waited for TJ to talk again.

"I'll pick you up tomorrow at seven o'clock, okay?" TJ said and then paused. "Don't think too many naughty thoughts of me tonight."

"I'll see you tomorrow night, TJ," I said and hung up. I walked to my bedroom and flopped down on the bed. Never in a million years would I have thought that I would be in a situation like this, and with TJ Walker of all people. It was like I had entered an alternate reality. An alternate reality where all my dreams had come true. I sat up and reached over to my night table drawer and pulled out my diary and grabbed a pen. I paused before writing as I realized that I wasn't quite right. This reality I was living was exciting and thrilling, but it wasn't quite a fulfillment of all my dreams. I wasn't sure what it was, really, but I knew that only time would tell me exactly what I was getting myself into.

"YOU'RE VERY PUNCTUAL." I answered the front door with a smile.

"Actually, I'm early." TJ grinned at me. "It's six fifty-five p.m."

"Don't tell me that." I grinned back at him. "Or I might think you were eager to go on this date with me."

"I wouldn't want you to think I was eager," TJ said, as he looked me up and down. "You look very beautiful this evening."

"Stop it." I blushed. "You're just saying that."

"I never just say anything." He shook his head and touched my blouse. "I like it."

"Thanks. I got it at a little old store called Old Navy." I winked at him. "Cheap and cheerful."

"What, no shopping spree?" He looked shocked. "No fancy dress for our dinner date?"

"I thought jeans and a top would do?" I smiled at him. "You weren't planning anything fancy, were you?" I looked at TJ in his dark grey slacks and white button-up shirt and cringed. "Am I underdressed? I can change, you know. I have five minutes left before I'm late."

"You don't have to change." He shook his head. "Frankly, I'm glad you didn't dress up."

"You are?" I was surprised. I'd dressed casually both for myself and for him. I knew that if I'd put on some ball gown or sexy outfit, I'd be putting both of us in the mood for something more seductive, and I didn't want that. I wanted us to just hangout and relax.

"Yeah." He nodded. "Somehow a picnic in the park would have felt off if you were in your Sunday best."

"We're going on a picnic in the park?" I gazed at him and studied his face. "You don't strike me as a picnic guy."

"Okay, so maybe we aren't going on a picnic in the park." He laughed. "Maybe I'm going to cook you dinner at my place."

"Really? You can cook?"

"Mila! You've known me for how many years now? Of course I can cook."

"Ha!" I laughed. "This I have to see. I hope you have a fire extinguisher."

"Very funny." He grabbed my hand. "I won't burn anything if you help me."

"If I help you?" I put my hand on my hip. "You're supposed to be treating me to dinner, not me treating you."

"A man can only hope." He winked at me. "You ready to go?"

"Yeah, just a second. Let me get my bag." I hurried to my room and grabbed my handbag and made sure my phone, wallet, lipstick and a box of mints were in there. I hurried back out of the room and paused as I saw him standing in the doorway. "What're you doing?" I asked him suspiciously as he just stood there, not moving out of the way to let me pass. "We're not about to play tonsil hockey on my bed, you know?"

"I know." He grinned as he stared down at me. "I was just watching you in your natural habitat."

"Um, okay."

"Are they peppermint or minty green?"

"What's that?" I asked, embarrassed.

"The mints you put in your purse."

"None of your business, TJ Walker." I pushed him back, my fingers enjoying the feel of his hard chest. "Let's go."

"Okay, we're going." He stepped back. "I like it when you get bossy."

"Really now? You never seemed to like it before."

"There was nothing you could boss me around to do before that I would like."

"And there is now?"

"There sure is." He flicked his tongue at me and then laughed as I blushed. "Come on, my innocent little flower. Let's go and eat."

"I hope you tidied up." I laughed. "I wouldn't want to tell your dad that your place was a mess."

"Tell my dad?" He looked down at me with hooded eyes. "You've been in contact with my dad?"

"Of course not." I wasn't sure why he looked so annoyed, but I figured that he was fed up of women trying to come on to him to get to his dad. "I was just joking."

"I knew that." He laughed again, but it seemed to me as if his laugh was forced. And I wondered why. He couldn't really think I cared about the Walker millions, could he? "Let's go, Mila. No more small talk."

"You want the big talk instead?"

"I don't think you really want to know what I want, Mila." He winked and then tapped me on the ass as I walked down the hallway in front of him.

❤

"NONNO'S CALLING ME, DO you mind if I take it?" I asked TJ as I pulled out my ringing phone.

"Of course not." He shook his head. "We'll be at my place in about ten minutes."

"I know," I said and smiled, and then answered the phone. "Hello, Nonno."

"Mila." He sounded happy. "I haven't heard from you."

"It's only been a few days, Nonno." I said, exasperated.

"Well, the last call had you and Sally in tears. I want to know what happened."

"We weren't in tears." I laughed. "And Sally will be fine. I think she realizes now that Cody is an asshole and not worth her time."

"And you?"

"I'm actually in a car with TJ right now, Nonno. He's taking me to dinner." I didn't bother mentioning that dinner was at TJ's house. I was pretty sure Nonno would not approve of that tidbit or of the fact that I'd almost lost my virginity to TJ at the lake house.

"With TJ?" Nonno sounded suspicious. "Cody's friend."

"Yes, the one and only."

"You're going to dinner with him?"

"Yes, Nonno." I sighed. He wasn't sounding as delighted for me as I'd hoped he would.

"How did this happen?"

"How did what happen?" I could see TJ looking at me from the driver's seat and I gave him a small smile.

"How did you go from being upset that he had another girl at the lake house, to you going to dinner with him?"

"Nonno, can I call you later?"

"Fine." He sighed. "I was calling to tell you about your parents. Things aren't going so well."

"What do you mean? Are they getting a divorce?" My voice sounded shrill, even to my own ears.

"No, no," Nonno said quickly. "I mean the business. It's not doing well. I'm worried for them."

"Oh, no." I bit my lower lip. "I'm sorry, Nonno."

"It's fine," he said, but I knew it wasn't. The business was Nonno's life. In fact, he still owned the majority share. I knew he would be crushed if it failed. "I just need you to make more of an effort to help out at work, okay?"

"Yes, Nonno. Of course."

"Don't let yourself be sidetracked."

"I won't."

"I don't know about that TJ." His voice was low. "Be careful."

"Nonno." I moaned. "You've never had a problem with him before."

"Mila, do you have to be so loud?" Nonno sounded exasperated now. "Call me when you get home from your dinner."

"It might be late."

"I don't mind. I'll be waiting up."

"Okay, I love you."

"I love you too, mia cara. I love you too," he said and hung up. I put my phone back in my bag and looked over at TJ, who was grinning. "What's so funny?" I said as I looked at him.

"Nonno doesn't want me dating you, does he?"

"He didn't say that." I shook my head and clasped my hands. "Though I'm sure if he knew what happened last night and the night before, he wouldn't want me dating you."

"What happened last night?" he asked with a small smile.

"I'm not going to bring up the contract or anything like that. Tonight is meant to be a causal date."

"And that it will be." TJ grinned as he pulled up to his high-rise apartment complex and into the parking lot. "We're here."

"Yes, we are." I got out of the car and all of my nerves suddenly hit me again. I couldn't believe I was going to dinner at TJ's place and it was just going to be me. No Cody, no Sally, no parents, no nothing. Just the two of us.

"Let's go." TJ took my hand and led me to the building. "Are you nervous, Mila?"

"Of course not. Why would I be nervous?" I said and I ignored the feeling of his fingers squeezing mine as he escorted me to the elevator. We walked into the elevator and I tried to ignore the look he was giving me. Was he deliberately trying to look sexy as hell?

"This is my floor," TJ said as we got off on the twenty-first floor and walked towards his sumptuous loft apartment.

"What's for dinner?" I asked him, grinning as he opened his door.

"Me," he said with a raised eyebrow as he ushered me in.

"Very funny," I said as my stomach flipped over. I walked into his apartment and looked around in awe. TJ had redecorated since I'd last been there. His walls were all a light sand color and he had a huge dark-brown sectional in his living room, opposite a grand fireplace. "You have a fire burning?"

"I wanted to set the mood," he said softly as he stood next to me. "You approve?"

"It's gorgeous in here." I nodded, admiring his taste as I walked farther into his apartment. I noticed the bottle of champagne on his coffee table, sitting in a silver bucket of ice, and two flutes next to the bucket. "Champagne?"

"And strawberries." He grinned. "And chocolate."

"Are you trying to spoil me?" I laughed.

"Something like that." He nodded and he reached over and ran his fingers across my lips. "But before I spoil you, you must eat."

"What are you cooking?"

"I have steaks." He looked down into my eyes. "With a red wine cream sauce and mashed potatoes."

"Sounds yummy." I licked my lips.

"Good." He kissed the tip of my nose. "Have a seat on the couch and I'll start cooking."

"Are you sure you don't want any help?" I asked him as he walked to the kitchen. "I can make a mean salad."

"No, that's okay. Put on some music. My stereo is next to the TV."

"What shall I put on?"

"You choose." He grinned and looked back at me from the kitchen. "Just no One Direction or 'N Sync or whoever the cool boy band is today."

"I don't listen to boy bands," I lied. Of course I still listened to boy bands. They were awesome. I walked over to his stereo and my jaw dropped as I gazed at his flat-screen TV. It was huge, at least 65 inches. I'd never seen a TV so big before. I turned to his speakers and saw an iPod sitting on a Bose dock. I nodded, impressed. I picked up the iPod and searched through his music to see who he listened to. I was surprised at the range of musicians that he had on the player and quickly pressed play on a Beatles song I'd loved as a child, "Hey Jude."

"That's not baby-making music," TJ called out from the kitchen, and I laughed and walked back towards him to see how he was doing.

"How goes the cooking?" I asked as I walked into the kitchen and burst out laughing at the huge mess. There were plates and pieces of food all over the countertops. "Or shouldn't I ask."

"It's going fine." He laughed. "It looks worse than it is."

"Uh huh." I shook my head at him. "What can I do to help? Peel the potatoes?" I looked down at the half cut potatoes that still had most of the skin on them.

"You don't have to do that!" He shook his head and dropped the butter knife that was in his hand. "I want you to relax."

"So what should I relax and do?" I asked him softly as he walked up to me, his green eyes gleaming.

"Come with me." He grabbed my hand and led me out of the kitchen and down a hallway.

"Where are we going?" I asked him suspiciously.

"I want you to relax in a bath while I cook."

"Relax in a bath?"

"I have a spa tub." He grinned. "I'll put in some relaxing salts and oils and then I'll come and get you right before dinner's ready so you can put some clothes back on."

"Are you sure?" I asked him as he opened the door to his bathroom and I stared at his huge tub.

"I'm positive." He nodded and walked over to the bathtub and started running it. "I'll let you decide on the temperature," he said as he walked to a cupboard and pulled out a box and bottle of something. I watched as he poured them both into the tub and then put them on his marble countertop. He then opened another drawer, pulled out two candles and lit them and turned the lights out.

"TJ," I said, looking at him in surprise. "This is really thoughtful of you, but I would feel really bad to take a bath while you're cooking."

"Don't." He grinned. "I want to spoil you and show you what could be yours if you lived here too."

"TJ," I admonished, and he just chuckled.

"Relax, Mila. Have a bath and I'll be back." He gave me another quick kiss on the nose and then walked out of the bathroom. I stared at the door for a few seconds and then started to take my clothes off. Who was I to say no to a luxurious bath in TJ's home? He had insisted, after all. I placed my big toe into the water to check the temperature and almost melted when I felt how warm the water was. I climbed into the bath eagerly and lie back, loving the feel of the hot water and soft bubbles covering my skin. I closed my eyes and let the water seep into my bones. I reached to the side and pressed in a button and the water started whirling in the tub. I could feel it shooting from the side of the tub all over my body. I sighed in happiness as I lie there and smiled to myself.

Knock knock.

"Hello?" I called out, feeling sorry for myself.

"Can I come in?" TJ asked softly as he opened the door and walked in.

"You didn't wait for my answer." I pouted at him from under the bubbles.

"Enjoying the bath?" He smiled down at me and it was then I noticed the glass of wine in his hands. "Here you go," he said and handed it to me, crouching next to the tub.

"How long have I been in here?" I asked as I took a sip of the red wine. It slid down my throat eagerly and I felt a warm feeling inside my belly.

"Thirty minutes." He grinned as he watched me sipping the wine, his eyes intense on my face.

"Wow, that felt like ten minutes." I sighed. "Is dinner ready?"

"Nearly. Are you hungry?"

"Not really." I shook my head. "I'm just enjoying being in here and relaxing. This tub is amazing. It almost feels like I'm being massaged at the same time."

"I can make that happen," he said and he stood up and went behind the tub. "Lean forward," he said and I felt his strong hands on my shoulders, squeezing and massaging the tension in my bones.

"Oh, TJ." I sighed as I placed the glass of wine down.

"Do you want me to stop? Am I hurting you?" he asked, his hands resting on my shoulders.

"No, it feels amazing," I said honestly.

"Stand up," TJ said and I watched as he grabbed a big, white, fluffy towel.

"What?" I frowned up at him.

"I'm going to dry you off and then take you to my bedroom to give you a proper massage."

"TJ." I looked at him with wide eyes. "Are you sure that's a good idea?"

"No." He grinned and he flicked the towel. "But I'm going to do it anyway. Now stand up and let me dry you off."

I stood up then and let the water fall from my skin back to the tub. TJ's eyes narrowed as he took in my soap-covered breasts and I stepped out of the bath and directly into the towel. He patted me down carefully and slowly, ensuring that my entire body was dry. I was surprised and disappointed that he didn't try and touch me intimately, but I supposed that he was on his best behavior.

"What are you doing?" I asked as he picked me up and held me in his arms.

"Carrying you to the bedroom for your massage," he whispered as he walked out of the bathroom and down the corridor and into his bedroom. I noticed immediately that the lights were off and that there were at least ten candles burning in his bedroom. I gasped as I stared at his king-sized bed, for it was covered in red rose petals.

"TJ?" I said, looking up into his face as he placed me down on the bed. "What's going on?"

"What do you mean? I'm about to give you a massage."

"With red rose petals on the bed?"

"That's the best way."

"TJ, you said we weren't going to talk about the contract or the fake engagement tonight." I sighed. "I thought this was just going to be about us."

"It is." His eyes crinkled as he looked down at me. "Tonight is all about us." He pulled the towel off of me and pushed me down on the bed on my stomach. I felt him shaking the towel out and throwing it on the ground. "I'm going to give you a full body massage now, if that's okay with you?"

"It's fine," I said breathily as I waited, light-headed, for my massage. His bed felt soft and comfortable, and I closed my eyes as I waited to feel his strong hands on me once again.

"Let me get my oils," he said and then I heard him walking away. Within a few seconds I heard some music playing in the room.

"What's this?" I asked, not wanting to open my eyes.

"Just some music to help you relax," he said and I felt his hands on my back again. I sighed in contentment as he squeezed my shoulders and then I felt a warm liquid on my back and his hands rubbing it into my skin.

"TJ." I giggled as I felt his hands rubbing the oil over my bottom and I moaned as I felt his hands working down my legs and to my feet. TJ's fingers felt like magic on my body and, as he kneaded the knots out of my muscles, I felt myself growing more and more relaxed.

"Turn over," TJ said and I rolled over right away. I moaned as I felt his hands on my breasts, kneading and rolling before he moved down to massage my stomach. My heart was racing as he massaged me all over and I could feel myself growing wet. TJ's hands slipped past my belly button and continued lower until they were inside of my legs and massaging my most intimate of spots.

"Oh TJ." I moaned again as his fingers rubbed back and forth on my clit.

"Is this the first time you'll come from a massage?" He grinned down at me and I reached up and grabbed his hair and pulled him down on top of me. "Mila, what are you doing?"

"You don't think you're going to have all of the fun, do you?"

"Mila, your dinner is ready." He groaned as I ran my hands down his back and wiggled my body against him.

"You said you would be my dinner." I winked at him and then kissed him hard. I'm not sure how long we were making out before I realized that we were both naked on the bed, my breasts crushed against his chest as he sucked on my neck. I squeezed his ass as he rolled me around on the bed and I could feel his hard cock pressing against me.

"I want to make love to you, Mila," he whispered in my ear as his fingers played with my nipples.

"I want you to make love to me, TJ," I answered back and grabbed his right hand and put it between my legs. "I'm ready for you," I said as I rubbed his fingers in my juices.

"You're such a tease." He groaned as he rolled me over on top of him. I sat astride him, his cock underneath me and I grinned down at his darkened lust-filled face. "Are you sure you want this?"

"Are you sure this wasn't the very reason you decided to have me over to dinner tonight?" I laughed and he growled and rolled me over again.

"I have a condom," he said and reached over to the night table and grabbed a packet. "I'll go slow, so that I don't hurt you."

"You won't hurt me." I spread my legs beneath him. "I just want to feel you inside of me."

"Oh you'll feel me all right." He ripped open the condom packet and I watched as he rolled the rubber on top of his hard cock. I swallowed as he placed it between my legs. "Hold my hands," he said as he grabbed my hands between his and leaned down to kiss me. "It might hurt a little bit." He groaned as he inched his cock inside of me little by little. He slid in easily and I cried out as I felt him breaking through my hymen. "Are you okay?" He looked concerned and I nodded and wrapped my legs around him tightly.

"Please don't stop." I whimpered as I felt him moving slowly inside of me. "You can go faster."

"Are you sure?" He groaned as he increased his pace and I nodded. His lips crushed back down against mine and I felt his cock sliding in and out of me, moving faster and faster as he sucked on my tongue. I couldn't believe how amazing it felt having him inside of me. I'd never known sex would feel like this, so powerful and pleasurable. TJ's eyes gazed into mine as he continued moving inside of me and I felt him stilling before thrusting into me hard five more times and then shuddering inside of me. He collapsed on top of me then and rolled over, holding me in his arms and kissing me all over. "Did you come?" he asked me, his eyes glittery as he stared at me.

"I'm not sure," I breathed out as I felt his cock leaving my body. I felt empty without him inside of me, yet I felt powerful that I'd made him orgasm.

"That means you didn't." He looked annoyed with himself. "Some women don't come the first time. Give me ten minutes and I'll be good to go."

"Oh?" I asked, yawning slightly. "I'm not sure if I will be."

"You will be." He grinned at me as his fingers slid between my legs. "Trust me when I say that."

◆

"TJ!" I SCREAMED OUT his name as he slammed into me from behind. "Oh please, TJ."

"What, Mila?" He grunted as he grabbed my breasts while he

continued to fuck me hard. "Do you like this hard cock?"

"Oh yes," I screamed with abandon as I felt each and every thrust deeper and deeper inside of me. "Why didn't we start off with this position?" I cried out as I felt him hitting what I could only assume was my G-spot once more.

"I didn't want you to lose your virginity doing it doggy-style," he muttered as his right hand reached forward and rubbed my clit.

"Why not?" I moaned as his cock slid completely out of me while he was moving in and out so quickly.

"Because." He groaned as he slipped back inside of me. "It's not a romantic first position."

"I don't care," I cried out as I closed my eyes and felt my body shuddering as a huge orgasm hit me, and I felt my body trembling on his hardness before I fell forward.

"I don't think I need to ask if you came this time." He laughed as he moved his cock in and out of me a few more times before I felt his body shuddering behind me.

"No, you don't." I felt exhausted as I lie there and TJ pulled out of me and pulled me into his arms. "By the way, I've made my decision," I said sleepily as I laid my head on his chest.

"Oh?" he said, his body stilling as he gazed down at me.

"I'll be your four-week fiancée, TJ," I said as I reached down and squeezed his still semi-hard cock. "I'll do it." I smiled as I heard him groaning and then closed my eyes to sleep. I was excited to see what the next four weeks would have to offer.

Nineteen

TJ

MY COCK STILL FELT hard as I watched Mila sleeping, though I knew our relationship was too fresh for me to fuck her while she was sleeping. That might scare her to wake up to me inside of her, though that was exactly where my cock wanted to be. I held her in my arms and I felt satisfied and worried. Satisfied because she'd given herself to me and she'd seemed to enjoy it, but worried for what would happen when she found out exactly what all those clauses in the contract meant that she'd been so worried about. Frankly, I was surprised that she'd agreed to my terms without more of a discussion. She was too trusting, which I both liked and disliked. I was glad she trusted me, but it made me angry with her. She had no clue what she'd signed up for.

I slid out of the bed and watched her sleeping. I had two phone calls to make. I made the first call and received a voicemail. I hurried into the hall so that Mila wouldn't be woken up, speaking quietly into the phone. "It's done. Mila has agreed to be my fiancée." I hung up quickly and called the next number. I received another voicemail and left the same message. "It's done. Mila has agreed to be my fiancée." I closed my phone and walked to the kitchen. I wasn't feeling proud of myself, but I knew that I had to do what I had to do. I decided to put the food away when my phone rang—it was my dad returning my call.

"TJ," he said, his voice surprisingly alert for such a late call.

"Dad."

"Good job. I'm going to send some papers over to you tomorrow. I need you to go over them."

"What papers?"

"You know what papers."

"How did you get them?" I frowned into the phone.

"How do you think?" My dad sounded annoyed.

"Dad, I think you're—"

"I'm not paying you to think. I'm paying you to get the job done. The papers will be in your office tomorrow morning. Don't fuck this up."

"I won't," I said dully as my heart slowed.

"Good." My dad sounded pleasant again. "I always knew that Mila had a thing for you. Just keep her satisfied for the next four weeks and the plan will be fine."

"Uh huh," I said, hanging up the phone and flinging it onto the couch as I walked into the living room.

"TJ?" Mila walked into the living room, wrapped in a sheet, her long hair a tousled mess around her shoulders.

"What are you doing up?" I frowned at her, wondering what she'd heard.

"I woke up and you weren't there and I heard your voice." She squinted at me as her eyes adjusted to the light. "Who were you on the phone with?"

"No one." I shook my head. "Come, I have something for you."

"Oh, what?" She looked excited and I laughed as I led her back to the bedroom.

"Sit on the bed," I said and walked over to my bag. I pulled out the jewelry box and another small bag. "This is your engagement ring." I pulled out the large diamond ring and placed it on her finger. "I hope you like it."

"I love it." Her eyes were wide as she stared at her finger. "Thank you."

"Now you can open the other bag," I said to her with a smile, my eyes never leaving her face as I watched her pull out the handcuffs.

"What are these for?" she asked, all shocked as she gazed at me.

"This is just a reminder that while these four weeks are going to be a lot of fun, they are going to be crazy as well." I took the handcuffs from her hands and walked over to a drawer and dropped them in before turning back to her. "The more you get to know me, Mila, the more you will see that the boy you thought you knew is not the man I am now. I like to have fun. I like to get down and dirty. I'm going to take you on a ride that you will never forget."

"And you need the handcuffs to do that?" she asked nervously and I could see her fingers trembling as she held the sheet to her body.

"I don't need the handcuffs to do that." I shook my head and walked back towards her. "In fact, I'm not the one who will need the handcuffs at all." I stopped in front of her and pulled the sheet off of her beautiful body.

"You're not?" she asked, confused, as she looked at me with parted lips.

"You're the one who will need the cuffs, Mila." I pushed her down on the bed and rolled her onto her knees. "You're the one who will need the cuffs," I said again as I entered her swiftly from behind, all guilt gone from my mind as I once again showed both of us just how much pleasure our bodies could give each other.

Twenty

MILA

OCTOBER 1, 2010

DEAR DIARY,

When I marry TJ Walker, I'm going to have a big wedding and invite all those girls in school that made fun of me for having a crush on my brother's friend. "He'll never be with you," they said. "He'll never want you," they said. I'll show them. One day, he'll be mine and they'll be eating all of their words.

Mila

XOXO

"Sally, I'm telling you that TJ has been the perfect gentleman since I said yes," I whispered into the phone during my lunch break.

"It's only been a week, Mila." Sally didn't sound impressed. "I would hope he'd still be a gentleman in the first week."

"He's a perfect lover." I sighed as I thought about the previous night's lovemaking. "So giving."

"I should hope so," Sally said and I knew that she was slightly jealous because I kinda had TJ and she had nothing with Cody.

"He wants me to move in with him," I said and bit my lower lip. "Hold on, I think Cody is coming," I said as I saw my brother approaching my office. "What can I do for you?"

"TJ's here," he said with a small frown. "Are you going to bring him to dinner tomorrow night? I think our parents and Nonno deserve to know that you guys are engaged now?"

"I guess I'll ask him." I sighed, not really wanting to have to lie to my parents and Nonno.

"Is Sally coming?" Cody asked almost indifferently. "I haven't heard from her in a while."

"I don't know." I shrugged, my eyes narrowed. "Why do you care?"

"I don't." He looked away. "I was just wondering."

"Okay," I said and whispered into my phone as he walked out of the room. "TJ's here, I'll call you back in ten minutes, Sally," I said and hung up quickly. I jumped up and hurried out of the office to look for TJ.

"There you are, darling," TJ said as he walked towards me with a large bouquet of flowers.

"Hi." I smiled shyly, still not quite believing that I was sleeping with and dating this amazing man. I leaned up and gave him a quick kiss on the cheek. "What brings you by?"

"I wanted to say hi, see your pretty face and ask you to dinner tonight."

"Okay." I smiled. "That sounds good."

"It's a work dinner." His eyes bore into mine. "With my dad. And the board."

"Oh, okay." I nodded, reality hitting me. "An important dinner, then?"

"Yes." He nodded. "Real important."

"Okay." I nodded again. "Can you come to my family dinner tomorrow night as well? Cody thinks we need to tell everyone about our engagement."

"I can do that." His lips thinned and my heart dropped.

"Unless you don't want to, of course."

"I want to." He smiled, leaned forward and kissed me lightly.

"Of course, I want to."

◆

"YOU DIDN'T HAVE TO buy me a new dress," I said as we drove to the restaurant to meet his dad and the board of directors. "I have cocktail dresses."

"I wanted tonight to be special," he said, reaching over to squeeze my knee. "I want you to make a good impression."

"Okay," I said, feeling slightly peeved. What did that mean? Did he think that my own wardrobe wasn't good enough? "Is there anything you want me to do or say?"

"Just pretend that you love me." He shrugged. "Act all lovey-dovey and pretend you want more than my body."

"Okay," I said, my voice stiff. How could I tell him that I did love him and I did want more than his body?

"Okay, we're here," TJ said with a small smile as he gazed at me. "Just act natural and be yourself. Everyone will love you."

I smiled at him as I got out of the car, not knowing how to tell him that I didn't want everyone to love me, only him.

Twenty-one

T J

I COULD TELL THAT Mila was unsure of what was going on. Dinner had been uncomfortable for both of us and my father had acted in a lecherous way towards her that had made me want to beat him down. Though of course, I couldn't do that. I could feel my pent-up energy and I knew that I needed a release. I needed a high that I hadn't had in a long time and I needed it from Mila. I wasn't sure how she'd react. I wasn't sure if she'd go running for the hills, but I needed to see. I looked over at her and smiled as if I didn't have a care in the world.

"I want to tell you about the sexiest moment I've ever had in my life." I sat there still as a statue as I stared at Mila, her face looking confused. She was dressed in a T-shirt and shorts, having taken off her dress as soon as we'd gotten in.

"I don't want to hear about it." She licked her lips nervously as she looked away from me. She was still pissed from what had happened at dinner and I didn't blame her.

"I want to tell you about it, though," I said as I stood up and walked towards the wall.

"What are you doing?" She frowned.

"The night I'm going to tell you about starts with the lights being turned off," I said as I flicked the lights off.

"Why are you turning the lights off?" she squeaked as I walked towards the coffee table.

"Setting the mood for my story," I said and pulled a lighter out of my pocket and lit three candles that were on the coffee table. I looked over to Mila, still sitting on my couch, and she shifted slightly, her gaze looking slightly scared as she gazed at me.

"There were three candles burning that night," I said as I headed back towards her. "All three of them smelled like honeysuckle." I took a deep breath and smiled as Mila did the same and smelled the sweet scent of honeysuckle in the air. "The air that night was rife with sexual tension. It was so palpable that I swear someone could have cut through it with a knife."

"Okay," she said and nodded. "I don't know how air can be rife with sexual tension," she said with a slight edge to her voice.

"Oh?" I said and raised an eyebrow at her. I sat next to her on the couch, so close that our thighs were rubbing against each other. I placed my hand on her shoulders and ran my fingers down the slight curve of her back. Mila shifted again, trying to stop my touch, but she didn't get off of the couch. "I remember I touched her, my fingers fleeting on her body, not even touching her skin. That didn't matter though, because she still wanted me."

"You sure think a lot of yourself," she said, her voice soft as she stood still.

"I remember that I touched her leg." My hand moved from her back to her thigh and my fingers moved gently up and down, enjoying the slight trembling of her muscles as she sat there waiting to see what was going to happen next. "I remember that her legs parted slightly," I said as I gazed into her eyes and smiled as her legs parted involuntarily. "She wanted me to touch her. She wanted me to feel how wet she was for me already."

"She sounds like a slut." She swallowed hard, her eyes not leaving mine. She froze as my fingers ran higher up her thigh, close to her private place, the place I knew was burning in need for me.

"She wanted me to touch her." I ignored her comment, knowing she was trying to diffuse the situation. "And I very badly wanted to touch her."

"So why didn't you?" she said. I could see her eyes gazing at my fingers and she sighed slightly, the sound coming out as a soft moan. I felt myself growing harder as I sat there, teasing her with my words.

"I needed to make sure that she knew that the moment was special," I said and removed my hand from her legs.

"I see," she said stiffly as she sat back and looked away.

"That night was special because I played her a song. A song that had special meaning to me."

"What song?" she asked.

"'Let Her Go' by Passenger," I whispered. I pressed play on my phone and the song started playing through my speaker via Bluetooth in the room.

"You didn't have to play it," she said and I grabbed her hand.

"I had to play it," I said simply. "Then I took her hand and held it," I said. "I caressed her fingers and then sucked on them gently, one by one." I took her pinky finger and put it in my mouth and sucked. She gasped as she stared at me, but she didn't pull away. I pulled her pinky finger out of my mouth and pulled her up off of the couch with me.

"What are you doing, TJ?" She gasped.

"I'm going to tell you what happened next," I said and unbuttoned my shirt slowly before pulling it off and throwing it on the floor. "Put your hands up," I said to her and took a step forward.

"Why?" she said, her eyes widening.

"Because the next part of the story has to be shown to be believed."

"TJ." She gulped. "I don't know what you're saying."

"Yes, you do," I said as I nodded. "You know exactly what I'm saying."

"TJ." She shook her head. "I don't."

"Go to my closet drawer and get the handcuffs and then come back."

"What handcuffs?" she said and blushed. As if she could have forgotten!

"The handcuffs we're going to use tonight."

"Where?" She looked shocked. "Here?"

"No." I laughed. "That would be way too easy, Mila. You should know by now that I'm anything but easy."

"So where?" she said.

"Go and get the handcuffs and then come back to me."

"You think you're hot stuff, don't you?" She glared at me. "You think you can just boss me..." She stopped talking as I pulled her towards me and kissed her hard.

"Put your hands up," I commanded as I pulled away from her. She put her hands up obediently and I smiled as I pulled her top off. "You can keep your bra on for now."

"Why, thank you." She rolled her eyes at me.

"Go and get the handcuffs," I said as I stared at her beautiful body. "And then come back to me."

"What are you going to do?" she asked softly, gazing at me in wonder.

"I'm going to do all of the things that your brother, your father, and your grandfather have worried about."

"What things?" She gazed at me with her mouth half open.

"I'm going to take you to new heights." I smiled at my apt choice of words. "I'm going to possess your body and soul and I'm going to make you come so hard that you'll wonder how you can ever survive without me inside of you."

"TJ." She blushed.

"You'll be screaming my name a lot louder than that." I smirked at her. "You'll be screaming my name into the wind as the city sleeps, and you'll wonder if you'll survive the passion of the night."

"TJ, I thought this story was meant to be about your sexiest night."

"Oh, it is." I grinned at her. "And it's about to start right now." I licked my lips slowly and I growled as she reached over and touched me. "Tonight, I'm going to make you believe that your body was made for me and me alone. Tonight, my dear Mila, I'm going to show you just how dark and dirty I can be." I spoke lightly and stared at her, wondering if she knew just how true my words really were. Tonight Mila would see just how this man of the night rolled. Tonight Mila would see that being with me was not just about fun and games. Tonight Mila would soar and I would be there with her. I just hoped that what was about to happen wouldn't scare her too much. "Go to my room, take off your panties and your bra. Put on a skirt and a top, grab the handcuffs and then come back out to me," I said and stood back, waiting for her to do as I said.

"WHERE ARE WE GOING?" Mila's voice was breathless as I parked my car.

"To my office."

"You brought me to your office at night to have sex?" She looked at me with a questioning look as we got out. I stood there, staring at her in her short black skirt and loose white top, and grinned.

"Kinda sorta," I said as I reached my hand down the back of her skirt and pulled it up to slap her naked ass.

"Ow, what are you doing?" She gasped as I slipped a finger between her legs.

"Making sure you don't have any panties on."

"You know I don't have any on. You're the one who took them off."

"Oh, yeah." I laughed and pulled the back of her skirt down. "Come, let's go inside."

"To your office?" she asked again.

"Not exactly." I shook my head and smiled, my heart racing a thousand beats a minute as we walked into the office building and towards the elevators. "Do you have the handcuffs on you?"

"Yes, T.J." She nodded and held them up to me. "They're here. Are you going to tell me more about this sexiest night or am I just supposed to wait and see?"

"I think experiencing it is better than hearing, don't you?" I said as I pressed the button to the top floor.

"I wish I knew." She shrugged, but I could tell from her eyes that she was excited. "Where are we going?" she asked as we got off at the top floor. I took her hand and led her to the side door that led to the stairs. "Sex in the stairways at work?" she asked curiously, her eyes wide.

"No." I shook my head and led her up the stairs. "Come with me." I almost ran up the last few stairs as we made our way to the door. I opened it and took her outside to the roof.

"Sex on the roof?" she said, her eyes looking at me shrewdly. "Wow."

"Not just on the roof," I said, my heart racing even faster now as I led her to the edge. "Sex on the edge of the roof."

"Are you joking?" She shook her head and took a step back. "I'll fall." She looked over the ledge and shuddered. "Hell no."

"Remember how the contract said you had to trust me?" I said softly. "Even when you thought your life was at risk?"

"You put that in your contract so you could fuck me on a roof?" Her voice rose as she looked at me incredulously. "Are you out of your mind?"

"I'm not out of my mind." I took a step towards her. "And I promise you that you won't fall."

"How can you guarantee that?"

"You have the handcuffs, right?" I grinned at her. "I'll cuff you to this railing." I pointed to the pole next to the ledge. "You won't fall."

"TJ." Her breath caught as she gazed at me. "I can't do this."

"You can," I said, my hands reaching up under her shirt and caressing her breasts. Her nipples were hard already and I could tell from her demeanor that she was still considering it. "You'll feel like you're flying. Trust me." I gazed out at the city lights and took a deep breath. "Look at the skyline, Mila. Do you know how powerful you'll feel if you let me fuck you up here?"

"Don't you mean make love?" she asked, her voice nervous as she looked out at the night sky.

"No, I mean fuck," I said coarsely as my hand slipped in between her legs again. "Because that's what I'll be doing, Mila. Have no doubt about that. You will feel every inch of me as I slide in and out of you, and you will scream out my name to the night sky, as we reach new highs together. You will know in every fiber of your being that you're being fucked. Hard and deep, and you will love every second of it."

"You're serious about this, aren't you?" She moaned and her legs parted slightly. My fingers rubbed against her clit roughly.

"Yes, I'm serious." I stepped back and pulled my shoes off and then my pants. I stood there with my hard-on and my shirt, and she just gazed at me wordlessly. I grabbed her hand and reached her wrists up to the bar.

"Hand me the handcuffs," I said softly, my hands held out to her.

"I don't know." Her lips trembled as she spoke.

"Hand me the handcuffs and get up on the ledge," I said, my voice commanding this time. I grinned as she moved forward and bent over the edge.

"I'm not getting on the ledge," she said and shook her head. "But I'll bend over it." She leaned forward, so that her hands were resting in front of her, touching the air and her ass was up, ready and waiting for me.

"Are you excited?" I asked as I grabbed my hardness and rubbed the tip of my cock against her clit. I felt a gush of liquid touching me and I laughed. She was more than ready. "Now you see why I wanted you on the pill. No one has time to worry about a rubber in a moment like this," I said as I thrust my cock inside of her. She moaned loudly and moved slightly forward. I grabbed a hold of her hips and pulled her back. "This is why I wanted you cuffed." I growled. "You can't keep moving."

"Sorry." She gasped as my cock hit her G-spot and stayed there for a few seconds. I pulled my cock out slowly and then slammed back inside of her, enjoying her moans in the night sky.

"Open your eyes and look at the buildings," I said hoarsely as I continued moving inside of her. "Look how high up we are—it's almost like we're fucking and soaring in the air at the same time." I thrust into her hard again as I felt the cool air slapping me in the face.

"TJ." She whimpered. "I think I'm going to come already." I could feel her lips tightening around my cock and I stopped moving.

"Not yet," I said, not wanting the moment to be done so quickly. I knew that she would want to stop as soon as she came. She'd want to move back from the edge and that would take away part of the fun.

"TJ," she cried out. "Please."

"Not yet." I slapped her ass and then rubbed her swollen clit as I waited for her orgasm to subside. I stepped back as an idea hit me.

"Hold on," I said as I pulled her up. "I need to go and get something. Wait for me here or I can handcuff you first."

"What are you going to go and get?" she asked me, her voice hoarse with longing.

"You'll see." I grinned as I thought about the vibrator I had in my office. If she thought the pleasure was too much to bear now, she wouldn't be able to stand it when I was sliding deep inside of her at the same time her clit was being massaged. I quickly grabbed my pants and pulled them on, then I hurried back to the doorway and the stairs and took the elevator back to my floor. I couldn't stop myself from grinning as I made my way to my office and it was only when I saw the light on in my dad's office that I faltered. I walked over to his office lightly, trying to be as quiet as possible. The door was slightly ajar and I could see that he was fucking someone over the table.

"Do you like that?" He grunted as he moved and I could hear the lady in question crying out.

"Oh yes, big boy, fuck me harder, Hudson," she squeaked out in delight and I froze in disgust as I watched them.

"Who's your daddy?" My dad moved forward and my lip curled in disdain as I watched them.

"You are," she screamed. "You know I'd do anything for you."

"I know you would, Barbie. You've already proved that to me." My dad growled as he pulled her blond hair, and I was about to turn away when I heard him say my name. "There's no need to leave, TJ." My dad turned to me. "Don't you want to say hello to your soon-to-be new stepmother?" He pulled out of her and she jumped up, her callous blue eyes gazing at me in delight.

"Why hello, TJ." She grinned at me. "I guess we're both working late tonight." I stared at her for a few seconds before turning around and heading to my office. I walked in, grabbed the vibrator and headed back up to the roof, my heart pounding. As I walked out of the door and saw Mila standing there, I knew that I'd gotten myself into something more complicated than I should have. Someone was going to get hurt. I should stop everything now before it was too late. I could walk away and still manage to fix some of the things I'd done, but as I walked out and stared at Mila's naked ass, I knew that I couldn't just walk away. The four weeks were just beginning and I was going to make sure that my four-week fiancée lived up to her side of the bargain in every way. No matter the cost.

Thank you for reading Four Week Fiancé, part I. This is a two-book series and the second book will be out in September 2015. To be notified as soon as the book is released, please join my mailing list: http://eepurl.com/bpCvd1

Please think about leaving a review and recommending this book to a friend as this really helps me as an indie author. You can also connect with me on Facebook: www.facebook.com/J.S.Cooperauthor

Or send me an email at jscooperauthor@gmail.com. To be notified of all new releases.

Thanks,
Jaimie
xoxo

Made in the USA
Lexington, KY
09 September 2015